The
Topography
of Love

Also by Bernice Morgan

Random Passage

Waiting for Time

The
Topography
of Love

~Stories~

Bernice Morgan

BREAKWATER
100 Water Street
P.O. Box 2188
St. John's, NF
A1C 6E6

Cover Photo by Sadie Vincent Vardy.
Design and layout by Carla Kean.

Canadian Cataloguing in Publication Data
    Morgan, Bernice
        Topography of Love
        ISBN 1-55081-157-6
    I. Title.
    PS8576.0644T66 2000   C811. '54   C00-950100-2
    PR9199.3.M638T66 2000

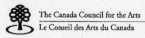
The Canada Council for the Arts
Le Conseil des Arts du Canada
We acknowledge the financial support of The Canada Council for the Arts for our publishing activities.

Canada We acknowledge the financial support of the Government of Canada through the Book Publishing Industry Development Program (BPIDP) for our publishing activities.

for George
who makes writing possible

Author's Acknowledgements

Foremost I want to express my gratitude to Anne Hart, whose thoughtful editing greatly improved this book.

I am grateful to Patrick Kavanagh for kindly giving me permission to use words from his wonderful novel *Gaff Topsails* for my title.

For background information essential to Celie's story I am indebted to Patricia O'Brien for her history of the Waterford Hospital, *Out of Mind, Out of Sight*.

I thank Penny Dickens of The Writers' Union of Canada who held my hand and talked me through a crucial stage in the completion of this book.

To Joan Clark and Helen Porter, who read the manuscript, and to my friends in The Newfoundland Writers' Guild, who workshopped much of it, my thanks for your support and your suggestions. I also want to thank Carla Kean and the staff at Breakwater for their work on the finished product.

The stories in this book are fiction but like most fiction they each contain a seed of truth. I am deeply indebted to the many friends, relatives and strangers who, knowingly and unknowingly, presented me with the seeds from which these stories grew—chief among these are my Vincent aunts and uncles, people who left but never forgot Cape Island.

In particular I give grateful thanks to my dear brother-in-law Leo Reddy, whose "lies" are an inspiration and a resource I continually draw upon. Without Leo could I have imagined a Catholic boyhood in downtown St. John's? Without Leo's introduction would I have encountered a character as amazing as Gertie Perkel?

Contents

"This is what God sees:
this is the topography of love..."

— from *Gaff Topsails*
a novel by Patrick Kavanagh

Part One

Folding Bones

Moments of Grace

$\mathcal{N}$ot only is Beryl half sick with the heat, she is bored, tired and dispirited, feelings she has managed to keep at bay for most of her life. She leans forward, peeling her bare back away from the sticky car seat, smoothing out the skirt of her white sundress, which had looked so crisp an hour ago. Knowing it is a mistake, she eases her feet out of the high-heeled red shoes and for a few minutes feels better.

When Maud disappeared into the office building, Dot had gotten out of the car right away. Muttering "the frigger turned off the air conditioning again," she'd gone to sit on the concrete curb of the parking lot, in the small spot of shade provided by a rotating sign listing the many departments of the greater Los Angeles taxation office.

Except to light one cigarette off another, Dot hasn't moved since. She squats on the curb, her tired old face resting on her knees, her arms wrapped around her legs. All her energy is concentrated on drawing in smoke from the cigarette clamped firmly into one corner of her mouth. Dot doesn't use her hands to smoke; she keeps the cigarette between her lips, shuts the eye above the smoke and, if talking, speaks out of the other side of her mouth. Years of this has set her face askew so that her left eye stays half shut and her mouth pulled down on the right even when she is not smoking. Studying her friend, Beryl thinks of the troll guarding the bridge in a book she used to read to her grandchildren.

The minute they arrived in Los Angeles, Maud made it clear that Dot was not to smoke in her house or in her car. Maud's husband Wilfred had been a great smoker. When he died Maud had everything fumigated and didn't intend to have things stunk up again.

Each night before bed, Dot drags the only chair in Maud's guest room across the floor, kneels on it and sticks her head and shoulders out the window. Talking all the time, she puffs smoke into the California night and Beryl, in the room behind her, lies on the faded chenille spread, giggling and munching Canadian chocolate bars smuggled through customs as protection against the anticipated frugality of Maud's housekeeping.

This hour just before sleep has been the best part of the trip. Lying there looking at Dot's big rump covered in flamingo net, listening to her gravely voice, watching her arms wave around on the other side of the glass, makes Beryl feel almost happy.

Dot is a real card. Always was. During the war years when the three of them shared a room down at the bottom of Brazil Square, Dot had been the smart one, the townie who showed Beryl and Maud around the dirty streets of St. John's when they arrived green as grass, from the Cape. Dot had dragged them up to LeMarchant Road, introduced them to boys who lounged against street lights with their jackets unbuttoned. It was Dot who found them jobs at Purity Factories. It was Dot who told stories that kept them awake, laughing and squealing until Mrs. Stowe began thumping on the wall with her slipper.

Later Dot joined up with the Canadians, went to work over at Lester's Field driving huge Army trucks. The money was better, and there were lots of fellows. She tried to persuade Beryl and Maud to join her, but they stayed on at the factory. They used to bring home smashed candy to suck while they lay in the dark listening to Dot tell about the fresh Canadian soldiers she'd outsmarted.

No wonder we all got false teeth, even Maud who says she spent a fortune trying to save hers, Beryl thinks.

She doesn't want to go sit beside Dot, who looks like a half-mad old bag lady squatting there on the parking lot curb. Beryl lowers the car window but it doesn't help. The air here has an unair-like substance, like the yellow waxed gauze that used to cover cheese, as though it might press against her face, into her nose and mouth and suffocate her.

People crossing the parking lot are staring at Dot, but Dot doesn't see anyone; her open eye seems fixed on the motionless cloud of smoke suspended just above her face.

Beryl has always thought of her friend as saucy and sure of herself. "Hard" was how Beryl's mother had described Dot all those years ago when she'd brought her home to Bonavista North for a visit. And Maud's mother, Beryl's Aunt Rosie, hadn't liked the tall, quicktongued townie either: "It's not like you, Beryl to have such a loud friend! You mind she's not a bad influence on our Maud."

Beryl could understand now what her mother and aunt had meant. Dot must have had the bold good looks that were so in style back then—a look that perfectly matched the uniform, a kind of khaki coverall and perky little hat that Dot wore on the side of her head. It was about that time Dot started smoking and she probably had looked hard—hard and happy and confident.

Through the years Beryl had enjoyed imagining Dot like that—cocky and sure of herself. Not scared of the snooty Toronto sales clerks. Marching through the big stores, fudging around for the presents she sometimes sent, bossing Eric and her children and grandchildren and doing, as she often said, "Just what I damned well please."

After last night Beryl will not be able to think of Dot that way again.

Last night Dot hadn't told funny stories. Suddenly, without easing into it at all, with her head still out the window and her rear, like some great overblown flower, pointing towards Beryl, Dot said: "He beat me, you know—for years he beat the bejesus out of me every Saturday night."

At first Beryl didn't understand, thought Dot was making some kind of joke. She'd even giggled a little. "Ya I bet. Him and who else?"

But it was true. Eric Cooper, the gorgeous Canadian Sergeant who looked so much like Clark Gable that Beryl almost fainted with envy the first time she'd seen him: wonderful Eric who'd brought them stockings and chocolate bars, who told them he loved them all and one night, with the three of them standing around him on the sidewalk outside their rooming house, had sung "But You Can't Marry Three Pretty Girls"—Eric, who had married Dot and taken her off to the fairyland of Canada, this same Eric had beaten her black and blue!

"It didn't start right off, not til after young Eddy was born. After we moved to our own place. And what could I do—go home with Pop workin longshore and five other kids in that little house on York Street, the place I got out of the first week I went to work? No, by God! I'd rather grit me teeth and stick it out—and that's what I done."

Beryl listened in shocked silence as Dot told about beatings from a man everyone saw as an indulgent husband, a genial man who lived, it seemed, in the glow of his wife's good humour.

"He was all right in some ways, always good to the kids. It was just me he wanted to slap and punch. Sometimes when we was out somewhere and I'd be talkin and laughin, he'd look over at me and I'd know then that I was gonna get it when we got home."

There had been a long silence, during which Dot leaned out the window blowing smoke rings into the humming night.

"Now, of course, the poor old bugger's too weak to do anything except grouch. It's hard to say, Beryl girl, which of us came off worse—you grubbin your guts out on that fuckin potato farm, junkyard, whatever it was, with sweetie pie Tom, or me livin with Eric's lousy temper all these years and now tryin to be half decent to him til he pops off and I gets his army pension. I'll have some fling then, I can tell ya!" Dot laughed her great cackling laugh and flicked a butt into the dark garden. "I won't be like Maud spendin me days running back and forth between accountants and lawyers, tryin to double me millions. I'll just have one friggin good time!"

Dot had pulled her head in from the window, climbed down from the chair, rolled onto the bed and stared at the ceiling, planning how she would go to Las Vegas and gamble all night. "You won't see me for dust. You come too, Beryl—we'll have a ball! We won't ask Maud—poor old bat would flip right out if she lost five cents. Me and you'll have some time rubbin shoulders with all them rich muckie-mucks!"

Beryl didn't think it would happen. In Toronto she had stayed with Dot and Eric for a week. They seemed a contented enough couple despite the stroke that had left Eric unable to get about, and with days when he was so irritable that he'd ask Beryl what she was doing there and how soon she was going home. Dot ignored her husband's moods, jossed him along, tended him cheerfully and just as cheerfully patted him on the head as she rushed off to the delicatessen down the street where she worked part time and from which she brought home white paper bags of spicy salami, strange salads, flattened bits of chicken rolled around some wonderful green mixture. When Eric was cheerful Dot would run out for a six pack and they'd play 45s until midnight. If he was crooked she and Dot went to the movies or walked up and down Yonge Street looking in shop windows and at weird people.

On the day they left for California, Eric seemed like his old self. While Dot drove over to pick up Beverly, who was coming to stay with her father for the week, Eric and Beryl had sipped coffee at the round plastic table in the bay window of the second-storey apartment. Down below, a Chinese man in a long white apron sprinkled water over pots of flowers he'd carefully arranged on the sidewalk in front of his shop. It was a warm morning, and the smells of the little shops along the street drifted up, the garden smells of celery and apples, the flowers, the smell of baking bread, of curry and pizza, all mixed in with the smell of exhaust fumes and the noises of people and traffic. It was lovely, Beryl thought, so unlike her own house back home—half hidden by weeds and the rusting remains of wrecked cars, shabby and awkward among the pastel bungalows that now encircle it. She had envied Dot that morning—what a good life her friend must have had with this wonderful street to look at, with Eric's comfortable income to keep her safe.

Then Eric told her about Dot's lungs. Pre-cancerous according to the doctors. "I been telling her for years to give up smoking, telling her it would kill her, but she says she'd rather be dead than without her fags." Eric started to cry and Beryl cried too.

"She says it's all foolishness, that she never felt better in her life, that Dr. Lemann is nuts—but he told me her lungs are black as tar." Eric wiped his eyes and gave Beryl a warning look when they heard Dot and Bev coming up the stairs.

His depression returned when they were leaving for the airport. He told them they must be half cracked: "Don't go making fools of yourselves— three old women out chasing men. Never had a brain between you even in the best of times."

Beryl recalls that Dot tried to kiss him good-bye but he'd turned his face away.

Maud has been in the tax building for almost an hour. Beryl decides she cannot stand the car another minute. Painfully she forces her feet back into the spike-heeled shoes. She pulls a plaid blanket from the back seat of the car, walks over to Dot and spreads it on the curb before sitting down.

"I could wring that one's neck. Us here on a visit and her usin every morning inside some office talkin about her money. I can't get over it—comin all this way to sit in fuckin parking lots." Dot speaks without turning her head, the cigarette dangling between her lips, her eyes on the cloud of smoke.

"Maybe she's not all that well off," Beryl says. "Maybe all that talk about Wilfred havin money was just a put on."

"Na, she got money. Look how mean she is. Mean people always got money—she gets three cups outta a god damn tea bag for frig's sake! I expect to wake up one morning and find her hangin tea bags out on the line to dry. Know what Ruth Freeman next door told me? Told me she pays rent to Maud. Oh Maud's got money all right. Old Wilfred took care of that!"

"Dot, remember when Wilfred came into St. John's after Maud?"

The memory of Wilfred standing in the hallway of the house on Brazil Square brings a grin to Dot's face. "Christ yes—I can see him now, like something on a calendar, a bunch of flowers in one hand and a box of chocolates in the other—Pot of Gold they were. We ate em in bed that night."

"Remember how he hung around for weeks beggin Maud to go back to the Cape with him and help run his father's grocery store?"

"Ya, and us makin fun of him to Maud. Him with his queer haircut and his salt and pepper cap—some different from your Tom with his two-toned jackets and his big Chrysler—some different from my Clark Gable. More fool us!"

Beryl wonders if Maud had taken account of Wilfred's money when she married him. Beryl hadn't thought so then, but Maud was shrewd. Maybe she'd seen that Wilfred had prospects. She and Dot had certainly never considered the expectations of the boys they went out with. Only thought about how handsome the boys were, about what fun we were having and how pretty we looked in print dresses with our hair curled and tucked into snoods. Like something right out of the movies we were, like Rita Hayward.

How wonderful it had been to walk down the street with your arms linked, to go to movies, to ride around town in Tom's shiny car, with the taxi sign unscrewed from the roof. Later, when the tires wore out, and there were no more to be had in wartime St. John's, Tom just parked the car behind his father's house. Her darling Tom's been dead these five years but the car is still there, right where he left it, in the shadow of a row of dogberry trees. Beryl sees the car every day, rusty and rotten, its once smooth fenders crusty with holes, mice running around in the mouldy tufts of stuffing that still cling to springs of seats that had been covered in deep blue plush. Beryl remembers herself and Tom parked up on the hill in the moonlight, the town below all blacked out, her and Tom making love on those plush seats.

Dot was right, life with Tom had not been easy. Every year the same problems—never enough fodder to get the few animals through the winter, always some bit of machinery broken down in one of the fields. Tom hadn't wanted to farm, he'd wanted to drive cars, to fix cars, to own cars. Only the cars had gotten more and more complicated—and poor Tom hadn't. Strange, Beryl thinks, how some people always miss out while others seem to have things fall right into their laps.

"What happened to us?" Beryl doesn't realize she'd asked the question until Dot answers.

"I don't know, girl—if I'da known Wilfred was gonna be Smallwood's bag man I'da gone after him. Bay-whop or not, I'da snatched him right out from under Maud's nose and run off with him meself!

Your crowd down in Bonavista woulda had some fit—Maud's feller runnin off with a Mick!"

"Go on, Dot, Wilfred was a real stick-in-the-mud! You or me wouldn'ta been caught dead with him."

"Yeah—and look what we got caught with instead." Dot jumps up off the curb and begins pacing.

"If I had the friggin keys we'd go for a spin in this car—we'd go out to see that ranch ourselves. Let Maud have her fit. She's the worst driver I ever seen."

Dot kicks one of the whitewall tires on the aqua Plymouth. "Just look—all them years and she only got forty thousand miles on her—what a pisser! I'd put more miles than that on a car in one year. I bet I could hot-wire this baby—wonder how far it is out to that ranch...."

Neither Beryl or Dot can bear to think they might miss seeing the ranch.

Within hours of their arrival at Maud's, Dot had become fast friends with Ruth Freeman next door. Ruth, a homesick exile from New York and a chain smoker, invited Dot over for a puff any time she couldn't stand the purity of Maud's house.

"She talks some queer, I could listen to her all day, you'd just love her," Dot said when she came back that first day.

So Beryl was lured into the smoky kitchen to sit and listen to complaints loud and loving about Dot's Beverly and Ruth's Tracey—daughters who never took their mothers' good advice.

"My Tracey got a good heart, but smart she's not, perceptive she's not. 'You'll love it on the coast, Ma,' she tells me. Listen, this place is my idea of nowhere. I'm hot footin it back to the city as soon as the sub-let on my apartment is up. That daughter of mine can stay here if she likes, bein a glorified nursemaid to a bunch of horses. Horses, for God's sake! For this we sent her to college?"

Yesterday they finally met Ruth's daughter. A leggy, tanned, not-quite-young girl, as friendly as her mother, Tracey had invited them to see the ranch she was caretaker of out in Hidden Valley.

Beryl almost fainted with excitement when she found out who owned the ranch: "Sylvester Stallone! Will we get to see him, to meet him? Maybe I can get his autograph for our Tommy!"

Tracey dashed such hopes. "Oh he's not there. Fact is, I've been working for him for almost a year and haven't seen him yet. Come on out anyway and see how the other half lives. Ma won't come, she pretends she's allergic to horses." Tracey drew a map and told them to come out in time for lunch.

"It's almost noon, not one speck of shade!" Dot gives Maud's car another kick, lights a cigarette from the one in her mouth, shakes the pack, holds it up to her eye and peers inside. "Shag that! Only one left!"

She rejoins Beryl on the curb. They sit in grim silence surrounded by an ocean of shimmering metal.

Beryl is afraid she might cry. She's looked forward to this trip for so long. For years. And here she is, half choking in the heat and smoke, her new

dress crumpled and damp. She'll probably never
get away again and this is what she'll remember, this
parking lot, sitting here beside poor Dot with her
lungs rotting away, trying to keep from crying. She
can feel sweat beading along her hairline, on her
upper lip, between her breasts. It's all too mean; she
doesn't think she can stand it. Tears trace a slow
path down through her makeup and plop onto the
red vinyl purse she holds in her lap. Dot pretends
not to notice.

They sit in the silence and heat, a great cloud
thicker than the polluted air, darker than the cigarette smoke, hangs over them. They will never be
young again, or pretty; they will never again walk
out on a spring night and know that anything might
happen, know everything is possible. Never again
feel sure that all they can ever want is there, just
around the corner. That will not happen again.

The silence is broken by the sound of Maud's
heels clicking towards them. Sullen eyed, they
watch her cross the parking lot. How can she wear
stockings in this heat?

For the first time since their arrival Maud looks
cheerful, "It's all settled! I don't have to come back,
and I don't have to pay the estate assessment. He
found a way of delaying the reappraisal...."

Undeterred by their sour expressions she babbles on about "internal deferment funds" and
"rebates on property maintenance cost." She might
be chanting Latin for all the sense her words make
to Beryl and Dot.

"We'd better get a move on if we're going to get out to Hidden Valley in time for lunch," Maud says, as though they have been the ones holding her up.

Beryl doesn't say a word, she can hear Dot's teeth grinding. When the car begins to move their spirits lighten. Dot makes Maud stop at the first 7-11 so she can buy cigarettes. She comes back holding three double decker ice cream cones in dripping pink, yellow and green and they ride in silence, savouring each lick. They pass the switching yards, drive out onto the freeway between miles of huge signs extolling the virtues of Summersea swim suits, Kimmer Beer, Foresight Funeral Vaults, Cool deodorant. They leave the fast food restaurants, the coffee shops and service stations behind and turn up a valley of orange and lemon groves. Beryl wants to stop, to take a picture of them picking oranges, but Maud says they can do that coming back when it's cooler.

Their first sight of the ranch is disappointing. Acres of grey-brown grass strung around with barbed wire. The road, narrow now, leads to white-washed fence posts and a wide gate with "SS" burned into the wood. Just inside the gate and to the left a long trailer is parked.

A young Mexican man sits reading on the steps of the trailer. When the car stops he strolls over to the gate. "You the ladies coming to see Tracey?" His broad handsome face still holds the softness of boyhood. He opens the gate, smiles and waves them through: "Just drive on along here about a mile. See that clump of trees? The house and paddocks are in behind there."

Dot pokes her head out of the back window, "Where are the cows?"

"We don't keep cows. This isn't a working ranch, just polo ponies and horses—we've got beautiful horses." Still smiling as if something about the three women gives him immense pleasure, the young man takes a few steps back from the car.

Beryl notices that his finger is still in the book and that the book has a cover picture of what looks like a man with no skin. Not very nice. She hopes he isn't one of those perverts you hear of who read about how to chop people up, then one day go off and do it.

"Who stays out here besides Tracey?"

"Only her in the house—but this family, a man and his wife and son, live in the trailer. The man does the outside work and the wife keeps the house clean. Tracey hires extra help if they need it," Dot says.

"Who's chummie back there, then?"

"The son, I guess. Tracey said he's a medical student just stayin with his folks for cheap rent—helps with the horses."

As they drive nearer, they can see the low house through a break in the trees. Circling it are green lawns where dozens of sprinklers send rainbows of water spiraling up. Tracey is standing near the door, shading her eyes with her hand. Barefoot, wearing jeans and a white shirt, she looks like a long-haired boy.

"Come on in. I'm out back with the horses. The man who cleans their teeth is here."

She leads them into the house through a wide cool hallway and out the other side. "I'll give you a tour later, right now I'll have to get back to the barn—I bet you've never seen horses having their teeth cleaned."

The house is built in a large "U" with the open end enclosing a swimming pool and multi-levelled wooden decks across which they pick their way between lounge chairs, white iron table and chair sets, and dozens of big pots overflowing with droopy scarlet flowers. Beyond the pool and the deck is a row of trees, and beyond the trees are barns and paddocks where the horses are exercised.

Tracey tells them there are eight horses—three really, two white palominos and a big thoroughbred stallion; the others are polo ponies. The horse dentist, who Tracey calls "Val," is scraping the teeth of the stallion with a file the size of a carpenter's saw. The horse, gleaming black, stands as still as if he had been cut out of coal, his head resting awkwardly on the man's shoulder.

Tracey explains that the horse has been tranquilized. She runs around talking to the animal and patting it as she passes Val swabs and disinfectant. She seems to have forgotten the three women, but when the dentist moves to another horse she sees they are not interested and waves them away.

"Go on back to the pool and sit at that nice shady table under the awning. I'll get Lene to bring you drinks. I'll be along when we're through here."

As they go out into the sunlight Tracey picks up a telephone, and before they cross through the trees they see a short, fat woman in a striped dress and white apron walking onto the deck. The woman smiles and nods at them but doesn't speak. A wire leads from her ear to a small transistor radio clipped inside her apron pocket. She places a tray of frosted glasses on one of the tables, smiles again and walks away, swaying slightly to music they cannot hear.

Beryl sinks into a chair and kicks off her shoes. "Ah, this is the life!"

They sip the drinks, which are pale pink and taste of lemon, coconut and some fruit they do not know. The trees and the white of the house throw dappled shadows across the warm brown wood, across the blue water and red flowers. The only sound is the tinkle of ice in their glasses.

"Some place, what? Imagine havin a place like this!" Beryl says, but cannot imagine it herself. She has often dreamed of owning a nice new bungalow like the ones in the subdivision, or even an apartment like Dot's, but she's never dreamed of anything like this. Hardly thought such houses existed outside of movies and television—not like this for people to sit in and use every day. The idea overwhelms Beryl.

Maud interrupts her reflections, "This guy Stallone, a good actor, is he?"

Dot and Beryl cannot believe that Maud doesn't know who Sylvester Stallone is. "He's Rambo, girl, Rambo! Just think, he's probably sat on these very chairs!"

Beryl has seen each Rambo movie twice with her youngest grandchild. She and young Tommy had screamed and yelled for Rambo although she had not been perfectly clear what all the shooting was about.

"He's gorgeous, you should see his pictures, Maud—they'll give you the hots!" Dot leers.

Maud chooses to ignore this remark. "No, I never seen his pictures, but now you mention it, I do believe I saw his name in some magazine. He made fifty million dollars last year—I guess he can afford all this."

Beryl thinks she could sit here forever, sipping citrus juice, watching the water and flowers. But after only a few minutes, when Dot says: "We shoulda' brought swim suits—bit quiet isn't it?" she has to agree. It is a bit quiet.

She jumps up, pulls out the little Instamatic Jean and Kevin gave her last Christmas. "Let's take all our pictures. Here, first I'll take you two, then Maud can take me and Dot, then Dot can take me and Maud."

After the pictures are taken, Dot pulls her shoes off and dangles her feet in the pool. "Ah it's lovely, just right. I wonder—if I stripped off would anyone come along?"

Maud is shocked: "Don't you dare, Dot Cooper! Suppose that woman's husband comes along, or that guy Val. He'll probably come right through here when he's done with the horses."

It is the wrong thing to say. Within a minute, Dot has pulled off her orange slacks and blouse and is stepping gingerly down into the water wearing only underpants and a bra that has seen better days. Dot's arms and legs are thin, white and blueveined. She has narrow shoulders and small breasts, but at the waist she balloons into a pear shape that puffs out against the thin pink underpants.

Beryl thinks of the tall slim girl in the trim uniform, the girl with the square shoulders, the tiny waist, the smooth hips and pointed breasts. What in the world happens to our bodies as we get old? Everything sags down, eyes, mouth, breasts and bum. Her mother and Maud's mother now, you never thought of them as sagging. They'd been stiff, upright and well-braced until the day they died. But then, she reflects, they never got to float around Sylvester Stallone's swimming pool.

"Come on in you two." Dot, floating on her back, reaches over the edge of the pool, fumbles for her cigarettes, sticks one in her mouth and lights it. She paddles away, eyes closed, cigarette pointing towards the blue sky.

Maud clicks her tongue, then grins, "I can't come in, girl. Know why? Mom wouldn't let me go near the water til I learned to swim."

Dot hoots, her cigarette slips and she begins to choke. A look of panic comes over her face, she flounders.

"Do something—she's drowning!" Maud screams, doing a kind of dance at the edge of the pool.

Beryl searches for something she can toss to Dot who has now flipped onto her face. Only the dome of her round, pink bottom is showing above the water. No pole, no rope, no life preserver in sight, Beryl grabs one of the chairs and flings it in the direction of her friend.

The iron chair hits the water three inches from Dot's bottom, then it sinks. Dot rolls over, sputters, spits out the cigarette, says, "You friggers! Some help you two are!"

Laughing again, they drag her up onto the deck and pound her on the back until she recovers.

When Tracey comes from the barn, alone, Dot is afloat again. She has salvaged the chair and is flicking water at Maud and Beryl who sit on the edge with their feet in the pool.

"If you want to go in we have swim suits to fit all sizes—or we can eat right away if you're hungry."

They decide they will see the house first. Tracey tells them to go ahead, while she checks on lunch, but first she brings a striped towel for Dot to wind around her head and a terry-cloth robe to pull over the pale body and dripping underwear.

The house sprawls off in two long wings. The walls are whitewashed adobe, the furniture all cream and pale fawn. Huge windows fill the rooms with light which reflects back from golden wood floors.

In the doorway of Sylvester Stallone's bedroom they stand in awed silence until Dot yells, "At last, a chance to climb into a movie star's bed!" She dashes across the room and bounces onto the middle of the largest bed any of them has ever seen: round and fitted into a circular window.

They take pictures of each other draped across the bed pin-up girl fashion, one knee bent, head demurely tucked into one raised shoulder, eyes looking invitingly towards the camera. Even Maud has her picture taken.

Shamelessly, they explore every inch of the house, even the drawers and closets. Amid coarse comments, Dot changes into a pair of wine coloured shorts and a tee shirt, both monogrammed "SS." Maud insists that Dot put the bathrobe back on over the underwear. Beryl takes pictures of everything until at last her film runs out. They go back to look at each room one more time.

Having left their shoes beside the pool, they pad around the honey-coloured floors in bare feet. It's like walking through light, Beryl thinks. Like walking in a dream. She cannot remember ever being so happy. Oh, she's going to enjoy telling her friends about this—imagine what Vera will say! She resolves to get a piece of the underwear Dot is wearing to take home to young Tommy.

In the kitchen Lene has set out a tray of cheese and a big fruit salad before leaving for the day. Tracey piles hot croissants into a basket and pours coffee. They are hungry and eat great amounts of bread, fruit and smelly white cheese not even Tracey knows the name of.

While they eat, Tracey tells them how she's always loved horses and how she'd got this job through a friend who raises polo ponies. "I don't think I'll ever go back East, the weather is so great here!"

She asks Beryl about Newfoundland but cannot see how people live in such an uncomfortable place. They are forced then to make her understand, to regale her with stories about their childhoods, about winters with snow up to rooftops, about slid- ing down great hills, jumping across ice pans, skating over frozen ponds. They tell her about strange lights, shipwrecks, ghosts, about berrypicking—about everything. They tell her about the grand times they had when they were living on Brazil Square together during the war.

Tracey urges them on, asks questions, opens a bottle of wine, confides that the boy at the gate is her boyfriend. They will marry, she says, as soon as she gets the nerve to tell her mother. She says her mother is the world's greatest bigot.

They rush to Ruth's defence. Oh no, they say, Ruth will love the boy once she gets to know him. Tracey should just bring him over to meet her mother. What is he like, they ask, how long has she known him, are they—you know—sleeping together?

The four women huddle around the table, leaning towards each other, their voices rising, falling, one minute wet-eyed, the next shrieking with laughter.

They make confessions: Beryl, that it was she and Tom who siphoned all the gas out of the army truck that night Dot parked it outside the boarding house; Dot, that she once burnt a big hole in a satin slip of Beryl's, then cut it into little bits and flushed it down the toilet; Maud confesses that she's always—always—been in love with Dot's Eric—"That was the only reason I went back home with Wilfred, I couldn't bear to see you with Eric!" Dot says she'll mail him down to her.

By the time they get up to leave it is dark. In bare feet they walk across the wet grass to the car. Dot is still rigged out in the turban and white robe.

They line up by the car and sing "The Squid Jiggin Grounds," then, when Tracy requests another song, they sing "The Ode to Newfoundland." Maud thinks they should sing "God Bless America." Dot says fucked if she will. Still arguing, they climb into the car.

Dot gets behind the wheel and Maud doesn't object. They call their thanks to Tracey who stands in a shaft of light and waves as they drive away. They blow kisses to her young man when he comes out of the trailer to close the gate behind them.

The car speeds along the narrow road, its lights make a long tunnel in the blackness. Beryl could swear the engine sounds different, happier, with Dot at the wheel. They drive with the windows open; down past orchards, through the scent of lemons and oranges rising in the cool air, on down towards the lights of the city, the soft night slipping past.

They sing all the songs they know: war songs and love songs, cowboy songs, folk songs, commercials and rock, and old Methodist hymns only Maud can remember all the words to.

Dot holds the wheel lightly, steering the big car with easy confidence. "Ya know what we're gonna do? Ya know what we're all gonna do next year? We're going to Jerusalem. Ruth Freeman told me she's goin. We'll go too—all of us. They do some kind of special dance there called the Hora." Dot lifts both hands from the wheel and whirls them above her towel-covered head.

The car barrels along. Garish signs, transformed by speed, spin into long ribbons of light.

Inside the car three women, heads thrown back, sing: "Shall we gath-er at the riv-er, the beau-ti- ful, the beau-ti-ful the riv-er; gath-er with the Saints at the riv-er that flows by the throne of God."

Not A Face You Know

From the second floor of the Wabush Inn I'm looking straight across the street to Valu-Mart and I can
see Mr. Coveyduck was right. More customers are
goin in and out of the store today—more than any
day since I came to Lab City. There are even more
people than usual on the street. Right this minute
two old men and a woman are stopped outside the
store talkin, every now and then one of them looks
over at the hotel. I got the chair pushed back a bit
so they can't see me up here in the window.

I only spoke to the man twice—that first night
when he came into Valu-Mart and next morning at
the coffee shop. I keep tellin myself it don't matter
to me. And God knows, apart from their bein curious, it don't matter to anyone else around here. For
all that, I been hours now tryin to remember everything I can about him. It's the least I can do.

Usually I don't mind workin past closin time but
that night I was wild to get away. I wanted to take a
bath, put on my makeup and change into the green

dress before Trev got back to our room. This would be our last night together for months and everything had to be just right.

Also I was dyin for a smoke. I had a pack of cigarettes in the pocket of my smock. I got one out and held it under my nose while I watched this Chinese-lookin man fill grocery carts. I'd never seen anyone buy so much. As each cart was filled he lined it up beside my checkout—takin his own sweet time—never lookin my way or sayin he was sorry to have come in so late.

The bounce was gone out of my hair, too—which meant I was goin to have to wash it before we went out. I didn't even want to go to Mavis's that night. I'd have much rather stayed home—just me and Trev in our room at the Wabush Inn—havin a bit of fun, laughin, gettin beer and sandwiches brought up from downstairs. I still can't get over how nice it is livin in a hotel. Pure heaven, sendin downstairs for meals, havin a maid come in every day to clean up, make your bed, even take away the dirty towels.

Trev tells me I'm gettin spoiled. He says I'll have to learn to cook if we ever find an apartment. Mavis and Denis aren't even livin together and she cooks him supper every night—or so Trev says. Still, he hasn't suggested we look for a place of our own, so I'm not too worried. What's the sense, anyway, when Northern Tel is willin to pay most of his hotel bill?

Apartments are scarce up here and Trev says the ones advertised are real dumps. For all that I was sure Mavis's place would be smart. Probably have modern furniture and those light wooden floors you see on TV shows—all the lamps and cushions colour coordinated.

"We'll have to take somethin to drink," Trev told me that morning. "Here—get a nice bottle of wine and some beer from the back place. Maybe Old Coveyduck'll let you have a special price." He pushed a fifty dollar bill into my hand. Trev is good about money.

Whenever Trev and Denis talk about their job it sounds like there'd be just two of them up at the satellite station. But when I asked Trev which of them would do the cookin, he gave me that look, like I'm after missin some bit of information everyone else knows.

"Don't think me or Denis will be doin that shit work do ya? Na, Charlie Chan cooks and cleans for us," he said. "Gets lost between shifts, Charlie do. Queer stick, pure hates it up here. Still, he'll be back. Them Chinks loves money too much to give up a good payin job!"

I'd never seen the man before but I guessed the customer I was watchin must be this cook. He'd stopped loadin carts and was just starin at the spice shelf. His face had a strange, blank look, as if he was asleep on his feet. By rights I should have gone over and asked if I could help. But I didn't. I just leaned on the counter and sniffed the cigarette. I would have lit up but for Mr. Coveyduck bein out in the stock room and dead set against smokin in the store.

Pushed under the cash register by my feet I had the Valu-Mart bag of beer and the bottle of wine I'd bought lunch time in the profit place. The profit

place is what Mr. Coveyduck calls the room attached
to the back of Valu-Mart. It's really a liquor store but
you have to come in through the supermarket to get
to it. On IOC paydays there are more customers in
the profit place than in the supermarket, but most
of the time it's empty.

I was worried about the wine. While I waited for
the man to finish his order I lifted the bag onto the
counter and looked at the bottle—"Ambience" it
was called. It might be the wrong kind. Mavis, who's
a school teacher, will know all about wine—Denis
Poirier too, him bein French Canadian.

The label on the wine had a picture of a green
valley with a castle in it, a creamy castle outlined
against purple mountains. It reminded me of the
covers of those books Mom reads. Only there's
always a woman in front of the castle on the book
covers—a beautiful woman wearing a dress that
floats around her like mist. Sometimes there's a
man, too. The men are usually dark like Trev—and
he's either kissin the woman or standin behind,
gazin down at her bare shoulders with a half starved
look on his face.

Can you imagine? Someone my mother's age
readin that romantic shit about women bein swept
away, livin happy ever after? Still, who can blame
her? What a life—stuck in a Newfoundland outport
with my father! And here was I, her daughter, wonderin if I bought the right wine—and in a few minutes I'd be runnin across the street to a hotel where
I got maid-service and a real silk dress hangin in my
closet!

The thought of how far from home I was cheered me up. I just wish the girls back in Davisporte could see me and Trev. See us leavin the hotel, him in his white shirt, me in that green dress, arms linked, laughin, steppin into the night. Going out to dinner just like real people.

I decided that if Trev didn't mind, I'd take my camera to Mavis's—get a picture to send home. Trev probably won't want me to do that, though. He said it was hokey the time I asked the desk clerk to take a picture of us in the lobby of the Wabush Inn.

"What you gonna do with a picture—prove to mommy you're not barefoot, pregnant and in an igloo?" he said. Trev gets along fine with Dad and my brothers but he don't like Mom.

Mom's not keen on him either. First when Trev went away she told me that was the last I'd ever see of him—good riddance too, she said. Then, last spring, when he comes home drivin a Chevy Blazer and with money in his pocket, she's still not satisfied—couldn't believe Trev had this good job with the telephone company or that he'd kept his word and come back for me like he promised.

"If what he's tellin you's true, then he's the first Fowler ever amounted to anything." Mom's got this way of twitchin her nose when somethin don't suit her.

Mom's right, the Fowlers are a rough crowd. But Trev is different. For all he was five grades ahead of me in school he was always nice to me. Once, when we were all out at Ochrepit Pond, I remember watchin him dive—jumpin off the cliff—his body slicing down into the water, hardly makin a splash.

I was only thirteen but I think I wanted him even then.

Afterwards, when we were goin out together, I asked how come he could swim so good. He told me when he was eight his father threw him out of the fishin boat.

"I did somethin stupid and the Old Man just flung me over the side. It was late in the year—bitter—still he let me flounder around in the water til I thought I was gonna drown. Then, just before I gave up, he shoved an oar at me and hauled me into the boat."

I cried when he told me that story. Imagine, tossin a little boy into the sea, a child—most likely wearin a heavy jacket—gaspin for breath in that icy water.

But Trev just laughed, like he thought what his father done was all right. "The old fucker don't mess around," he said.

I never told Mom that story—maybe if I had she wouldn't be so hard on Trev.

When I told her I was leavin home, drivin up here with Trev, Mom was so mad I thought she was goin to hit me—or even lock me up, like I heard tell of people doin to their daughters in olden times.

"Well Miss, I hopes you knows what you're takin on. I hopes all them foolish ideas you got about away comes true. Hope you don't find out there's worse places than here, worse jobs than guttin fish!" she said when she saw I was set on goin.

Just before I got into Trev's car she gave me this quick kiss on the cheek and pushed an envelope into my jeans pocket. Wasn't until we were crossing the Gulf, sittin at one of them little tables in the bar of the Caribou, that I opened the envelope. Inside was a note and ten twenty-dollar bills.

"Dear Vicki, You're going to find it hard living in a strange place. I remember what it was like when I worked in St. John's—people everywhere and not a face you know. Put this money away just in case you need it for coming home."

The words didn't sound like Mom even though it was her hand—round even letters I used to try and copy when I was little. The note and the money started me crying. Trev said I shouldn't be such a sook—I knew him didn't I? Besides, everyone was friendly in Lab City and I'd love it.

Trev and I spent Mom's money on a night in a big hotel in Quebec City—the place that looks like a castle. How could I keep money to myself when Trev was bein so good, payin for all the gas and food and buyin me things? Doesn't have a mean bone in his body, Trev doesn't.

Anyway it didn't matter because Trev had cheques from Northern Tel waitin when we got to Wabush. Then, Trev and Denis bein good buddies, I met Mavis. She's Mr. Coveyduck's niece and it was her got me this job in Valu-Mart.

"Trev's old girl friend, Danielle, worked for my uncle too—but she took off just after loverboy left. Broken hearted, she was!" Mavis told me the very first night the four of us went out together. Mavis tucked her head into her chin and looked up at Trev through her eyelashes—I think she tries to copy

Princess Di. But Trev gave her this dirty look as if to tell her to shut up.

Later, back in our room at the Wabush Inn, Trev lay on the bed watchin Sports Round-up while I brushed my hair and watched his reflection in the mirror. I was tryin to work out in my mind how to ask him about this girl Danielle. Finally I just said, casual like, "Is Danielle French?"

You never saw a person move so fast. He came up off the bed like a spring was under him. He grabbed me, pulled me around so I dropped the brush.

"Is Danielle French? What's her last name? What do she look like? Who was she? What did you do with her?" He made his voice high and squeaky, copyin mine, and he jerked at my wrist, twistin my arm back. "A bit of advice, Victoria—don't get like your old woman!"

I started to cry. Trev realized he'd frightened me. He stopped then, right away, put me down on the bed and began kissin the finger marks around my wrist.

"Don't mind that Mavis, she's a real bitch! Been tryin to get Denis on the hook for years. Jealous of how you got me wrapped around those little fingers of yours." He kissed all my fingers. "Jealous of your pretty eyes, your pretty hair, your pretty tits."

Trev laughed. He talked and kissed me until I was laughin too. I said I was sorry—and I was—I know how he hates bein quizzed about things. Then we made love and I haven't mentioned Danielle since. Not even to ask Mavis about her.

"Please Miss, can you find the oregano?"

The Chinese man finally pushed his fifth cart into place and stood beside the checkout, smilin at me—a kind of half-smile as if he wasn't sure he should. From what Trev said I expected the cook to be old and fat, but he was young. The skin of his face looked smooth—as if he had never shaved. And he was good lookin—real good lookin for a foreigner.

"It should be down here," I said and led him back to the shelf he'd been starin at earlier.

I knelt down and began to sort through the bottles of spice and herbs. Some of them looked like they'd been there since the Flood. Right at the back I found the oregano.

"You must be Mr. Chan, the cook for the satellite station. Trev Fowler is my boyfriend," I said when I passed him the bottle.

This queer look came over his face. He was still smilin but his eyes changed. "My name is not Chan but I am the cook at the station."

I knew I'd said something wrong, "I'm sorry, I must have got the name mixed up—I don't know Chinese names," I told him. Then, seeing my apology had only made things worse, I said, "I'm sorry," again.

He took the bottle. We were almost the same height. He stood studyin my face, as if somethin about me puzzled him.

His skin was toast colour, browner than the Chinese I see on television. His white shirt was tucked into grey pants. Although both his shirt and pants were plain as could be there was somethin about him that reminded me of men you sometimes see in late night movies dancin behind the singer.

"Of course you would not know. Don't apologize," he opened his hands, palms outwards in a way I've never seen before.

"I am Vietnamese, not Chinese. My name is Guyen Van Thom."

"Mr. Thom," I said. I tried to copy the sound.

"No, I would be Mr. Guyen—Guyen is my family name—but you should call me Thom." He smiled and made the graceful movement with his hands again.

"My name is Vicki Soper," I said and held out my hand. I felt big—awkward as a cow. His hand was narrow and cool.

Then the steel door from the stockroom clanged shut.

"Hallo Tom. Back again then? Despite all?" smiling to himself, Mr. Coveyduck came in and began to pile bags of potatoes under a sign that said "Today's Special."

"Back again," Mr. Guyen said. He did not stop to talk to Mr. Coveyduck but followed me to the checkout where we started unloadin the first cart.

I called to Mr. Coveyduck, askin if he wanted me to lock up. On the way back I grabbed six empty cartons from a stack beside the door and put them on the counter.

"You didn't take any of our wonderful potatoes?" I said, tryin to make a joke, like I would with any customer.

"I have learned that the new ones will be in a week after Mr. Coveyduck marks the old ones down—until then we will make do with rice," he said in this solemn voice. He spoke slowly but not with that funny accent I expected. He sounded something like Denis, as if he might speak French.

"But how will you get the new potatoes?" I asked. I was really not talkin to him anymore—just passin time.

"Oh the telephone company is very generous, they have an open account here. I phone for anything we run out of and Mr. Coveyduck puts the order on the IOC train."

"What's it like up there—up at the station?"

Fact is, Trev's right, I am a nosey person. I likes to know about things—and after all my boyfriend'll be livin up there for the next three months. Almost the only thing Trev ever told me about the station was that it somehow bounces phone calls and television shows off a satellite and back to communities along the Labrador coast—and that tomorrow morning he and Denis Poirier would take the Iron Ore Company train to the end of the line in order to get there.

True, Trev and Denis sometimes chat about their job when we're out havin a drink. But it's almost like they're talkin in a kind of code—Anik, Telesat, Intelsat. Mavis says it sounds like Innuktituk.

I think myself the men don't want us to understand what they do. Whenever we ask anything they laugh and tell us it's just a job. Good pay, but they earn every cent of it, day and night watchin a panel of lights and dials. Then they grumble about bein stuck up in the bush.

"Hard work, but someone's gotta do it," Denis usually says and they click beer bottles as if there's some great secret, as if it's so important me and Mavis couldn't possibly understand. I've heard my father and brothers talk the same way about the sea and boats.

None of us said so, but I could see by then that Trev and Denis were both bored with their long holiday, tired of goin to movies, playin afternoon cards, watchin hockey games—tired even of me and Mavis. "Playin house," Trev calls it.

The Vietnamese man didn't answer my question—just kept piling groceries onto the counter.

I decided to try again, "How many shifts have you done up there, then?"

"Twelve." He was stacking things one on top of the other, carefully, in little groups: the soup, the milk, the cereal, the tinned cream, the meat. I could see that he'd bought the best of everything.

"I've completed twelve. This will be the fourth shift I've done with your friend and Denis Poirier—it will be my thirteenth."

"You should be careful, then," I said.

His hands went still all of a sudden, his head jerked up. His face had this terrible frightened look.

I pulled back so fast that a pile of Bic lighters behind me fell to the floor. "The thirteenth—the thirteenth, you know—it's only old foolishness—it's supposed to be unlucky." I could hear a kind of panic in my own voice.

"Ah yes, the unlucky day. In my country there is a saying, 'for the coward all days are unlucky.' " He bent forward to lift a case of tinned peaches onto the counter. I couldn't see his face.

Suddenly I felt tired of talking to him. I couldn't think of one more thing to say. All I wanted was to get rid of him, rid of the strain of tryin to understand what was goin on behind his smooth face. Wasn't fair his comin in so late—it was almost six and I wasn't goin to have time to wash my hair. I looked over at Mr. Coveyduck, but he seemed not to have heard a word we'd said.

I started to slam the groceries through, jabbin at the keys, pushin tins and bottles along the counter, droppin them any old way into the cardboard boxes until the man moved to the other end himself and began packing things carefully.

We didn't say another word. It seemed forever until the register spit out the total.

Mr. Coveyduck came over then, "You go on, girl—this is a big night, isn't it?" He winked at me like he do sometimes. Then he pulled off the tape and said, "$968.75—the best of everything, Tom. Well, I s'pose Northern Tel's good for it."

I took off my smock, ran and hung it in the stock room. When I got back they were talkin. Neither of them looked my way. The Vietnamese man was leaning forward like he was tryin to explain somethin to Mr. Coveyduck who just let out with this big laugh.

"Oh go on with ya—there's not a bit of harm in that young feller," Mr. Coveyduck said as I went through the door. I looked back and saw him clap Mr. Guyen on the shoulder in that nice, fatherly way he has when he's not bein a dirty old man.

Next morning, the very first person I saw when I came out of our room was the Vietnamese. As I stepped into the hallway he was comin out next door. I know I must have turned beet-red thinkin he could have heard me and Trev durin the night. Before either of us could speak, Trev called me back into the room—only to tell me I shouldn't bother to bring up any coffee. "I'll get another forty winks—bye, love," he waved his hand at me without even openin his eyes.

By then the Vietnamese man was gone. I went on down to the hotel coffee shop where I usually eat breakfast on work days. I can watch the front of Valu-Mart from the window booth and just go over when Mr. Coveyduck comes and unlocks the door. The restaurant seemed empty but I could hear Pam in the kitchen talkin to someone. I poured my own coffee and took it to my usual booth.

I was just puttin my cup down when I saw him sittin there. He was slouched in one corner. His face had that same blank look I noticed the day before. Both of us were startled. I stepped back just as he began to stand up, between us we sloshed most of my coffee across the table. Makin more fuss that was needed, we pulled handfuls of paper napkins out of the dispenser.

"Two early birds, are ya? Havin breakfast, Vicki?" Pam swooped down like she does, spongin up the coffee as she talked.

"How goes it, Tom? They told me you was back—have a good holiday, then? All ready to go up in the woods with them other two? I hear tell the company's changin back to six week shifts next year.

Crowd here's the same—always movin shifts around. Don't s'pose it makes much difference one way or t'other, do it?"

Pam brought more coffee, and then, still askin and answerin her own questions, went back into the kitchen.

"Maybe someone is joining you for breakfast?" Mr. Guyen picked up his cup as if to move to another table but put it down when I told him Trev was dead to the world and wasn't comin down.

For some reason I didn't want to look at his face, so I kept staring down at his hands. I never noticed hands before but his were narrow, long fingered and always moving.

"I am sorry if I said anything to offend you last night. I was very tired." His index finger outlined a wet circle on the table.

"What did you do on your holiday?" The way I said it sounded like a school assignment, but I couldn't think of anything else to ask.

"Oh I do not do much. I visit my mother in Montreal." Then he asked if I visited my mother often.

I said that I'd never been away from my mother until last month. I told him about my father and brothers, how they fish for whatever's on the go, and about Tina and Doss workin in the plant: "I'm that glad to get away from the place, I can't believe my luck!" I said.

He said he had a friend in Newfoundland, a young woman from India who is studyin at Memorial University: "She tells me to come visit her—she loves it there."

I felt queer then, thinkin he knew more about Newfoundland than I did, more about a lot of things maybe. "I never been to St. John's; they do say it's all right in there if you got a job. I s'pose goin to university is different from workin in a place. You ever been to university?"

"I go to McGill—I have an arrangement—I study on my time off."

"You didn't have no holiday then, not really?" I asked.

"Oh no—it was a holiday! The best kind of holiday. Doing something so different it seems like being in another world."

He didn't seem to mind answerin questions about himself so I kept on. After all, how often would I have the chance to talk to such a stranger? He told me he'd been in Canada since he was nine. After that war in his country him and his mother were the only two left in his family. He said this quickly, and then, not givin me another turn at a question, asked if I liked Lab City.

I told him yes, I liked it fine and slipped in a question about whether the friend at Memorial University was his girl friend. It was like talkin to a child—like he was obliged to answer anything I asked.

"I don't know, I do not think so—we write many letters but we have not seen each other for almost two years." He smiled, then shrugged and made the graceful movement that reminded me of dancers on television, so I asked if he danced.

"I have danced—once or twice I've danced—but there are many dances I do not know." His voice had gotten tense again and I began to feel like I had the night before, trapped and stunned—like he was looking for some answer, only he hadn't asked the question.

"There are many things I do not know—I have concentrated too much on music, I think," he said.

Just then I saw Mr. Coveyduck pull into the parking lot across the street. I jumped up, muttered something about the boss killin me if I was late again and rushed out. I didn't even say good-bye.

Mr. Coveyduck was putting a new tape into the cash register when I came into the store. Instead of goin over to the checkout I started tidyin this big pile of cardboard boxes by the window. That way I could keep my eye on the door across the street.

At 9:30 the blue and white telephone van with Denis drivin pulled up outside the hotel. Thom came out right away and crawled in behind with the equipment and boxes of groceries. It looked to me like there wasn't a word between them. Denis waited about one minute before tappin out three loud blasts on the horn.

I don't think I like Denis Poirier, he got a sneaky little face. I wondered where he and Mavis said their goodbyes. Mavis says the two of them can't live together because she's a school teacher. She says things like: "Teachers get tarred and feathered if they shack up." But Trev told me Denis don't really want to live with her. Denis was certainly set to stay on last night, though. I noticed his hand down Mavis's blouse before me and Trev got out the door.

"Looks like the cat that ate the cream, you do— s'pose you'll last without it?" Mr. Coveyduck came over and stood gachin out the window. I stopped even pretendin to stack boxes. Denis blew the horn again.

"I allow loverboy's beat to a snot. Still, he better get a move on—they got to be down for the train before ten."

"You ever been up to the satellite station?" I asked before he got a chance to get back to his favourite subject.

"Once. They had a bush fire up there three years ago—half the men in the place were up helpin put it out. Pretty good it was—the phone company paid us all double time."

"What's it like up there?" I said. Then, seein I'd made the question sound too important, I giggled, "Oh you know—will Trev be comfortable?"

"It's okay, I s'pose. None of the comforts of the Wabush Inn, of course," he leered. "But it's a decent enough place. There's only the two buildings, an office where the transmitter and equipment is, and a modern bungalow with four bedrooms and a big common room and kitchen. Everything in the way of convenience—small TVs in the bedrooms and a big one in the living room, video player, books, tapes, even a billiard table and exercise bike. Just about anything you'd want—except booze and women!" he patted my behind.

I didn't slap at his hand like I usually do, just moved away a bit and asked what the outdoors was like.

"The outdoors—well, that's not so comfortable. Jeezely bleak. They built the station on this big bald rock with bush all around, spruce and scrubby pine.

They got a rope stretched between the front door of the house and the door of the office 'cause in winter there's times you can't see a hand in front of your face, not even in daytime."

I tried to imagine it. The wind howlin, Trev holdin onto the rope, seein nothin, inchin forward through all that whiteness. I was glad it wasn't winter.

"What's it like now, this time of year?"

"Sunny—friggin hot a good part of the time. Still and all, I thinks I'd rather be up there in winter." The horn sounded again, "If that boyfriend of yours don't come down soon they're gonna miss the train—the crew they're relievin'll be some pissed."

The way Mr. Coveyduck talks you'd think Trev was retarded or something! "He'll be down in a minute—the track's only at the end of the street, for Lord's sake," I said.

Still, I was startin to wonder what was keepin him. For all Debbie who comes to clean our room is about forty and got three kids, I seen Trev more than once sizin her up. Useless, even to think about stuff like that. I asked Mr. Coveyduck what's wrong with the station in summertime.

"For one thing it's harder to get in and out of. When there's a good snow down they can take the skidoo from where the train track ends up to the station, make it in less than an hour. But this time of year, on that old tank contraption it'll probably take half the day to go the twelve miles over bog and bush. Then there's the friggin flies."

"Worse than here?" Flies in Lab City can be a proper torment.

"Don't tell me Trev didn't tell ya what flies are like up in the country? Don't waste much time talkin do ye? Sure the air up there's black with 'em this time of year—bites like hell. I never seen the likes— big as dogs! The men got to wear nets over their heads and faces every time they goes outdoors— jacket things that ties down over their hands even, else they'd be et alive and I...."

Then the horn blasted, and Trev burst out of the hotel door, tossed his bags into the back of the van and jumped in beside Denis. They took off with a screech of rubber. Denis must have made some crack about how long he'd been waitin. As the van pulled away I could see that him and Trev were yellin at each other. My arm dropped down and I stood there feeling lost and a bit foolish. Trev had- n't even looked in my direction.

"Never mind, he'll be back before you know it," Mr. Coveyduck said, comin over all fatherly-like again. "And I tell you one thing, he'll eat well. That Chink is some cook."

"He's not a Chink—he's Vietnamese," I said, real crabby.

Had no effect on him, of course. He winked and went off to the stockroom singin, "What ain't we got! We ain't got dames!"

I wondered if I would miss havin sex. I didn't before. But then we'd only done it twice—once in the back of Cory Hefferton's van and once in the school gym. Now it's different, like we'd been mar- ried for a month. I wondered what I'd do after work, stuck in Trev's hotel room by myself.

Turned out it wasn't too bad. By the third week I had to admit that I didn't miss Trev half as much as I'd expected. I couldn't call him but he called me almost every night. The telephone company didn't mind. He would call late, after I was in bed, keepin me on the phone for an hour or more. First off I was worried that the girl on the hotel desk might be listenin, but after a while I just closed my eyes, curled down in bed and did whatever Trev told me to do. I never tried anything like that before and I was surprised what my hands and Trev's voice could do. Sometimes I thought it was better than him bein there.

With Trev away I thought about Mom and the girls more, pictured how nice it'd be if Tina or Doss would come up here to work. I started writin home every week.

I half expected Mavis to drop me like a hot potato once Trev was gone, but she didn't. We went to the movies three or four times and we made plans to go down to Quebec City for a weekend when I got some money saved. Trev wasn't keen on the idea but Mavis said I got to learn how to handle him. I didn't tell Mavis about the phone calls, of course. Still, I'd like to know if Trev did the same things with Danielle.

Then, the day before yesterday, when I came in to work Mr. Coveyduck was packin up this order of groceries to send to the station. I helped him stow things in boxes. Layerin in newspapers between the frozen food I saw two forty ouncers of Johnny Walker.

"I thought the company don't let them have booze up there," I said.

Mr. Coveyduck said it was his own little treat he puts in for the boys. "Just pretend you didn't see—makes sense to keep good customers happy."

I been wonderin how Valu-Mart got the Northern Tel business when there's a big supermarket over in the mall.

"Next time you sends an order up, can I put a cake in it for Trev?" I asked.

"Sure, long's it's not one them girls jumps out of. I can see you now, in your altogether, poppin out of a cake," he said. Mr. Coveyduck is all right—you just have to know how to take him.

That was Tuesday. That night Trev didn't phone but I wasn't worried, I guessed that he and Denis were havin a drinkin party. I wondered if Thom was drinkin with them. Trev never mentioned the Vietnamese cook, and I never told him about the talks we had in the store and the coffee shop.

On Wednesday morning I asked Mr. Coveyduck if Thom had phoned in the order we sent up to the station on the day before.

"No, that was only basic stuff put on the train every four weeks or so." He laughed. "Heard from the poor little son of a bitch last night, though."

I didn't say a word. The less interest I shows, the more Mr. Coveyduck is likely to tell me.

"It's the same every time—since your boyfriend got here anyway. The Chink is sure Trev is gonna murder him. Tries to persuade me not to send booze up to the boys—and I got the feeling he tries to keep them from drinkin it when it arrives.

Anyway it's like clockwork—after I sends up a bottle I can count on gettin an SOS in the middle of the night. 'You must come up here, Mr. Coveyduck, the crazy man is going to kill me—I beg you to come up,' he bawls over the phone. First time it happened I half believed him. Nothin ever comes of it, of course. Trev is good as gold, wouldn't hurt a fly. There's Dave now, I bet he got called out of bed, too," he said as a Mountie came in.

"Jesus, Warren, how many times do I have to get after ya not to send booze up to them fuckers?" The Mountie was Dave Williams. I seen him around, once he went bowlin with a crowd of us.

"Forget it b'y. No law's been broken and by now Tom is back in the kitchen none the worse for wear," Mr. Coveyduck told him.

"I wouldn't be so sure, poor bugger called me three in the morning, sounded like he was gonna have a heart attack. He'd locked himself into his bedroom, said Trev had a hammer and was beating the door down."

Then the Mountie turns to me, gives me this dirty look, "You should teach that boyfriend of yours some manners."

The nerve! But before I got a chance to say one word he turns back to Mr. Coveyduck. "Well I'm a bit worried—called up there soon as I signed in this morning but can't raise an answer."

"I'm not surprised. I daresay Trev's sleepin it off and Denis is barely able to sit upright—he'd be in front of that switchboard nursin the worst jeezely hangover you ever seen. Hope the phone company don't choose today to do a check," Mr. Coveyduck says. Then he gives the Mountie a shove, "Come on back and pick yourself a brace of rabbits—I still got ten froze."

Last night me and Mavis went over to the mall to see "Pretty Woman." I didn't say anything about the drinkin or about the Mountie. After the movie I told her I had a headache and came back here early, just in case Trev might phone. Only he didn't. I spent a good part of the night awake, wonderin what was happening up at the station.

Nine o'clock this morning Mr. Coveyduck still hadn't turned up at the store, so I went over and rang the bell by the door but no one came. I got no key, so I just leaned against the window and waited.

No one ever changes anything in the window. There's this old poster offerin a free ice scraper with every quart of antifreeze. All the writing and the polar bear holdin the ice scraper is faded to a pale blue. It was nice this morning with the sun shinin on my face and arms. I stood there havin my smoke, thinkin last night's worries were just as silly as that blue bear. Thom Guyen is all right. So is Trev. He'll phone tonight for sure. I was some glad I hadn't said anything to Mavis.

Must of been nine-thirty when Mr. Coveyduck drove up. The car swerved around and stopped right beside me, under the No Parking sign. After he got out he kind of held onto the car door like he was sick or drunk—though I never seen him either way. Then he looked up and I saw that bewildered look men have when they been shocked. I can remember the same look on father's face the day we found out Vern was drowned. As if his   daytime expression had fallen off, and there was nothing to replace it with.

Mr. Coveyduck unlocked the store and I followed him in. He didn't even move to turn on the lights. "He's dead. They got him down at the train station rolled up in a blanket," he said.

I didn't say nothin. Just stood there runnin my fingers along the metal edge of the counter. I knew he was talking about the Vietnamese man. But he said, "Oh Trev's all right, wasn't Trev, don't think that. Trev had nothin to do with it. Tom went out of his mind—them foreigners gets like that sometimes. He run off—was out in the bush for a day and a night—roamin around, probably couldn't find his way back. He was et!"

"Et?"

"The skin on his face and hands is practically gone—ate off him by flies. Worst thing I ever seen." Mr. Coveyduck kept on talking. Somethin about the police contacting the company's head office, about an autopsy. His voice seemed far off.

"He was studying music," I said. I felt sick, like I was going to throw up.

"Later today they're sendin a new shift in, so Denis and Trev can come out. They'll have to swear a statement about what happened...."

"Trev good as killed him," I said.

This time he heard me. "Don't talk such crap! The fella killed hisself. Cracked, some of them people are. Not like us—afraid of their own shadows. Trev's all right—there's no harm in Trev."

I didn't say anything. Mr. Coveyduck was tellin me what a busy day we were goin to have. "Anything

like this brings people into the store," just as if he
expected everything to be normal. He switched on
the long fluorescent lights.

"We all good as killed him," I said. Then I really did start to bawl. Loud, like I always do, not nice
and ladylike the way you see in movies. "No one listened to him. You sent up that whisky—we could
have done something—could have sent the
Mountie up. We didn't do one thing to help him!"

Suddenly Mr. Coveyduck was standin right in
front of me, shoutin like I was deaf. "Now look here,
miss! You'd just better calm yourself down—better
start thinking about your boyfriend's job—about
your own job, too, comes to that!" He took me by
the shoulders and shook me—which made me bawl
all the louder.

Then the door slammed and two women came
in. They just stood there lookin at the two of us. He
gave me a little push towards the door. "Go on
home—get Pam to make you a cup of strong tea."

He walked me towards the door. "And for
Christ's sake calm down," he whispered, "just think
about Trev—think about what I said."

"She's a bit upset," he told the women, "I'll be
with you ladies in a minute." He opened the door
and stepped out onto the sidewalk with me. "No
more of this foolish talk about blame. Mind now, no
one's to be blamed except the man himself! Always
said there was something soft about him—afraid all
the time! Worse than a woman."

By the time I got up here I'd already stopped
cryin. But I can't stop thinkin. All morning I been
sittin in this chair just lookin down on the street,

thinkin about how scared he must have been out in the woods—alone all night and all day. How long did it taken him to die?

After a while I got up and phoned the airport. They told me there's a seat still left on the midnight flight. I'm pretty sure I got enough money saved to get as far as Quebec City. The very thought of going off by myself frightens me—it frightens me a lot. I pulled the old brown suitcase Mom used to take into hospital down off the closet shelf. It was half-full of things I been savin since I got here—swizzle sticks from my drinks on the boat, a plastic lobster from that restaurant in New Brunswick, tags off my silk dress, even my Bad Bowler Award, stuff like that.

Finally I dropped it all into the wastepaper basket, everything except the label off the bottle of wine we had that last night Trev was home. I was cryin again, just lookin at the wine label and rememberin all the good times we had and cryin, when Mavis phoned.

"Hi—you sick or something?" She was callin from the school, I could hear kids' voices in the background.

"No. Yes. Well, I don't feel so good."

"Yeah—I called the store. Uncle Warren said you were home sick. Better perk up quick, girl! There's dancing tonight!" she hummed a bit of some song. Then, when I didn't say anything she asked if I knew that Denis and Trev were comin home tonight. "You do know, don't you?"

I said I was feelin pretty bad about what happened up at the station.

"About the poor guy getting himself killed? Why should you feel bad about that? I mean sure, I'm sorry—but no more than if I saw it on TV."

"We didn't see it on TV, though," I said.

"Oh grow up, girl—these things happen. It's awful, but it's got nothing to do with you or me—Trev or Denis either. I don't think they even liked the Chinese guy much. Things are always happening to foreigners—we people can't be all the time bawling over their troubles."

I couldn't think of a thing to say.

Mavis's patience ran out, "Look, they'll be here by dark. And for all we know they might be back up there again tomorrow, or the day after. So we'd better make the most of tonight. Get a grip on yourself girl. Go take a bath, fix your hair and put on that gorgeous dress—Okay?"

She didn't wait for an answer, just hung up, and I went back to the window. There is a crowd of teenagers outside Valu-Mart now, boys and girls foolin around, drinkin Pepsi and tormentin each other.

I still got the wine label scrunched in my hand. I smooth it out, lick it and stick it on the window glass—like we used to do Christmastime with paper snowflakes. Light shines right through the purple mountain, through the green fields and cream coloured castle—such a pretty place, a place you'd like to walk into and live forever after.

Unfinished Houses

For years the thought of going back—"coming home" her mother would say—ran like a subtext through their marriage. Lenora and Dave talked about it every time they visited, agreeing that St. John's was more interesting than it had been when they were growing up. Nowadays the town had art galleries, theatres, even a symphony orchestra. Still, returning was just a thought—a nice way to end a visit. "We'll be back to live some day," they would say as they waved goodbye. Then Dave got the job offer.

By now Dave had been with DeChem Canada for twenty years. They were financially secure, owned a small sailboat and a condo overlooking the lake. In summer they sailed and played golf, in winter Lenora taught flower arranging three afternoons a week just for the fun of it. They had a congenial circle of friends in Mississauga. Dave had been President of the Chamber of Commerce twice and that year he was also on the board of the Society

of Ontario Chemical Engineers. There was no reason, really, to move, nothing except a vague restlessness, an awareness of being in their fifties, of
Dave's having gone as far as he was going to go with
DeChem. And the children were gone, their son
transferred to California, their daughter married
and living in Vancouver.

"Besides, it's a hell of a compliment to be asked
to head up a new government laboratory," Dave
said. Lenora knew then that he wanted the job,
knew he was thinking how it would be to return to
St. John's, move into a big house in the old part of
town, buy a larger boat, join the yacht club, enter-
tain, show old school pals how successful he was.
Success, she imagined, must be sweeter in a place
where people know how far you've come.

Aware of her husband's unspoken wish, Lenora
flew down to join him in St. John's as soon as he
accepted the job. On her second day in town she
went scouting around with her sister Pam, looking
for a house she and Dave might buy. They were due
to move permanently in two months, and Lenora
hoped she would have an appropriate house ready
and waiting. "Appropriate" was a word she held
onto during four hours of house hunting with her
sister. It seemed like a good word to use, inoffensive
but understandable. It had not been understood,
and the afternoon had not been a success.

Still, an hour back in the hotel room, a bath and
a fresh application of makeup had restored
Lenora's confidence. Expertly recurling wisps of
blond hair, she reflected that the unsuccessful afternoon was her own fault, she should never have

asked Pam along. Looking at houses together only
confirmed how different she and her sister had
become. Pam just assumed Lenora would want to
live within walking distance of her and their mother—although there wasn't one house in the
Pennywell Road area she'd consider buying. And
she could imagine what Dave would say about the
one bathroom, two storeys Pam had dragged her
through—handyman's specials, these square box-
like houses outport carpenters built in the 1940s.
Lenora could have found her way around in any of
them blindfolded.

If Dave had not insisted on taking a shower
before they went down to join the Deputy Minister
and his wife for dinner, Lenora would never have
seen Marion Fifield on television. To pass the time,
she'd poured herself a weak drink and flicked on
the television set. From the bathroom, Dave, his
voice fogged by steam and water, was telling her
about the new lab. Located just behind the university, he said, and more up to date than anything
he'd seen in Ontario.

Lenora kicked off her shoes and, taking care not
to wrinkle her dress, slid back on the hotel bed.
Half-listening to Dave, she sipped her drink and
watched the announcer's lips as he delivered the
day's dose of gossip, news and propaganda to the
citizens of Newfoundland and Labrador. Her opti-
mism started to seep back. She decided that tomorrow she would call one or two real estate agents, go
around by herself. There must be something available on Rennie's Mill Road or out Waterford Bridge
way—houses she would really enjoy looking at.

She might not have recognized the blur on the TV screen if the grey haired woman coming out of the court house had not paused and blinked into the sun, surprised, apparently, that it was still day. "Good God, it's Marion Fifield!" Lenora shouted.

Marion, as if she'd heard her name called, turned and looked right into the camera. There was no mistaking those eyes, blue and stupid, like the eyes of women who gaze out from old paintings. Eyes that accept the world without understanding a thing about it.

In the bathroom Dave stopped singing. "See any decent houses?" he called over the sound of running water.

Lenora didn't answer. On the screen a police woman took Marion's arm and led her gently, almost protectively, to the van—a modern version of the vehicle she and Marion used to call the Black Maria.

From Grade Five, when the Fifield family moved to Pennywell Road, until the second-last year of school, Lenora and Marion had been best friends. For those six years they had told each other every-thing—which boys they liked, when their periods began, what they thought about God, about sex, about other girls in the class, what they wanted to be when they grew up, when they washed their hair, even which shampoo they used. They had owned one tube of lipstick between them, Pond's Harem Orange. They baby-sat together and shared the money fifty-fifty. One year, in the final exams, Marion had slipped Lenora the solution to three algebra problems. Another year, Lenora made Jim

Tobin choose Marion as partner in the square dancing sessions that, for some reason, had replaced school skating that winter.

The girls sat beside each other in class, walked home together. Two afternoons a week they went to Lenora's house, to the bedroom she shared with Pam, to work on what they called "projects." The bedroom had no lock, but Pam, who was five years younger, could be excluded by simply pushing the bureau against the door.

Lenora and Marion spent hours in that icy cold bedroom cutting pictures of movie stars out of old magazines and pasting them into scrap books. They had books for each of their favourite stars—June Allison, Paulette Goddard, Elizabeth Taylor— women smiling from the arms of handsome men, women pressing their footprints into wet cement, sitting before gold framed mirrors, sweeping down marble stairways. Other projects included the construction of toy houses out of apple crates and the making of fragile furniture from match boxes and scraps of cloth. Sometimes they simply looked at old pattern books that Lenora's mother—who took in sewing—kept under the stairs.

Once, with some idea of setting up a display in the bedroom window, the girls made a Victorian street. It took weeks and weeks to contrive shops and houses from old Christmas cards, to arrange the tiny buildings along a fence paling covered with cotton wool to look like snow. The plan was to have horses and sleighs on the street, lampposts and children and Plasticine shoppers looking into store windows. But one day, after Marion had gone home,

Lenora stood in the cold room staring at the rickety arrangement, and suddenly saw how ugly it really was. She put her foot down on one of the tiny red houses and crushed it. Then she jumped up and down on the other buildings until they were all smashed, reduced to bits of coloured cardboard ground into cotton wool and glue. Afterwards she splintered the paling, gathered it up and took it to the basement where she tossed it into the coal bin.

"We'll be finished the Christmas Street pretty soon—what'll we do then?" Marion asked after school the next day.

Although Marion was the one who understood Algebra, the one who got 100 percent in spelling every week, the one who could twist crepe paper into flowers and paint intricate patterns on toy furniture, she always asked what they would do next—as if she didn't have an idea in her head. The way she asked—so meekly—sometimes made Lenora want to punch her friend, hit her. Make her fight.

"How do I know what we'll do next? Anyway, I threw the Christmas Street out," she said.

"Threw the Christmas Street out?" Marion hadn't seem particularly surprised, or even angry. She just stood there on the school steps in her old rust jacket with the too-short sleeves, waiting for an explanation.

"It was under the window and the rain came in. It got all wet—the colours ran together—it was a mess!" Lenora said, and Marion nodded, seeming to accept the lie she was surely too smart to believe.

During the school year the girls allotted certain activities to each day. It gave a pattern to their lives.

Every Friday they went downtown after school and walked the full length of Water Street. They started on the water side, going into the big stores, gaching at the dresses and shoes, feeling the yard goods, knowing to the minute how long they could linger before some brisk clerk would approach asking if she could help. When they reached the Sally Shop they would cross and walk back east on the other side past little stores they dared not go into, but stood outside of, studying the windows.

Sometimes they would ride home on a bus because Lenora's father worked for the Golden Arrow Coach Company and drivers let each other's children on for free. Usually though, the girls walked home, dodging slowly up Long's Hill in the half-dark, trying to decide which—of all the things they had seen—they would buy if they had the money.

On Saturday afternoons Lenora and Marion always went to the Paramount. They arrived early, picked the best seats: not too near the front where little kids dashed around changing comic books, not at the back where grade elevens sat necking in the shadows, but just far enough back so they could wave to classmates, see what girls from the big schools were wearing, note which girls arrived with boys and which couples had changed partners during the week, watch and whisper about the boys who came in groups, choose the boy they thought most handsome, the one they would go out with if they were asked.

Once the lights went out and the big double curtains, gold and red, swung majestically apart, not a word passed between the girls until the last credit rolled up on the screen. Then the lights came on, blindingly, and with great crashings and bangings the fire exits were pushed open, and hundreds of children stumbled blinking into the street. Lenora and Marion walked home, their heads so filled with visions—of girls (not much older than themselves but infinitely more beautiful) dancing along neon-lit New York sidewalks, flirting with boyfriends on leaf-shaded verandas, or running, often through snowflakes, beside trains, calling farewell to handsome men—that they were hardly aware of each other or of the narrow streets they walked through.

Saturday night was usually hair washing, skirt pressing, shoe cleaning night. But once or twice a month the girls babysat for Lenora's Aunt Marge and Uncle Jim, who paid twenty-five cents an hour, their main source of income.

On Sunday night Marion and her twin sisters, Ruth and Roma, were obliged to go to Bible Chapel under the supervision of their father. Marion's mother did not go. Lenora's family, who were not church people, could never understand why Lenora was always waiting, dressed and ready, when the Fifields came out Pennywell Road. As Lenora ran out of her door Marion would drop back; they would wink at each other and fall into step, walking sedately behind Mr. Fifield and the twins.

These were the only times Lenora ever saw Marion's father. Mr. Fifield worked at a place called the Ropewalk. But each spring he bought a piece of land on which he would immediately begin building a house. In the long summer daylight after supper and on Wednesday afternoons (in those days a half holiday) the sounds of Mr. Fifield pounding and sawing could be heard all over the neighbourhood.

"The man works like a nigger," Lenora's father, who played darts in his time off, said; "Mark my words, he'll be rich as Dan Ryan one of those days."

Because of Mr. Fifield's house-building, Lenora and Marion didn't often see each other during the summer. When school ended, Marion, her sisters and their mother had to help with the new house. Each morning, before he went to work, Mr. Fifield allocated jobs for the day: sort nails, throw rocks into the foundation, stack wood, or scrape concrete off boards that had been used for cribbing—horrible, dirty work, worse, even, than the floor scrubbing and baby tending expected of other girls during school holidays.

As soon as he had the walls up and roof on, usually just before school started again, Mr. Fifield would sell the house his family was living in and move them into the house he was working on. Through the winter he worked inside the house at night and on half holidays, installing partitions, flooring and stairways around his family. Despite her father's predictions, Lenora could never see any change in the way the Fifields lived or what they owned. The house they moved into was always identical to the one they had just moved out of—except it was an unfinished shell.

Mr. Fifield was a short, stocky man. Lenora thought he looked as if he'd been stuffed into his dark serge suit and starched Sunday shirt. His face, shiny and red, was cheerful enough, although he

never spoke on the way to church, only nodded at
Lenora and tipped his hat to her mother if she happened to be watching from the window.

After church Mr. Fifield stayed on for something
called private testimony, so Marion, Lenora and the
little girls were free to walk home on their own.
They would almost run up the steep hill from the
Bible Chapel, then slow down at the top, detouring
along LeMarchant Road with Ruth and Roma trail-
ing behind. Every church in town got out about the
same time so the lower side of the road—the side
with street lights—would be crowded with boys and
girls, pushing and jostling along past each other. It
was like a play, or a movie, Lenora thought: little
groups meeting, merging, gathering in coveys,
exchanging jokes, then moving on, overflowing
onto the street and into the front yards of irritated
homeowners who would yell from windows that the
police had been sent for.

On a Sunday night in summer, with every young
person in St. John's strolling along under the trees,
Marion and Lenora wouldn't have exchanged
LeMarchant Road for any street in the world, not
even the sidewalks of New York. They would walk
slowly through the warm evening, arm in arm, pre-
tending not to notice boys leaning against fences or
sitting on gateposts, snatching tams and whistling at
every girl who passed.

If they had babysat the night before, the girls
would have money and could buy chips, chips
drenched in salt and vinegar and piled in twists of
brown paper, from a van at the bus terminal. They
bought chips for Ruth and Roma too, part of an

understanding that nothing would be said about this buying and selling on the holy day, or about beating the streets on the way home from church.

When she thinks about Marion, it is hard for Lenora to remember the order of things they did together. Impossible to know, for example, if they'd been twelve or thirteen when they made the Victorian street, or to pinpoint which had been the square dancing grade, even to be sure what year they had begun breaking into Fifields' house to act out dramas after school.

In memory, Lenora thinks of the dramas as going on for a long time, months of unhooking a makeshift shutter, of squeezing through the glassless basement window and dropping onto the dirt floor. The foundation of the house would be still damp, would smell of raw wood and concrete and something else, something dank and unpleasant that had been dug up before the footings were poured. Feeling their way along rough concrete walls that left white dust on their fingertips, the girls would move slowly, silently, towards a faint light glimmering down from the floor above. It seemed to take hours. Could they have done such a thing for months? Or had it been one of those adolescent fads that lasted only a few weeks, or even just days?

When they came to the ladder they would climb up through the hole into the stillness of the first floor hallway, pulling their legs up quickly, suddenly sure something was watching from the shadowy pit of basement down below.

The bright emptiness of the main floor always shocked Lenora. Only the kitchen had canvas, clean shiny squares of cream and red. Only the kitchen had furniture—a stove, a green wooden table and five cream-coloured chairs. There was no kitchen couch, no rocker, no mats on the floor, no calendars on the unpapered walls, no toys, no dirt, no litter anywhere.

Lenora and Marion would pull their boots off and pad in stocking feet to the pantry next to the kitchen. In the pantry doorless cupboards and top-less counters had been studded in around a sink. Below the open counter sacks of potatoes and turnip, bags of beans and peas sagged against the wall. Marion would take a handful of split peas, dribble a few into Lenora's hand and toss the rest into her own mouth as if they were peanuts. They would then walk back into the hall and climb anoth-er ladder to the second floor. This ladder was homemade and nailed at the top; it went straight up, a separate ladder but directly above the first, occupying the space where the stairs would be. They would climb very carefully, knowing one mis-step would plunge them into the black basement.

Since no windows had yet been cut into the walls of the top floor, the bedrooms were quite dim. There were no ceilings either, so the girls could see the wide planks holding the slope of the roof. Small beams of light shone in at the corners of the rough, red brick chimney that came right up from the ground. Rooms would not be properly partitioned off, only separated up to eye level by green sheath-ing paper tacked around the studs. Even here, everything would be tidy. Woodhorses, lumber, tins of nails and Mr. Fifield's tools would be stacked in corners. In the doorless rooms beds would be neatly made, clothing hung on four inch nails driven into the outside walls. Although the floors were always gritty, no shavings or wood chips could be seen.

Having decided they must have bit players and an audience, Marion and Lenora had reluctantly admitted their little sisters to these dramatic presentations. The three younger girls got out of school earlier but were told never to go into the house alone. They were usually waiting impatiently by the basement window when Lenora and Marion arrived. Although Ruth and Roma were twins, Ruth was thin and plain and Roma plump and pretty. Roma knew the power of beauty; she lorded it over her twin sister and over Pam; she even tried to boss Marion and Lenora around.

One day, for some reason Lenora could not remember, she and Marion had been alone in the house. It was November, already dim at four o'clock. Marion, finger to lips, had led Lenora into her parents' bedroom. This room had a vanity with a heart shaped mirror and a little curved stool where you could sit and look at yourself. Marion eased open the drawer on the left of the knee hole. It was a deep, square drawer and, as Lenora leaned forward, Marion reached in and quickly pulled out a dead animal. Lenora screamed before she realized the thing was just a fur. Marion draped the animal around her neck and snapped one small paw into the hinged mouth. They stood then, side by side looking into the mirror, admiring the gleaming fur, the same blue-black colour as Marion's hair. Above the fur her friend's face seemed unreal, pale and misty as the faces of movie stars, her eyes startling blue in the dimness of the room.

"Marion! You're pretty as Elizabeth Taylor!" The compliment came unbidden. Lenora had always thought of Marion as unredeemably plain.

"Not me—Mom's the pretty one." Marion seemed embarrassed. She pulled off the fur and stuffed it back into the drawer. "My mother is beautiful," she said softly, formally. She smoothed down the fur and closed the drawer.

For all their shared confidences, that comment was the only one Lenora remembers either of them ever making about their parents. No one talked about parents. Parents were just there, the unknowable, mysterious foundation that supported their lives.

"Want ta see something else?" Marion whispered. "Swear not to tell?" She waited until Lenora wet her index finger in her mouth and crossed her heart, then she pulled at the drawer on the other side of the vanity table.

Only it was not a drawer but a door that swung open revealing six separate drawers. Marion opened them one by one. The drawers were narrow and lined with red satin—like little coffins—each holding one item: a pin with a red stone, a pair of white kid gloves, a jet and turquoise necklace, a gold locket, an atomizer painted with tiny violets. Marion squeezed the gold-laced bulb of the empty

container and a breath like the memory of violets
wafted across Lenora's face.

When Lenora pointed to the remaining
unopened drawer, Marion shook her head. It was
locked, she said. Unlike the others, it did have a tiny
key-hole but Marion didn't even try to open it.

"What's in it?"

"Promise not to tell!"

When she nodded, Marion leaned forward, her
mouth touching Lenora's ear: "There's a gun in
that drawer!" She made her voice deep and dramatic like they did when they were acting.

Lenora pulled back; she could smell split peas
on Marion's breath. "That's foolishness—nobody in
St. John's got guns! Where would you get a gun to?"

"Uncle Derm had it in the army—twas in his
stuff that got sent home."

"They don't send dead people's guns home—
the army keeps em!" Lenora said with assurance.
She was recovering from the surprise of seeing such
things as a fur and jewellery in the Fifields' house.
Sensing that she'd lost some advantage over Marion
by being so impressed, she reached out and yanked
at the drawer. But it truly was locked.

Suddenly they had heard giggles from below.
Marion pushed shut the door hiding the six little
drawers. They moved quickly out of the bedroom
into the hall and slid down with their backs against
the wall, facing the hole where the stairs should be.
They waited. Within a minute Roma, followed by
Pam and Ruth, climbed up the ladder and rolled
over onto the floor in front of them.

Roma jumped up and, with one hand pressed to her eyes, screeched, "Sweet Mercy! What will Lord Roland say? I've promised to marry Keith!"

"Stop that this minute, Roma Fifield!" Lenora was indignant. "We didn't leave off there—you're s'posed to be thirteen in this play—you can't promise to marry anyone for weeks and weeks yet!" She pointed dramatically at Roma: "Begone from my sight, wretched child!"

"Oh mother dear, don't send Camille away— that rich Mrs. Jamieson has promised to leave her a diamond ring, and we'll be able to rescue father from jail!" Marion declaimed. And they were off.

Following no script, the five girls flung themselves around the hallway, sobbing, laughing, screaming—suddenly unconcerned that their voices bounced off bare walls and echoed up from the cavernous hole at the centre of the house.

Thinking back, Lenora wonders if there was any sense to it all. If someone had written the words down or taped them, would they have found some gem of dramatic creativity in their histrionics? Or had it all been an outlet for something else? Some kind of sexual hysteria? She remembers having dull headaches each day when the dramas were over.

When it was almost dark, when only a faint light fluttered up from the lower hall, the little girls would falter, go suddenly silent. They would move back, sit on the floor close together and watch their sisters. Lenora and Marion would flail around for a few more minutes, determined to wrestle some order into the plot, to force it back to their will so that tomorrow they would still be the powerful mothers, the controlling wives, the Scarlett O'Haras of the story.

But soon the chill silence gliding up from the lower hallway would swallow even their voices, and the girls would all creep down the ladders, back down into the dark basement. Fumbling their way towards the window they would climb one by one out into the cold blue twilight.

Once outside, Marion and her sisters would go without a word and sit on the back steps to wait for their mother. Lenora and Pam would start across the field, hurrying toward their own house.

Often, then, they would see Mrs. Fifield walking in the road. She walked slowly, not hurrying or carrying packages. A woman by herself, walking as if she didn't have a husband coming home to supper or children waiting on cold back steps. Lenora and Pam always stopped to watch. So self-contained, so alone she looked walking in Pennywell Road. Lenora would reach out and take her sister's hand, glad to hold onto something alive and warm. They would stand in the darkening field and watch until Mrs. Fifield reached the house. There were no steps leading up to the front door and, without pausing, without seeming to look at the house, the woman would turn, walk around to the back, step between her daughters and unlock the back door. They would all go in. Lenora and Pam always waited until the kitchen light came on. When they could see the light, a small sun dangling on its black cord, they would turn and run across the field to their own untidy, cluttered house.

Lenora can remember the precise date of one event—the last day of November the year they were in Grade Ten. They had been walking home from school when Marion said: "I won't be in school no more."

Lenora stopped, but Marion had just walked on, explaining matter of factly that she'd gotten a job serving in Thorne's grocery store on Golf Avenue. "Edith Pye's leavin to get married—I got her job. Old Mr. Thorne told my father that he'd pay me ten dollars a week—fifteen after the first year."

Lenora was angry. She could not credit such a thing was happening—and without Marion having said one word. Without them talking it over! The two girls had walked all the way in Pennywell Road without speaking. Outside Fifields' house they stopped, stood facing each other. Marion kept her eyes down, watching her boot make a pattern of hearts in the slushy snow.

"But we promised to take Commercial together when we finished Grade Eleven!" Lenora said. "We was gonna work in a big office—travel around the world!" She was on the edge of tears.

Marion looked up, her face blank. "Yes, and we was gonna be movie actresses too, and write books, and design dresses! All just foolishness—pretend stuff—like that old fashioned street you broke up, like them plays we used to do!"

This house didn't yet have steps, front or back. Marion had to climb awkwardly up onto the slab of concrete, school books falling from her arms into the wet snow.

Lenora began to pick the books up. "Don't be botherin with em—I don't want em—I'm sick of school anyway," Marion said before she turned and went into the house. Lenora piled the books against the door and went home.

Lenora's family dealt at Thorne's Grocery, so for a little while she and Marion talked each time she bought bread or milk. But there wasn't much for them to talk about, and after awhile Lenora refused to go. "Make Pam go," she'd say whenever her mother tried to send her on a message to Thorne's. Although the Fifields stayed in the same part of town, they moved each year. Soon Lenora wasn't sure where Marion lived, had almost forgotten her.

One night, in Lenora's final year of high school, Marion had phoned. She didn't say hello, just: "I thought I better tell ya I'm getting married tomorrow."

"No! Who to?"

"Who Too—the Chinese laundryman," Marion said.

For a second Lenora thought she was serious. Then they both began to giggle.

"Well!" Lenora had tried to sound the way she supposed you should sound when a friend tells you she's getting married. "Well! Aren't you going to tell me Prince Charming's name? Roland or Keith, I suppose!"

"No, his name is Vic—Vic Tulk," Marion said, keeping her voice flat, letting Lenora know she'd heard the false gaiety.

"Can I come and see you married?"

"No," she said, then again, "No!"

Lenora almost asked why she'd called but didn't because she knew. Marion could not have gotten married without telling her.

"Have a nice wedding!" she said. Then after a pause, "And Marion—have a wonderful life!" she made a kind of kissing sound and hung up.

She bought four china cups. Transparent things with pale green leaves circling the rims. She wrapped them carefully and took them over to Fifields' house one day after school.

Roma came to the door, took the package, smiled pertly and said: "Thank you, your ladyship." She didn't ask Lenora in. The house behind her seemed as empty and unfinished as any house the Fifields had lived in.

When she asked where Marion and Vic were living, Roma rolled her eyes. "They got this flat down off Long's Hill, alongside the taxi where he works. All Marion ever does is scrub and wax and paint and paper—she's at it all the time."

That June Lenora finished high school. She refused to answer to the name Nora anymore, saved enough money to buy a grey Gor-Ray skirt and pink twin-set. She registered for Commercial. By then she had a new best friend, and a boyfriend she'd met while working after school at a bike rental place. But he was only temporary. Lenora knew this because she had her eye on a handsome university student boarding in the house next door. She was enjoying herself so much that sometimes she wondered if she'd fallen asleep at a movie, if any minute the ghostly curtains might pull together, the lights come up and she and Marion would be shuffling out into Harvey Road.

About five months after the wedding, Pam told Lenora she'd heard that Marion had had a baby. The very next Saturday afternoon, without phoning ahead, Lenora went to visit. Marion lived one flight up, in the middle house in a row of three that had once been painted deep yellow but were now grimy with coal dust. There was no doorbell. Lenora stepped into a hallway so dark and damp it reminded her of the Fifields' basement. She called out but no one answered. Feeling uneasy, almost afraid, telling herself not to be silly, she climbed up the narrow stairway. At the top of the stairs there was a pink door. Pinned to the door was a page from a child's colouring book, a picture of two birds perched on a heart—birds and heart were encircled by ribbons. The picture had been carefully crayoned, and inside the heart Marion had written "The Tulks" in round swirly letters.

Before Lenora could knock, the door opened and there was Marion staring solemnly out at her. She'd put on a lot of weight yet her face seemed thin, almost sunken. Her hair was pulled back behind her ears and there were dark circles below her eyes. She looked so strange, so womanly, that Lenora had to force herself to stand there, not turn away, hurry downstairs and out of the house.

"Come in." Marion hadn't smiled, not even when Lenora passed her the beribboned package and congratulated her on the baby.

The flat surprised Lenora. It was nice, a pretty
kitchen and, Marion told her, a bathroom and bedroom. She did not show Lenora these other rooms
or the baby—a boy, she said, asleep in on the bed.

Everything in the kitchen was pink and pale
green; even the stove was green. A border of green
leaves had been stencilled all around the pink walls
up near the ceiling: "I copied them leaves from the
cups you gave us," Marion said. She was proud of
the kitchen and Lenora didn't wonder. They sat at a
half circle table whose flat end was pushed up
against a window. Marion pulled back the pale
green lace to show Lenora how she could see right
out to the harbour.

"Lucky you," Lenora said, "a husband, a flat and
now a lovely baby!"

"I guess so," Marion said. She seemed mystified,
a reaction Lenora didn't understand until months
later when Pam told her that the baby had been
born with something wrong with its brain. Pam had
been angry, said Lenora should have known.

The visit didn't last long. After admiring the
kitchen and the view there was nothing to say.
Marion didn't offer to get tea. They sat there looking down over the odd shaped roof tops out to the
harbour where the white Portuguese hospital ship
and several small fishing boats and were tied up.

Lenora had never seen Marion again. Over the
years, news of the Fifields came to her from Pam,
and sometimes from her mother. Mrs. Fifield had
died suddenly in her late forties. Ruth and Roma
had both married and Roma had moved away.
Marion and Vic had four more children, but the

first son was badly retarded and had never learned to walk.

Later, Lenora's mother told her that Mr. Fifield had moved to Florida to live year round. "So maybe he did make money on those houses he was all the time slavin over," she said.

Pam, who was still good friends with Ruth, reported that Marion had gone queer. Even when Vic Tulk could have afforded any house in town, Marion refused to move from their first squatty little apartment off Long's Hill. Eventually Vic gave up, bought the old row house and added rooms on back.

Then, a few years ago, just after their youngest got married, Vic and Marion broke up. Pam, having always maintained that Vic Tulk was "plain as an old boot and stunned besides," conceded he must have been smarter than she figured—after all he'd acquired a chain of taxi stands—and membership in Bally Haly Golf Club.

"Now," Pam wrote, "he's left, and according to Ruth, Marion never sets foot outside the door— won't even answer her phone half the time."

Pam had seen Vic downtown with some girl half his age. Ruth said they were living together in one of those big new houses out by Virginia Waters.

None of this had made much impression on Lenora. Her mother and Pam talk continually about people she can barely remember. She tries to look interested, says yes and nods, sips tea. But Lenora has lived in five provinces and met a lot of people. She's learned to play golf, to sail, has raised two children, managed a large flower shop and travelled twice around the world since she and Marion were friends. She can hardly be expected to remember someone she knew in Grade Ten, someone she hasn't seen for over thirty years.

It all comes back to her though, every bit of it. As Lenora crawls across the hotel bed to the television, spilling her drink, swearing, as she fumbles for the sound button, she remembers all about herself and Marion. If she doesn't get sound she may never find out why Marion, who is, after all, still young, has turned into this grey-haired old woman being led towards a police van.

The announcer's voice blasts into the room. Lenora twists a button and the voice moderates: "Mrs. Tulk had just come from the funeral of her eldest son. Apparently, she and other family members went straight to the airport to say goodbye to Mrs. Tulk's father who was returning to his home in Orlando. The following remarkable footage, taken just moments after the shooting, was filmed at the airport by our cameraman who was awaiting the arrival of the Premier. We apologize for the uneven quality of this clip."

The inside of Torbay airport appears on the screen—people pulling back, a baby crying, a tanned woman in a fur coat (could it be Roma?) screaming. The camera jerks downward, grey floor tiles, a man's hand curled inward. The camera travels up the sleeve of a dark blue suit, across the white shirt front, lingers on blood clotting along the edge of the tight collar. There is a split second view of Mr. Fifield's dead face, of his wide surprised eyes, his blood-spattered cheeks. The camera pulls away,

searches wildly and focuses on a woman sitting on
the edge of the baggage carousel. She has dropped
the gun; it lies on the floor near her feet. She reaches into her pocket, takes out a package of cigarettes,
sticks one between her lips and lights it.

"She smokes!"—for a moment Marion's smoking seems more shocking than the murder of her
father. Then the woman sitting on the carousel
looks up, straight into the faces of the people standing in a semicircle around her. She takes a deep
draw on the cigarette.

Back in Mississauga, trying to reconstruct the
events of that evening, Lenora is still not sure what
part Marion's murder of Mr. Fifield had in her
change of heart about coming back to
Newfoundland. Other things had to be counted
in—all those square houses, all that dull cosiness
between her mother and Pam.

Dave was annoyed at first. He told her she was
being hysterical, overreacting. He is over it now,
says they probably did the right thing after all. A
new job would have been very stressful at his age.

But it had lain like a rock between them for a
long time. "Look—a bit of shared past doesn't connect you with what someone does years later! Your
being friends with that madwoman in year dot has
bugger all to do with us!" Dave told her more than
once.

He is wrong. Lenora knows he is wrong. The
past can pull at you like bog water, haul you down
from any ladder you've climbed. She's never been
able to say this to Dave, of course, doesn't have
words to explain, doesn't want to explain either. But

she knows. The past is a dark hole, it can draw you
under until you don't know who you are, don't know
what you might do.

Touch and Go

*F*airy chimes fill the still dark hotel room, one line from a nursery tune that repeats and repeats. It becomes a part of the dream the woman on the bed is having, a dream in which ping-pong balls drop neatly into narrow plastic tubes that change shape, twist, melt, converge into each other in a kaleidoscope of fluorescent orange, green and yellow before smashing into a million coloured pieces.

The woman moans, rolls over, fumbles blindly for the bedside phone trying to stop the sound. But the dream wants her.

She knows it is her job to reassemble the pieces, to gather the neon splinters, sort them, press them gently into a shape that has meaning. The dream is familiar. She's been having variations of it since childhood. The coloured pieces used to be made of glass (the dream keeps pace with technology) but the sensation is always the same: a mixture of dread and terrible responsibility.

Lifting the receiver has not stopped the chimes. The woman says "Damn," stumbles out of bed and in the darkness locates a glowing wall unit that blinks 5:09...5:09...5:09. She hits the button with the edge of her palm, choking the merry tinkle in mid-note.

She pads across the carpeted floor to the window. The street, six floors below, is empty. Even the child prostitute, who had still occupied the corner at one o'clock, is gone.

Directly opposite the hotel there is an old stone post office. It must have high ceilings because its fourth floor windows, tall and curved at the top, come below the level at which she is standing. There are five windows and there are five people, sitting just as they had been four hours ago, back-on at a narrow counter, sorting mail.

Shivering slightly in the air-conditioned coolness of the hotel room, she studies the people across the way. There are two men and three women. Because they are slightly below her, their heads appear larger, out of proportion to their bodies. The men, one balding, wearing a red plaid jacket, the other sandy haired in a pale blue shirt, sit at the end of the counter. The women all look young. The one next to the men is a plump blond; her hair seems to be curled in old fashioned sausage rolls all around her head (can it be a wig?), and she is wearing a tight red dress. The woman beside her sits in a wheel chair; she has dark straight hair and wears a plain white blouse. The woman at the end is probably pretty; she has fair hair and is wearing a fluffy pink sweater. Each person is framed into a separate picture by the windows.

How strange in this day of computers and postal codes that people should be sorting letters all night. She wonders what it must be like to sit in a brightly lit room for hours, arms moving in slow rhythm, eyes focused straight ahead as the city outside becomes quiet, as the lights in surrounding office buildings go out.

The post office workers do not appear to talk. Maybe they've had a fight. In such forced intimacy almost anything could cause disagreement. Who should go for coffee? What kind of insulation is best? What hockey team? Can anyone smoke? She's seen it happen often in offices.

They are not people. She is sure they are not people.

Watching the cleverly-made backs, the life-like arms, the hair, she marvels at the skill. But the necks are wrong, they don't come out of the bodies at quite the right angle, particularly on the one in the wheel chair; maybe that one isn't finished. The woman watches for some time, becomes convinced they are robots, computers built inside bodies made to look like people. To trick the union maybe? She wonders who chooses their clothing, who dresses them, where will they be put when the day shift comes in?

She would like to watch longer. She would, in fact, be happy to drag a blanket off the bed and sit here in the dark window for hours, for days—certainly until the morning shift arrives.

But she has to be downstairs and checked out before the airport taxi comes. She hurries to the bathroom, wincing as one flick of the light switch sets ablaze two dozen bulbs surrounding a huge mirror. Holding onto the edge of the sink she studies her ageing face and waits for the wave of nausea to pass. She remembers the paint-by-number set her youngest son once had. Certain little numbered spaces on the face had called for astonishing colours: green, purple and a kind of mustard grey. She'd suggested that he paint the face a nice flesh pink but her son followed the instructions and it had worked out to be a recognizable picture of some hockey star.

If she were to tuck her hair into an old tam she could change places with the woman she'd seen going through the garbage outside the restaurant last night. She could disappear into the city without a trace, become one of these silent, disdainful old women one sees huddled in corners of subway stations or asleep on the heating vents of banks and office buildings.

She imagines Rex and the children dining at the window table of the little restaurant where she'd eaten last night, imagines them watching with fascinated horror, as she had, while a woman pulls bits of half-eaten food, sour milk containers and wet newspapers out of the sidewalk bin.

Would her family know her? Would some movement of her head, some gesture of her grimy hands culling carefully through the loathsome scraps, give her away? Would they recognize those hands as the ones that had cupped their faces, brought them aspirins, ironed their shirts and passed them a thousand plates of food? She thinks not. The idea pleases her. Not that she is romantic about poverty; she knows these women lead uncomfortable, often painful, lives. Still, it is an option that has not occurred to her before.

More and more often her morning face brings such thoughts. Just under the skin she can see the skull of her grandmother who some believed to be a witch. The sagging jaw, the jutting nose, the mad eyes are there each morning.

But she is a master of disguise. Dusty rose foundation and blusher, pale mauve shadow, brown mascara, sprayed over with magic dust blatantly labelled "Deceit" and the face in the mirror, although no longer young, is attractive, interesting, and, if one does not catch the eyes unaware, sane.

She stuffs the makeup and night things into her small case, flips expertly through the stack of papers on the bedside table, tosses most of them into the hotel wastebasket and deftly slides the rest into a narrow leather brief case. Then, dressed in a not too fashionable linen suit, she swings out of the room, shutting the door with a businesslike click, forgetting to make a last check on the plastic post office people.

She is early after all, and has to sit waiting in the glass and chrome lobby for the airport taxi. A silent, smiling young woman wearing the hotel uniform passes her a *Globe and Mail* and continues to arrange fresh flowers in tall black vases. She sits on a velvet chair and reads about murders and betrayals that have taken place while she slept.

After what seems a long time, the elevator door slides open and she is surrounded by twenty or more marvellously cheerful, noisy women. She estimates them all to be over sixty. From behind the newspaper she studies them, wondering at their buoyant good humour and at the variety of sizes

and shapes that women come in. None of them sit.
They swirl around the lobby like autumn leaves, yellow, red and orange. She can almost hear them
crackling. They come together in little groups, then
swish off to remind someone in another group of
something, to show pictures taken yesterday, to
exchange jokes and bits of information about
today's schedule. Drifts of chuckles waft from group
to group.

They are joined by a beautiful young prince
whom they obviously adore, though he fools none
of them. They know he has an equally beautiful
young princess stashed away back at the travel
agency. Indulgently, the women let him coax them
gently onto the waiting bus which has "Outermost
Ontario" and a larger than life Indian, hand shading eyes, painted across its side.

After the women leave, the lobby becomes quiet
again. Just as she begins to feel uneasy the taxi
arrives. She is the only passenger. The car is very
warm and smells of oil, old smoke and long eaten
chips. There is another underlying smell that unites
all the others; it takes her a few minutes to identify
it, the remembered classroom smell of unwashed
underwear and skin.

They drive through pre-dawn streets past dark
office buildings, past factories, then past houses,
some with a light in the kitchen where a shift worker is getting breakfast. Near her ear a speaker sobs
out a song about a man who promised his old mother to be good and hadn't been. The driver coughs
and coughs and wipes his nose daintily with two fingers.

She inches the window down and takes small gulps of the cool damp air, but the sick feeling will not go away.

When they pull up outside the airport she holds the money ready, pushing it into the driver's hand, saying "Keep the change." It's worth it not to have to watch as he fudges through his pockets.

Her generosity backfires. Although he is illegally parked, the driver now feels obliged to carry her bag not just to the door, but right to the check-in counter. There he stops and, in an outburst of misery, tells her he's had this cold for three weeks—and if it doesn't clear up soon he'll have to take time off. He wants to tell her about his wife, who has just been laid off from a wire factory, but in the face of her silence his voice dribbles away and he finally leaves, wishing her a safe trip.

She does not think of trips as being safe or unsafe. The possibility of minor catastrophes never occurs to her.

Only the front half of the airport coffee shop is open. She joins other grey faced travellers, slopping coffee out of her styrofoam cup as she squeezes into an immovable chair opposite a man in a dark business suit. His eyes flick over her, focusing for only a moment before dismissing her. The quick rejection causes her no grief; on the contrary she is relieved. It is not difficult to strike up easy conversations, and maybe more, in such places, but these encounters almost always lead to boredom and sometimes to embarrassment. She has developed a simple set of avoidance tactics that includes a book from which her head is raised only to stare into the middle distance as though pondering some deep truth just read.

In fact, she is an accomplished eavesdropper. A gatherer of odd tidbits from other people's conversations, a collector of what she thinks of as vignettes of Canadian life—rather like those produced by the National Film Board to fill the spots between unsponsored TV programmes.

She used to bring these fragments home, unwrap them for her husband and children like shells picked up on some exotic beach.

She doesn't do that any more. The stories she overhears are changing, developing sinister undertones. She senses, without being able to explain it, that the world of mindless bloodshed she reads about and sees on television screens is oozing into everyone's life, like chemical wastes that seep into drinking water, turn up in the bones of newborn children.

Last fall, sitting alone in a Black Angus restaurant in Vancouver, she'd listened to a conversation from the other side of a padded divider. She could see only the tops of two heads, one very black and one brown, both young males, both almost whispering. She'd moved close to the divider but could still hear only occasional words.

"No, no, I want to give you time to think this over..." the dark one was saying.

Then later, "...it's not as though you hadn't done the same thing before...and I can pay and I can get credit. That's what makes me different...."

She could hear nothing the other one said, just low murmurs. She'd decided they were probably gay until the dark one spoke again, "I hear you have one of those Wesson 5s, the kind that kicks off ten bullets in a row. That's ventilation, man!"

"Shut up!" the other's voice, suddenly clear, cold and quick, cut the first voice off.

Hairs stood up along the back of her neck. She had slid soundlessly to the far edge of the booth, carefully erasing the coffee ring with the sleeve of her coat.

They left a few minutes later without a glance at the next booth, two good looking, well dressed young men, boys really, not much older than her sons, wearing shirts and jeans carefully pressed by their mothers.

When she got home she told Rex and asked him if he thought she should have called the police.

He'd looked at her for a long minute before speaking. "You imagined it—or you misunderstood what was said. People don't hire murderers in restaurants." He made a laughing sound that was not laughter and turned back to the television.

The next day she took time to look up Wesson 5s in the public library. In a catalogue of small modern handguns she found: "Wesson 5—a very compact machine, developed from a larger prototype, designed but not used during the Vietnam war. Capable of firing ten high velocity bullets in quick succession."

She hadn't told her husband that, and she hasn't brought any stories home since.

But she continues to eavesdrop. It is impossible
not to. It keeps her calm, holds her in place in air-
ports, restaurants, in waiting rooms.

She is listening now, to a perfectly harmless
looking family at the next table.

The man, who has the plump rosy face of a
Santa or the kindly farmer in a children's picture
book, is wearing a shabby dark suit. His shirt is
unbuttoned and a necktie flops from his jacket
pocket. His entire attention is focused on his coffee
and on the doughnut in his hand. Three other
doughnuts are stacked like little car tires on the
paper plate in front of him. She thinks he hasn't
heard a word the two women with him are saying.

His wife is a little wire of a woman. She holds
her plastic cup in two hands and her eyes never
move from her daughter's face. She is willing something to happen, or not to happen.

The daughter, who is about thirty, has a flushed
look, the same round cheeks and big body as her
father. She is talking, has been talking for some
time. Her voice is high, shrill and childlike; it
matches her dress which is pink with a flounce
around the hem and coy little black bows at each
corner of the square neckline. She has taken off a
rumpled brown coat to display the dress, or maybe
just to enjoy the feel of it. Her pale fingers never
stop moving, smoothing the silken material, touching the puff sleeves, adjusting the little bows. She is
very happy about the dress, about the airport, the
people, the coffee shop. Her face shines with pleasure as she looks around.

"I like it here, it's nice, aren't the lights nice, look at them, look at the pretty shades. Did you see that poodle dog with the woman..." her voice gets louder and the words come faster and faster, like a tired child trying to distract adults from her bed-time.

"...and there are lights under the post, see, and on the tables too—they probably light them at night—when it gets dark...."

The child-woman's voice suddenly chokes on the last words and she clutches at her mother's sleeve, "Don't make me go home. I don't want to go home. It gets so dark there...."

The mother reaches to the daughter, at the same time jerking her head around towards the man.

The man raises his big head slowly. The kindly Santa face has gone. He gives the two women a long look of cold hatred. His wife pulls the daughter up and out of the seat. "We'll wait over by the gate."

The man doesn't speak. He is chewing. He continues to look at the girl. She has squeezed her eyes shut. The mother turns the girl towards the coffee shop door. She is trying to hold the coat around her daughter's shoulders as they go—but she is not fast enough to hide a spreading bloodstain on the pink satin.

In Halifax, where she has to change planes, it has just stopped raining. She can smell wet earth as she walks across the tarmac towards the Dash 8. The empty runway, the fragile silhouette of the plane against the lightening sky, evoke memories of old war movies, of innocence and hope.

She is beginning to feel very tired but knows she will have to go straight into the office when she arrives. She hopes to sleep on the last part of the trip but doesn't. The man next to her is much too large for the narrow seat and puffs like rising dough into her space. Holding herself as far away as possible she presses her forehead against the cool window, watches clouds pile over, onto and under each other. She imagines what it would be like to slide down cloud mountains into grey hidden valleys, into fleecy crevices.

A friend once told her of seeing a man try to get out of a plane in mid-flight. He had quietly gone over and started to unlock the emergency door, had told the flight attendant that he wanted to play outside. Unable to persuade him that this wasn't a good idea, the attendant hit him smartly over the head with her flashlight, eased him back into his seat and strapped him down. Most of the passengers had not even noticed, her friend said.

Half an hour before landing time she starts looking, she always does. The sky is bright now with scraps of clouds, below she can see black rock, the familiar filigree of lakes and sea.

Years ago, the second or third time she'd flown, the plane had been full of summer tourists and the pilot had come on the public address system to point out Ireland's Eye. "The back of beyond," he'd called it, giving the Americans their money's worth of Newfoundlandia.

The pilot told them that Ireland's Eye had been settled three hundred years ago by deserters from a British man-of-war; that it still had no roads, no electricity, no hospitals, no airstrip and, most years, no school.

She had not checked his facts—she didn't want to find out if he was wrong. She had known, even then, that she would need Ireland's Eye one day.

Whenever she comes back home she watches for it, always feels better as soon as she sees it: five or six houses clinging to a sliver of cliff, outlined by white breakers, the sea stretching away in front, and at the back mile after mile of forest, of bog, of vast barrens.

And there it is, right below. They are coming in higher than usual but it is still there, a place without roads, without newspapers, without electricity. Still there.

She is afraid that someday it will not be there. This is what she deserves. She has tried to work out a plan against that day. What will she do? She is not a very mechanical woman, and does not think it sensible to expect herself to undo the bolts on the emergency door before the flight attendant can stop her.

Secret Places

$\mathcal{G}$utted, head on. Gutted, head on. Gutted, head on. The beat alternates, ending on the left foot, then the right, left, right, left, left. Every five or six steps Nina unconsciously makes a little skip to prevent the phrase from ending twice with the same foot. This gives her walk a carefree, childlike quality strangely at odds with her Naturalizer shoes, neat fawn skirt and white blouse, with her thickening waist and short greying hair.

She has walked in a direction opposite to the one suggested by her daughter, has come to the last house on Main Street—a shacky sort of place where an Indian sits on the low front step, his back wedged against the door frame, his hands hanging limp on his knees. He stares at a boarded up garage on the other side of the street.

Coming up to the man she turns her head slightly, ready to speak. Susan has told her that everyone in Corby is friendly. But then, Nina reflects, they say that about Newfoundlanders, too —and God knows we're not. The Indian doesn't even blink although Nina passes directly between him and the garage.

Beyond the Indian's house is a grain elevator, apparently empty, its door fallen in, faded yellow

letters Sask Wheat Pool, barely visible. Beyond the
elevator, flat fields cut by a line of cracked asphalt
stretch away to the horizon.

Out here there are no sidewalks, but it seems
safe to walk on the dirt between the road and the
fields, or even on the road itself. Susan has told her
the younger farmers all live in town. They commute
out to their farms along the four lane highway at
the other end of Main Street where the shopping
mall and hospital are located. The only people
using this road would be old couples too stubborn
to leave their farmhouses.

Last night, as she chopped the supper vegetables, Susan told her all about Corby. Nina had sat
smiling and nodding, watching the rapid, angry
movement of the knife, knowing all this talk about
nothing can only mean things are not going well for
her daughter. Some man, she supposed. Probably
the one Susan mentioned in her last letter, the good
looking farmer who had helped her change a flat
tire. Nina has become adept at picking up casual
references, but after travelling through several time
zones she felt light headed, too weary to risk an
argument by asking who the man is.

Gutted, head on. Gutted, head on, over and
over. Nina wishes she had remembered her sun-
glasses. She sighs. She and Susan never have been
the way mothers and daughters are supposed to be.
Now it's probably too late. We're sure to get to know
each other better before I go home, she pacifies
herself.

She tries to make herself happy. Her friend Liz
says anyone can, it's just a matter of concentrating

on the right things. Nina tries to concentrate on how the sun feels on her face and bare arms, on the smell of baked earth, on the sight of fields, flat and endless as the sea, on the dry tinkling sound—some kind of insect, or maybe the wheat itself.

She wonders what it would be like to walk into a wheat field—to walk right to the middle and lie down. There's probably a law against it—for fear of damaging the wheat. Still, how pleasant to fall asleep surrounded by soft, yellow rustlings, with nothing to think about, nothing to look at but the patch of sky directly overhead. It would seem so remote, like being on a tiny island. I could die there, she thinks, and when the big combines roll across the fields at harvest time my bones would be crushed, blown into the hopper with the wheat. I'd be shipped off, made into bread in Russia, into Tim Horton's muffins back home.

My God, I'm crying. I must be mad to even think such things. Foolish words in my head and now walking along by myself, crying at the thoughts of Liz eating my ground-up bones. She searches her memory for female relatives who'd spent their last years afraid to venture outdoors or locked up in asylums. Nerves, it was called. "Aunt Jane Dawe got nerves," she can remember her mother saying.

"You may feel vulnerable for a few weeks," the doctor told her after the hysterectomy. "Take a month off work, and we'll see how it goes before prescribing anything." He'd peered at her sharply, and Nina had smiled back, bright as the buttons on her new red raglan, her hair gleaming with the mink rinse Liz had given her the night before.

"Gutted, head on—gutted, head on." The words had first come to her as she left the doctor's office, walking briskly past the bored patients, past the polished nurse (shell-like fingernails poised over black keys), down the stairs (grimy orange carpet matted with chewing gum), out the door and across Gower Street to where Ralph was double-parked beside a drugstore.

Once inside the car she'd given a great gulp, a terrible kind of gulching like the sound that comes up from a sink when you finally get it unplugged. It frightened her, that sound had. But Ralph just started the car, easing smoothly into the traffic, keeping his eyes fixed on the road. After a block or so she'd gotten control of herself.

"Want to be dropped off at the store? Must be time for Liz's break, you could have a coffee with her," he said after she'd been quiet for a few minutes. She had nodded, but the words had been there in her head—and they'd stayed. Some days Nina thinks they are getting louder, so loud that she cannot concentrate, so loud that she imagines thoughts hovering just above her—like planes in a holding pattern, unable to land because there is no room.

In the distance Nina can see something grey. It's a good ways off—hard to judge distances when you're looking at more sky than land. A large rock, maybe, or a barn? She decides she'll try and walk out to it. There'll be some shade, she'll have a rest and then walk back. She can take her time and still be home long before Susan, who's doing twelve hour shifts out at the hospital.

The prairie is like the sea, she thinks, except for the colour. You could drown in it. There are even waves, combing along through the wheat, bending it so she can see a different shade, a paler gold, ripple across the field. She wouldn't be surprised to see a fish jump.

By the time she gets near enough to see the building clearly, Nina knows she's come too far. Her knees are shaky and she can feel the skin pulling across her incision. She's relieved to see that two old trucks are pulled up on the circle of cracked concrete surrounding the grey structure. She'll ask for a drink of water and, if worse comes to worst, get someone to drive her back to town.

She approaches the place slowly, studying the flat overhanging roof, the colourless curved walls that seem to be made of sand blasted plastic, the roofed platform with three circular steps along the front. The building reminds her of the grounded hulks of old ships you see around Newfoundland. Sometimes they're even set into concrete like this, with steps leading up as if they were Noah's arks, waiting for animals to come aboard.

There is a door right in the middle. A large window to one side of the door gives the building a lopsided look. She has her foot on the lowest step before she sees the words Pink Poodle Drive-In snaking in dead neon above the window. She climbs the steps and walks across the concrete platform. A metal bar nailed across the door announces Where There's Life, There's Coke, Nina pushes on the bar and steps inside.

After the bright sunlight she can hardly see. She leans against the door peering into the dimness. All she can make out is a black arborite table silhouetted against the window beside her. She walks to the table, sits down on one chair and adjusts another so that she can put her feet up. The chairs are faded pink with a pattern of poodles. The poodles have turned grey with age, but the chairs and table are dustless—someone wipes them clean. She'll find out who in a minute, but first she'll have a rest.

It's so good to be sitting that she closes her eyes, lets her head drop forward easing her neck muscles. Then, from the windowless side of the room, comes a cough—the polite, dry cough of a patient male on the verge of impatience. Nina's eyes snap open. She removes her feet from the chair, arranges her cotton skirt neatly and sits up straight.

Three men, Ralph's age or older, are sitting at a round table in the far corner. Nina cannot tell which one coughed. Their faces, eyes hidden below peaked caps, turn toward her, three blurred, identical half moons above almost identical checked shirts. One nods to the others, scrapes back his chair and stands. He unfolds like the carpenter's ruler her father used to have, sections opening out one by one until his head is four inches from the ceiling.

He is the tallest person she's ever seen. As he comes towards her, a cold finger touches the back of Nina's neck. She cannot think why. His face, narrow and caved in below the eyes, as if he has no teeth, is completely blank. Beyond him, in the shadows, the other men watch.

There is a smell of rot and mouse droppings, that cold, damp smell you notice around places left unheated all winter—as if last winter's snow, blown under the door and frozen in drifts across the floor, hasn't really melted but seeped into the basement to wait. It is a smell Nina remembers from clubhouses her brother Clyde and his friends used to make. The boys would claim territory and partition it off with old doors: a corner of the cellar behind the coal bin or the dank crawl-space under the back porch.

Nina had been fascinated by such places, would hover out of sight, sneaking in as soon as the boys left. She remembers touching things with the tip of her forefinger, the way detectives do in movies. Touching things Clyde and his friends had abandoned in corners and on the rough shelves they'd nailed to the walls: a grey lump of putty, the insides of softballs, bits of an old motor, screwdrivers, the blood-like mixture clotted at the bottom of a Vienna sausage tin, a worn package of playing cards, a bread knife. Examining mouse-chewed piles of comic books, battered copies of Esquire (stolen by Clyde from their uncle's barber shop), rusting bike parts, a bag of alleys, the box of shredded newspaper where, briefly, a rabbit had lived. Smelling, beyond the damp and rot, the forbidden cigarette smoke, the burnt candles by which they studied pictures of half naked women, the oil they used to clean their bikes. Sniffing the cork of a vinegar bottle containing molasses water, the bag of sweet biscuit crumbs, the shrunken apple cores, the stench oozing up from a jam jar holding a tiny frog that floated in green slime.

Sometimes she would be so intent on the touching and smelling, so near to discovering her brother's secret life, that she would not hear Clyde and his friends coming. She'd be caught and made to pay a penalty: dropping the dead frog, soft and slippery, down her dress, or holding her fingertip to the candle flame until she said "Unconditional surrender!" or getting a dab of the red stuff from the sausage tin on her tongue. Once Gordie Best, the little creep, said he was going to feel Nina's titties. Clyde told him she didn't have any, so instead they made her close her eyes while Gordie peed on her socks.

Nina hears the patient cough again.

The man is standing beside the table, waiting. How long has he been there? Has she said anything? Has he said anything? He must have, he seems to be waiting now for an answer.

"Yes, yes please," she says, very loudly, nodding her head like a fool, agreeing to whatever the man has offered.

He turns away, goes to the counter that is just behind him and pours coffee into an oversize brown mug. He puts the mug on a plastic tray along with a paper napkin, a spoon, a small jug of milk and a bowl of sugar. The real milk, not sealed edible oil, surprises her so much that she doesn't even say thank you when he places the tray on the table.

He returns to the game. She can see now that it is a game. The table the men are sitting around is really a circular board with hardwood edging like the tables on ships.

The tall man says, "Your turn, Gord." He seems to be overseeing the game while the other two play. The man opposite lowers his head, squints along the board and, using his thumb and middle finger, flicks a wooden ring towards the centre. They have forgotten her.

Nina watches, trying to remember what this game is called. She and her brother used to play it at Christmas on the floor of their grandmother's living room. It was almost the only time she and Clyde ever played together. Sometimes one of the uncles would get down and play, too. The women never played. The board at her grandmother's house had flags painted all around the gutter, flags for countries Nina had never heard of. Her uncle told them that was because these countries had been swallowed up.

"Swallowed up?" She'd imagined a picture book village—green fields, houses with red roofs, neat streets and pink cheeked children—sucked into some vast mouth-like pit.

"Taken over. That's what unconditional surrender means, stupid," Clyde said.

She wonders what became of that board? Taken to the dump, more than likely, after her grandmother died and her mother and aunts gutted the house. Gutted.... Gutted.... Nina suddenly realizes that the sing-song words have ceased their treadmill through her mind.

"Gutted, head on," she whispers, "Gutted, head on—testing, testing." There is no echo. The words have been banished. In the kingdom of the Pink Poodle they have no power.

Rescued from madness, Nina leans back, sips her coffee and looks around the room. Not much to see: four more tables, each with two or three chairs, a high counter on which the coffee percolator stands, an old pink refrigerator behind the counter and, above the refrigerator, a pink poodle with a clock in its middle. The clock has stopped. Other pink poodles hang on walls. One, now frayed and faded, seems to have been crocheted out of stiff net. And there's a pair of plaster poodles, boy and girl joined at the neck with a chain. They simper at each other across a plaster heart.

Nina can remember when poodles were in. She had been thirteen. It was the year she stopped spying on her brother, gave up her investigation of male mysteries. She had made a friend, a girl named Thelma Rogers whose addiction was the maintenance of body surfaces: the polishing of nails, the painting of lips, the powdering of cheeks, the uplifting of breasts, the brushing of hair, the shaving of legs, the creaming of knees and elbows.

Thelma thought Clyde was cute. She and Thelma had matching poodle skirts. The skirts were pink and the poodles, down near the hem on the left side, had been made of a felt-like material. Charcoal grey braid circled the poodles' necks and looped up the skirt in big hearts.

Except for the display of poodles, the walls are empty—not even a telephone, although a water-stained bulletin board is nailed up beside the door where a telephone might once have been. There is nothing else to look at. Apart from the soft bubble of coffee, the only noise in the place is the click of the rings hitting the game board and the occasional word, "Your turn," or "Hell!" coming from the men.

This would be a good time to write Ralph, she thinks. But she does not move to take the paper from her bag. Instead she sits back, gazing vacantly out across the prairie.

"Dear Ralph, I'm in this place that looks like a boat—like Noah's ark for saving the animals. It's called the Pink Poodle. Susan likes working in the hospital lab. She tells me the annual rainfall of Corby is less than fourteen inches. Despite this I think a lot about drowning."

Would such a letter worry him? Would he phone Liz, ask her opinion of his wife's sanity? Would he rush out to the airport, catch the next plane for Saskatchewan?

The girl doesn't walk into view. She appears in the window, halfway between the horizon and the restaurant—a girl and a black dog walking right down the middle of the empty road where the white line should have been, almost as if they are keeping as far as possible from the miles of wheat stretching away on either side.

Nina doesn't take her eyes off the girl from the time she comes into sight until the door opens. And it will always be the same, even later, even on days when she is watching that very spot. Nina will never catch that moment when the girl and the dog are just two dots. The road will be empty and then they will be there, coming slowly towards her, the heated air shimmering around them so they seem to float just above the black asphalt.

Apart from never making a sound, the dog is ordinary enough. And the girl? It takes Nina several minutes to work out what is so unusual about her. It isn't her clothes (flat brown sandals and a pair of cut-off jeans over what looks like a black bathing suit), it's that there's nothing in her hands, no jacket, no scarf, no bag, no radio, no package. It's only when you see one like this, empty hands, hanging at her sides, moving slightly as she walks, that you realize women are always carrying something.

The girl's arms and her unusually square shoulders are dark brown. At first Nina guesses that the girl is an Indian. Her face is dark, startlingly dark, but surrounded by hair that is pale blond, so she's not an Indian. And she's not a girl either. The way she is walking, swinging her empty arms like that, her thinness and her straight hair, chopped unevenly around her neck, make her seem childlike, but her face is the face of a woman—and not a young woman. As she climbs the steps and comes into the shade, Nina can see deep lines around the woman's mouth and across her forehead.

Keeping as still as possible, Nina watches. The dog crosses the platform and lies down in the shade directly below the window. The girl-woman walks to the door. As the door swings open, Nina glances towards the men in time to catch the tall one tapping his head significantly. The other two nod. They are all smiling, but the smiles vanish as the woman steps inside. Their faces become blank, as blank as they had been when Nina walked in.

The woman doesn't even look at the men. She goes over and stands quietly by the counter. The tall man lets her stay there a good two minutes. Then he comes over. He pours a dollop of milk into a mug, fills it with coffee, takes a glazed doughnut from a plastic container, places it on a paper napkin. He is staring down at the woman, at the small mole just above the top of the black bathing suit. He returns to the game without speaking.

Nina is surprised to find herself trying to catch the woman's eye.

Completely unaware of Nina, the woman walks to the door and, with an awkward movement of her elbow, pushes it open. Outside she goes and sits cross-legged in the shade beside the dog.

Looking down on the woman's head, Nina can now see that the hair is more grey than blond, can see the bones in her neck, can see how the skin on her shoulders is spotted where it has burnt, peeled and burnt again. The woman crumbles the doughnut into small pieces on the concrete in front of the dog and then, with her back resting against the siding, she slowly drinks the milky coffee.

A low conversation is going on across the room. Without taking her eyes from the woman and dog, Nina strains to hear but cannot. The men might be speaking a foreign language; their conversation is a whispered blur. The bright sunshine and deep shadows outside fall into simple patterns of light and dark. It seems to Nina that she and the other woman, one on each side of the glass, are drifting in some timeless limbo. Floating, soft and pliable: waiting perhaps to be born.

Then the woman moves. She puts the coffee
mug down on the concrete, stands up and walks
down the steps the way she had come. The dog, who
must be thirsty, pads along beside her. Nina watches until they vanish into the line between sky and
earth. It takes a long time. When they are gone
Nina leans back; her neck is hurting again and the
hollow, empty feeling has returned.

She puts a tooney down beside her cup and
leaves. As the door closes behind her, she imagines
the sound of laughter. In her head the monotonous
voice begins again—"Gutted, head on, gutted head
on...." She walks home to its limping beat.

The sun shines every day and every day Nina
walks the same way. Every day she meets the same
people along Main Street—skittish, long-legged
girls sauntering up and down in coveys, testing the
brief power they have over boys who congregate in
doorways, old couples inching towards the library,
the crippled woman on the veranda of the big brick
house, the girl with fluorescent fingers pinching
leaves off plants outside the flower shop. Nina often
stops to watch. Nip, nip, nip, the girl's red nails dart
among the dark leaves, like the little fish you see in
restaurant tanks, always moving along the glass
walls, their mouths opening and closing, opening
and closing.

Once, watching such fish while Ralph paid the
bill in a Chinese restaurant, Nina had started to cry.
Then, for shame's sake, had to invent a pain. Ever
since, Ralph has maintained that she is allergic to
soya sauce. They don't go to Chinese restaurants
any more.

The girl with the fluorescent fingers never looks up or asks if she wants anything. Despite what Susan says, no one in Corby is friendly. They don't seem to see Nina but she doesn't mind. Even back home she's noticed herself becoming invisible to more and more people. The main street seems so quiet, so wide and sun bleached that it's like walking through a set for one of the old movies she and Thelma Rodgers used to go to on Saturdays.

Susan has stopped trying to fill every minute with talk. But Nina can sometimes see her daughter making an effort to remember what things are like at home—to recall someone she can ask after, her cousins, or the girls she went to school with. On the night her father calls (for Nina has still not written) Susan says, "Daddy'll be retiring soon—you'll be able to start doing things together."

Nina just nods. She's still holding the phone, fooling with the cord, trying to untangle it. Susan is making sandwiches, but when Nina looks up her daughter stands poised, knife held above the bread, just looking at her mother.

That's probably the same way I stare at her, Nina thinks. Like I'd be able to figure out everything about her if I looked at her long enough.

Susan has not said anything about the man, about any man, but Nina knows there is one. He calls sometimes, and her daughter takes the phone to her bedroom. She doesn't pry. Everything you read says mothers shouldn't pry into their children's lives, especially the lives of daughters.

Susan says they will have to spend a weekend in Saskatoon before her mother goes home. Nina wonders if this is a gentle hint, but decides not. She can see that her daughter likes having her there when she comes from work. Susan starts talking about the hospital right away, going over things that happened during the day, smoothing out the rough bits.

Nina has noticed Ralph doing the same thing, explaining why he failed a student, or how much better the timetable would be if only the committee had accepted his proposal. I suppose that's why people live together, to have someone you can make your life into a kind of story for, with yourself the main character. The idea seems like a revelation, proof that something must be working beneath the irritating voice in her head.

Nina visits the Pink Poodle every day except Sunday. Susan is off on Sundays, and they drive to the nearby sights, to Indian craft shops along the highway, to a wildlife park, the Ukrainian market in the next town, the huge church with the Russian-looking dome. But during the walk every day is exactly the same. The only difference Nina can see on her walk is in the deepening yellow of the wheat, the lengthening of the shadow under which the woman and dog sit.

By now the men at the Drive-In must expect her. Yet they still turn and stare when she comes blinking into the dark room. The tall man makes her wait longer now, not coming over to pour her coffee as quickly as he had on the first day. The men never speak to her. Thinking it might make them feel better about her sitting alone in the corner, she's taken to bringing one of Susan's magazines along—

though they must see she only sits staring out the window, never turning a page.

The woman and dog appear each day. The dog never barks, the woman never speaks and no one speaks to her. There is never the slightest variation in what happens. The woman picks up the coffee and doughnut and sits outside in the shadow of the roof. The dog eats the doughnut, the woman drinks the coffee, then they walk away down the road that is a black line into the sky. Nina cannot understand why she is so fascinated by this simple sequence of events. She begins to think she may drift forever, caught in this silent, timeless ritual. The thought doesn't frighten her.

One day, when the woman and dog have vanished, she rouses herself, calls, "More coffee, please," in the direction of the game table. Her voice sounds loud as a crow. All three men stiffen and stare as if she has made some terrible mistake in manners, but the tall one comes over and refills her cup.

"Who is the blond woman?"

"What woman?" Nina can see that he really doesn't understand.

"The one who comes every day with the dog."

"Oh Doll, you mean Doll!" suddenly the man seems almost friendly, relieved perhaps that she's not a lunatic imagining blond women where none exist.

"Used to work here way back. Read all about her if you like. Over there." He gestures with the coffee pot to the makeshift bulletin board and returns to the game.

Nina takes her time drinking the hot coffee. When the cup is empty she puts money on the table, picks up her bag and walks over to the bulletin board. She tries to flatten the scraps of paper, they feel gritty beneath her fingertips, curled and dusty as the moths Clyde used to pin on his bedroom walls.

"Mayor Newdorf Turns Sod," she reads from a yellowed clipping, "An ultra modern Drive-In is about to be constructed at the west end of Main Street by up and coming businessman Reg Koshman...." and so on. There is no date.

The next piece of paper she unrolls has "Call Judy 637-2900" written on it. The next is the twenty top tunes for July 1964.

Finally, the one she's looking for. It's a news story and it has a photo: five girls smile into the camera, their arms around each others' shoulders, their breasts pushed up and out. Five short skirts flare above five pairs of legs posed identically with one knee bent, the feet, in high white roller skates, turned at a flattering angle.

Nina has to hold the brittle paper flat with both hands, bend forward and tilt her head uncomfortably back to read the faded type. She knows how clumsy she must look. Her friend Liz, would have just unpinned the paper and take it over to the light.

The girls in the picture are standing on the curved concrete platform outside. Above their heads a neon banner blazes the words Pink Poodle Drive-In. Below is the caption: "Five lovely young misses have been selected to be hostesses at Corby's newest eating establishment, The Pink Poodle, owned and operated by Reg Koshman. From left to right: Valerie Ratushnick, Mary Obuck, Irene Novak, Dolly Galedorf and Betty-Jane Haychuk. 'The girls were chosen for their roller skating ability as well as for their great legs,' Mr. Koshman told your reporter."

Nina cannot see the faces; the photo is grey and the light poor. She glances around. The game has stopped, the men are turned towards her, watching.

She finds the courage to unpin the paper and take it to the window. Dolly Galedorf—the name doesn't suit, but maybe her real name is Dorothy. If it was not for the shoulders, Nina would not have recognized her. The wide eyes in the pale baby face, the smooth pageboy hairdo, the dark smiling mouth bear no resemblance to the woman who comes into the Pink Poodle every day.

The men are still watching as she goes back and pins the picture on the board. It takes time because the thumb tacks are rusty.

She moves towards the door—but, "There's another one just up above," one of the men calls. He is expecting something, what? His voice makes Nina uneasy, but she looks and finds the clipping. This bit of newspaper has come apart along the fold and been mended with the old cellophane tape, the kind that turns brown. There is a two inch band in the middle she cannot read.

"Miss Dolly Galedorf, the daughter of well respected wheat farmer Daniel Galedorf and his wife Evelyn," she reads, "chosen to represent North West Sask at a swimming meet, has placed first in an

open competition of all high schools in the region.
If this Corby high school senior places in the top
three in Saskatoon next week, she will be eligible to
try out for the Canadian Olympic team."

Swimming! Where in God's name did anyone
learn to swim in Corby? On the Sunday before,
Susan had taken her mother out to "The Lake"
which turned out to be a white encrusted hollow
encircled by blood-red weed. Not a drop of water to
be seen. The white shiny stuff was phosphorous,
Susan said. She didn't know the name of the weed.
To Nina it looked like a grotesque growth, like pictures in Susan's textbooks of things that had to be
cut out of people's insides.

That night Nina dreams of the girl in the picture. The girl is wearing the short flared skirt and
skating across the white lake. When she sweeps past,
Nina can see the skater's face, the dark blind face of
the woman with the dog. Air moves as the girl
whirls by and then she jumps, one of those little
jumps skaters do on television, only her jump turns
into a great arching dive, curving down into that
white glittering centre. It closes over her just as if it
were water.

Next day, when the tall man brings her coffee,
Nina asks: "What happened to her, then?"

He shrugs. "Nuthin I know of. Been taken care
of by some man or other all her life," and his mouth
clamps shut. Before moving away the man gives a
long stare, daring her to ask another question.

Nina recognizes the message. She's been given
all the information she is going to get. What isn't in
the newspaper clippings hasn't happened.

She continues to walk back and forth between the sea of wheat each day, sits each day looking out across the yellow waves. She likes it. How often has she done anything simply because she liked doing it? Inside the Drive-In her mind is free of the tormenting words. She feels on the verge of something, the answer to some question she hasn't dared ask.

The last day is exactly like all the others. The same people are on the street, the same Indian is draped over his front step, the grey hump of the Drive-In appears in the same place on the horizon, and the men are still shooting wooden rings across the board in the game she cannot remember the name of.

But the woman and dog do not come.

Even in this timeless place Nina knows she has been waiting much longer than usual. The men know too, restlessness, a continuous low rumble like an undertow, vibrates from their part of the room. Once, the tall one walks over and stands right beside Nina's table staring out the window. After a few minutes, without speaking to her or even glancing at her, he returns to the game.

When the dog comes padding down the road, Nina gets up and goes outside. The animal, seeming unconcerned at being alone, drops down in his usual shady place near the window. Suddenly the men are beside her, all four of them standing there, looking down at the dog.

"Jesus Christ," one man says softly, "Jesus Christ!"

"What's wrong?" Nina says, "What's happened to her?"

"Go on home!" The tall one grabs Nina's arm. Wrapping his long fingers around her arm, he turns her away, propels her towards the steps before releasing her.

She opens her mouth, then closes it. Too frightened to protest, she stumbles down the steps, hurriedly crosses the broken concrete parking lot. At the edge of the wheat she stops, she takes a deep breath, makes herself turn around and look back.

The men have forgotten her. They are still there in the shade of the overhanging roof, dark shadows looming above the black dog. Then the tall one mutters something Nina cannot hear. Suddenly they are off the platform and down the steps — three old men running awkwardly across the concrete, squeezing into the cab of one truck. The truck sweeps around in a wide circle and takes off with a screech, speeding down the line of black asphalt towards the empty sky.

Nina touches her arm. Tomorrow, on the flight home, she will notice a dark bruise shaped like a man's hand.

Folding Bones

"*N*ot all year around?" "Think of the winters!"
"Think of the isolation!" colleagues said when I told
them I was going to live in Newfoundland. For all
that, I could detect a certain relish, almost admiration, in their voices—as if my abandoning Ottawa
and the civil service mitigated somewhat their own
preoccupations with pensions and mortgages.

In fact, I am the most cautious of women. No act
in my life—apart from the conception of my son—
has been done impulsively. I gave up my job knowing I can always get contract work in Ottawa, and
my house there is leased, not sold. I remind myself
of these things each morning as I gaze down on the
mound of snow under which my car is buried. From
the window of my bedroom the shape looks more
like an upturned boat than a car. But car it is, and
with muscle power can be uncovered. Two hours
digging, a two hour drive to Gander, and a three
hour flight. Seven hours, and my son and I could be

back in Ottawa. Turks' Bight is not the Gobi desert,
nor a polar ice cap.

Reassured by this knowledge, I go downstairs. I
get Matthew's breakfast, make sure he is well protected for his short walk to school: cap, mitts and
boots pulled on, coat buttoned. My son loves it
here, thrives on the freedom. There are only four
children in his kindergarten class, but his summertime friendship with Todd Pardy next door has continued.

Despite Todd's being in grade two, the boys
walk back and forth to school together, play together on weekends and seem to agree on everything,
especially that Matthew must live in Turks' Bight
forever and ever. They have a plan—if I leave again
my son will go to live with the Pardys, he will sleep
in Todd's room. The boys have explained this
arrangement to me and to Todd's mother Ruby.
They never qualify, they speak in short, matter-of-
fact sentences, with a determined maleness that
seems rock hard, innocent and so irrevocable that I
find myself imagining Matthew being absorbed into
the Pardy household, becoming Ruby's and Dunc's
son.

Watching my son trot off down the lane—the
small, purposeful bulk of him, so eager to meet
Todd, to get to school, to start his day that he does-
n't wave, doesn't even look back—I feel bereft.
Telling myself that I should be pleased, that the
boy's independence reflects well on me, never
changes what I feel. When he disappears behind
that mountain of snow the plow has pushed up

between Velda's house and the street, I know this is just the first of many leavings.

"Days drawing in," Velda said Wednesday morning when I returned to the kitchen complaining of the cold, the dimness, this fading of light I never noticed in Ottawa.

She was fudging around under the sink for the saucer she and Ruby Pardy use as an ashtray. In all the summers Matthew and I have stayed here, I never once saw Velda smoking. "Only this time of year—once a day when Ruby comes," she said when I mentioned it.

Ruby must be twenty years younger than Velda, nearer my age really, but they have been neighbours and friends for a long time. In summer they trout, garden and berry pick together; in the fall they make jam, bottle moose, start knitting for the sale of work, reconvene their card group. In winter they team up for Christmas. Every morning now, as soon as Todd leaves for school, Ruby comes over. She and Velda sit at the kitchen table making lists, ticking off deadlines. They must strip floors, wax furniture, tackle windows, chop fruit for cakes; these morning conversations throb with verbs.

Mostly I just listen. I am amazed and mildly amused at the amount of work women here invest in Christmas, which has never been a big part of my life. In the years James and I were together he always spent Christmas with his children and I ignored the day. Even as a child I hardly noticed Christmas. My parents had married late in life, Christmas was not part of their past, or any past they acknowledged. We had no special celebration,

no rituals, no tree. My friend Doreen's family did
have a tree. I can remember the two of us sitting on
the wine plush chesterfield in Mrs. Pendergast's
front room. All the rooms in the Pendergast house
belonged to Mrs. Pendergast, except the basement
which was her husband's. I recall sipping some kind
of chocolate drink and gazing across the room at
the tree—a small, bare thing trimmed with a few
ornaments that had survived the onslaughts of
Doreen's older brothers.

Doreen's Aunt Angela was in the room, telling
us about Christmas decorations she remembered
from her childhood, "...blown-glass, blue and red
bubbles, light as tissue paper with elves and
snowflakes frosted onto the surface—made in
Germany—beautiful!" she said.

It was hard then to imagine Germans making
anything that was beautiful. For me, a child born
just as the war ended, the word German conjured
up black and white photos in mildewed issues of
Life magazines. Magazines Doreen and I snitched
from her brother's club house. Page after page filled
with shadowy pictures, concentration camps where
big eyed children crouched in corners, hands reaching towards food. Photos of skeletal prisoners lined
up, being shot, bodies pitching forward into holes
they had been forced to dig in the black earth.

Aunt Angela, who'd worked in the china department of Eaton's in downtown Ottawa, said that the
Germans had kept the secret of making these
Christmas ornaments safe all through the war. They
had now rebuilt their factories and trained new
glass blowers. She promised us that next year

Doreen would have a prettier tree, she'd make sure of that. Only by the next year Doreen was gone.

Velda notices when I'm not listening. She wants me here, now, taking part in the present. She has tried to draw me into this frenzy of Christmas preparation—not to help with the housework which she and Ruby have well in hand, but into some communal activity, the sewing of costumes or painting of a backdrop for the school concert, the baking of cookies for the church sale, for the seniors' supper, or for the dance that is planned for the young people who, Velda says, will all be home for Christmas. I refuse, pointing out that I already open the library every Saturday and teach art class at the seniors' home two mornings a week. Although they do not say so, I sense that Velda and Ruby consider these jobs insubstantial, frivolous. Sometimes I agree. Would anyone phone if I forgot to open the library on Saturday afternoons? Do the seniors come to art classes out of politeness—or out of curiosity as to why this mainlander has chosen to live in Turks' Bight?

People here are deeply curious about strangers. I did not know this when I was a visitor. For five summers I have imagined myself invisible—still did until last Tuesday, when I asked at the bank to have money transferred from my Ottawa account.

Located halfway between Turks' Bight and Greenspond, the bank is built onto the back of Shoppers Drug Mart. Only one employee seemed to be on duty the day I went in, a young woman who smiled, pulled a form towards her and filled in my name, occupation and address without asking a single question. I let her know I was upset by this, but later, when I tried to explain how much it bothered me, both Velda and Ruby thought I was being persnickety.

"Sure, that was Debbie Maidment," Velda said, as if this explained everything. Which it did. Debbie's father Cal is the school principal here in Turks' Bight, her uncle delivers oil and repairs furnaces all along the shore and Ruby's third son, the one at Memorial, is Debbie's boyfriend.

"It was unprofessional of her," I persisted, "letting a client see how much gossip she's picked up."

"We mightn't have big banks like you're used to upalong, but I can tell you Debbie Maidment is smart as a tack—and good at her job as anyone in Ontario! Was no need for you to get on at her like you did!" I knew by the way Ruby shot those words out that she must have been holding onto them, waiting for the subject to come up.

I should have shut up, but I didn't. It has come to me lately how much I dislike having people say "you're not from around here, are you?" whenever I open my mouth. It bothers me hearing them calling the new teacher "a green hand," referring to Nurse Johannsen, who has lived here half a lifetime, as "that Come From Away" when she recommends something a patient doesn't agree with.

"I value confidentiality," I said in the same haughty voice I had used to lecture Debbie Maidment. "The very fact you two know about a private conversation proves my point."

Ruby reached for her coat. "Got some nerve you have! Arse barely on the chair and you're tellin us people what to do!"

Ignoring Velda's "Now maid, now maid," Ruby slammed out the door, calling something over her shoulder about black strangers.

"Don't be bad friends with Ruby. She don't mean no harm—the poor mortal's sick with worry. She thinks they'll have to move away if Dunc don't get a crab licence." Velda peered at me, assessing my mood. "You're content here, aren't you?" she asked.

I told her I was. A lie, of course—as Velda well knows, as she knows everything. Having spent my childhood wishing for a mother who understood me, I now find understanding a burden.

Summer after summer I have been content here. Winter after winter in Ottawa, the thought of this place kept me sane, the thought of driving down this coast, taking the turnoff to Turks' Bight, driving until there was nothing before me but blue—endless blue stretching all the way to Ireland. I would sit in my hermetically sealed office and picture myself stepping out of the car with Matthew in my arms and all around us the smell of roses, the smell of the sea, Velda waiting in her shady garden.

I loved it all, then, without caution, without discrimination. As if feelings for my baby had overflowed to include Turks' Bight and everything in it, the plastic motels and ugly takeouts as much as the white churches and weathered wharves, the gouged-out gravel pits as much as the deep bays, the long sweeping beaches and fragrant marshes. And the

people, of course—what passion I had to protect
Velda and her friends, to protect everyone in this
place from the unkind appraisal of strangers.

I don't feel that way anymore. My impulse now
is to protect strangers from Turks' Bight, to take up
for Nurse Johanssen, to tell Mr. Richards he must
stop carrying that briefcase, stop wearing that
tweedy cap the men make fun of. It's myself I'm
worried about, of course, myself and Matthew. I see
now that one can be a stranger here forever. It does-
n't take much to be considered odd in Turks' Bight
and I'm already eccentric—likely to get more so as
time goes by. I remember my father, Matthias Stein,
who came to Canada after the war, when he was the
age I am now. I remember his lonely last years, wonder if I can live in a place where I will be considered
strange and a stranger for the rest of my life.

On Friday there is another snow storm. "Savage
weather," Velda says, looking out at the whirling
whiteness, not mentioning that Ruby hasn't been by
for two days, not since our argument.

I suggest we keep Matthew home from school
and we do. He and Velda make five batches of cookies, "One hundred and sixty three—for the mummers!" my son announces. He is in a fever of antic-
ipation, wound tighter each day by Velda. With her
own grandchildren gone, she has only Matthew to
make promises to: promises of a Christmas stocking, Christmas concerts, Christmas fireworks, now
Christmas mummers.

On Saturday the sun is out. I open the library
but no one comes, not even Angus Vincent to
replenish his weekly supply of science fiction. I con-

tent myself with dusting and indexing the four
boxes of books Velda found in the room she cleared
out for Matthew. The books are old, worn volumes
of poetry: Tennyson, Yeats, Shelley, English school-
boy adventures, a beautiful but tattered set of children's books called The Collins Crusader Series.

I would like to repair the books, to peel away
their broken spines, cut new covers, wrap them in
leather as my father used to do. I remember my
father lighting the gas ring under a pot of honey
coloured glue. It would be a winter's night, us alone,
me doing my homework and him reading, my
mother gone next door to visit Mrs. Pendergast. It
would be quiet, just the sputter of gas and, in the
snow silenced Ottawa streets, the occasional clank of
a loose chain hitting the undercarriage of a car. I
would know by the smell when the glue was soft,
when it was time for Papa to take the felt wrapped
package from the bottom drawer of his desk.

I remember my father's hands unrolling the
cloth, lining up his tools on the desk: the long curving needles, the ball pein hammer, square-tipped
knives and, my favourite, the eight inch strip of
worn ivory that he called a folding bone. He would
let me hold the cream-coloured bone, a small piece
of some animal, silk-smooth between my hands.

Slowly, carefully as a doctor uncovering wounds,
Papa would peel away the worn binding, expose
crystallized glue that looked like brown sugar. Old
covers falling away from the body of the book would
be used as a pattern for new covers. After cutting a
set of cover boards, he would pluck the round
brush, fat with glue, from the pot. Without getting a

speck on his hands he would spread hot glue over the new leather binding.

Then I would pass him the folding bone, which had grown warm in my hands, and watch as he folded soft leather deftly around the edges of the spine, over the cover boards, nudging neat corners into place with the little awl he cupped in the palm of his hand. He would turn then to the pages, stacked in what he called signatures. Using the curved needle, he would sew these together, restitching the spine before attaching a set of beautifully marbleized end papers. The last thing to do, before setting the book in his book press, was apply white paste to the backs of the endpapers. Then, with a magical snap of his hand, my father would wrap new covers around the book.

Papa often sang when he was repairing books. It was the only time he ever sang, a low chant in a language that was not English. Other times he recited poetry: Blake, "...and sands upon the Red Sea shone, where Israel's tents do shine so bright," and Yeats, "...and therefore I have sailed the seas and come onto the holy city of Byzantium." Sometimes he asked me to read poems out loud to him. Our tastes matched, or maybe his tastes became mine. "Where the great wall 'round China goes, and on one side the desert blows," I would read, or "Morning's all aglitter and noon's a purple glow...."

A wonderful thing for a child on a winter's night to stand in that warm core of safety, to smell glue and leather, to be surrounded by that whirl of words. Fingering old books in an empty library, I think of those nights with my father, remember them as the essence of happiness and childhood innocence. I wonder if I could recreate such times for my son. I still have the folding bone.

I am thinking this, wondering if I might be able to order bookbinding supplies from St. John's, when Matthew comes into the library. He scuffs in, complaining that his mitts are wet, that he has no one to play with. When I ask where Todd is he becomes cross, reminds me of the concert Todd is in. "I know the songs as well as Todd, but the teacher says I'm too small this year—they're all practising and there's no one outdoors," he whines.

I tell him about my father, about the bookbinding. He is not interested. I find A Child's Garden Of Verses, pull him onto my lap and read—"Where the great wall 'round China goes, and on one side the desert blows...." I am caught by the words but he is not; he squirms away. "Someone might come in," he says, "they'll think I'm a sooky baby!"

There is nothing for it but to lock the library and go home. Outside, where the evening really is all aglitter, with frost and sunset, Matthew becomes cheerful. He sings the Star Song for me. His voice is thin and off key. Still, I think, they could have let him sing. We smile at each other; he lets me kiss his red cheek, tells me that Velda has promised a little tree for his bedroom, a tree with lights. He lets me hold his hand until we come opposite Todd's house.

This week Matthew is coming straight home from school. "It's lonely," he says, lolling in front of the television, challenging us to coax him out of his sulks. We try. Velda makes toffee, finds an old Crokinole set her sons used forty years ago, teaches

him to shoot wooden rings towards the centre. I
read to him, tempt him outdoors, show him how to
make snow angels, how to draw in the snow with
food colouring. But we are dull, we cannot hold
him, cannot distract him from the hall where older
children are kings and shepherds, where Todd is
practicing the Star Song, where Mr. Richards has
promised he will take everyone out for pizza before
the concert.

"You're mean," the child says, and "I'm bored,"
and—I see Velda flinch—"I hate this place."

For the first time I have an urge to slap my son.
Yet I understand too, remember the summer my
friend Doreen and I were bored. We started meeting every afternoon inside a little shed in the
Pendergast yard. We were older than Matthew,
about twelve, but the boredom, the scorn of older
children, the heavy injustice of adults, days that lasted forever—those were the same.

It was the summer every boy on Dugan Street
suddenly owned a bike. But not the girls. Although
Doreen and I had learned to ride on bikes rented
for ten cents an hour from Wheelers', our parents
refused to buy bikes for us. The boys abandoned
their clubhouse, left home. Paper-wrapped sandwiches stuffed into pockets, inner-tubes and towels,
bats, balls and catchers' mitts attached to various
parts of their bikes, they went off on daylong trips,
out to Fairfield Park or downtown to Parliament
Hill—places Doreen and I had never seen.

Girls a little older than us were borrowing
babies that summer, babies in carriages which they
pushed slowly up and down Dugan Street, or

parked under the awning of our bookstore. These girls would stand in coveys talking, gazing into the store window, smiling in an unfocused, superior way when we walked past. They seemed to be waiting, expecting something. They mystified and infuriated Doreen and me; we withdrew from the street, began spending afternoons in the clubhouse, a place Doreen's brothers would not have let us near the summer before.

It was like another world inside the clubhouse, warm and quite dark when the door was pushed shut. Stretched out along rough wooden benches, that were really boxes built against the walls, we would talk, doze and smoke cigarettes I stole from my father's desk. Beneath us, inside the box-benches, Doreen's brothers stored things Mrs. Pendergast would not give houseroom to: half-eaten apples and packages of cookies, a tiny fossilized turtle, lurid comic books, magazines, mouldy copies of *Life*, *Esquires* that fell open to the pin-up centrefold, jam jars filled with unidentifiable liquids, rusty nails and rusty wheels, turpentine and tins of old paint the boys used to fix go-carts. Lying at right angles, the tops of our heads touching, we could smell the boys' lives rising around us, mixing with our cigarette smoke, hovering in long pinpricks of sunlight that jabbed down through holes in the rusting tin roof.

All that summer we hid in the clubhouse, whispering things we had never spoken of before: about where babies come from, about men's body parts, about the curse, which Doreen's mother had told her she will soon get. Mrs. Pendergast has explained that girls and women bleed between their legs each month, and Doreen will have to learn to take care of herself. It sounded too horrible to be untrue.

Our conversations, desultory and rambling, circled and circled, words drifting in dim, smoke-filled air. I told about the time I'd been grabbed by Mr. King the butcher, a man who chopped the legs off frozen lambs. It felt as if he had a frozen lamb's leg in the pocket of his bloody smock. The only thing that saved me was Mrs. O'Brien's coming in; her arrival sent Mr. King back behind his chopping block. Doreen disclosed that her brother Kevin and his girlfriend had had a baby together, that there'd been a big fight in the Pendergast house because of it. When I asked where the baby was now, Doreen made me cross my heart and hope to die. "Shirley's father made her give it away, give it to the orphanage," she whispered.

The lives of grown-ups, always remote, suddenly seemed mysterious, perhaps sinister as well. Could our own fathers have left children somewhere? Had our mothers given away babies before they married? Could we have brothers and sisters in orphanages? Doreen thought not, but I could imagine my mother having a baby and leaving it behind, forgotten as a pair of old shoes. We speculated about my mother, about why she was not like other women we knew, why she never cooked, or ironed, or asked people in, why she had married someone so much older than herself. I told Doreen about my father's other family, the woman and child in the oval frame on his desk. We agreed that Papa would not have left children behind, would not have forgotten them.

How extraordinary those enclosed afternoons now seem. That strange game of advance and retreat. Teasing the future. Perhaps all children do it? In three or four years will Matthew hide in some fish shed discussing sex? Perhaps not. It's hard to believe the power sex had then, the dark sting of words we now hear daily. What do children whisper about these days?

Velda and Ruby often speak of their sons' childhoods. Ruby says that her older boys talked of nothing but motorcycles when they were growing up. Talked endlessly, day and night, about carburettors and spark plugs and horsepower, bought old wrecks and took them apart in the yard, rebuilt them again and again. "Soon as ever they got one that ran properly they took off. I didn't sleep for four nights," she said, "not until they phoned from Toronto." She thought for a moment. "Tell the truth, I haven't slept the same since."

Two nights ago I dreamt that Matthew was leaving, saw him ride towards the highway on a motorcycle, passing 18-wheelers, spiralling off into the future while I stood beside Velda's rhubarb holding something—a scarf or book—some memento I'd never gotten around to giving him. I woke, knowing I had dreamt the future—for why should I be different from Ruby or Velda, from all women whose children go away?

As soon as I am alone in the house I phone Gander, make reservations for Matthew and me to return to Ottawa. I will tell no one until after Christmas. We are booked to leave on Old

Christmas Day—the day Velda says Christmas is really over.

Today is the day of the concert. Matthew does not come home from school. By three-thirty I have been back and forth to the lane six times. There is no sign of him on the road, or in the field where he and Todd sometimes slide. The Pardy house is empty. At four I phone the school but there is no answer.

"They'll all be over at the hall gettin ready for tonight. And I allow that's where our young lord is—bound and determined to be on that concert," Velda says. She is chuckling, recalling pranks her own sons played as she pulls on her coat. "You stay put in case he turns up—I'll phone from the hall."

The hall is right across from the school. The first floor, once a storage shed for salt cod, was converted some years ago into a recreation centre for teenagers. Since there are no longer many teenagers in Turks' Bight, the centre is now used as a community auditorium. It was almost five before Velda phoned. "Matthew's not here. Young Todd says he saw him putting his cap and jacket on when the rest of them left school." There is no humour in her voice now.

I grip the phone and listen. Around me, Velda's cream and green kitchen looks just as safe and shiny as it did before the phone rang. I know that I have stood like this before, struck by the impossible sameness of household objects, the permanence of walls, chairs and tables—the impermanence of flesh. I must have made some sound because Velda snapped, "Stop that!"

"He's around somewhere. Don't let yourself get all worked up," she says after a minute, then: "He'll be all right—he's just off somewhere sookin cause he's not on the concert."

"I'll come down. I'll circle around to the highway and loop back to the school," I'm already dragging on my coat, searching through pockets for my car keys.

Velda reminds me of the snow covered car. She tells me I must stay where I am, "You stay by the phone so's the people searching can check back," she says.

"Searching?" the word has a cold, news report feeling.

"Yes, searching," Velda says. She explains that Dunc and Ruby have gone out in their four-wheel drive, the school principal and several other men are out on snowmobiles, coasting around woods paths. Mr. Robinson and some highschool boys have been dropped off over at the old boy-scout camp back of the pond—they've taken snowshoes.

All this has been done without me knowing, done even before she called me. I feel grateful, yet resentful, "I can't stay here—I'll go mad," I said.

"No, bide there. Get yourself a cup of tea—scrub the floor—that's what I used to do," Velda orders, and I recall some of the stories she's told me, times when she'd turned to scrubbing floors to keep sane.

"Look," she says trying to sound cheerful, "we'll hear from the little imp soon. Everyone's out lookin. Ruby even called the RCMP road cruiser—they got flares and spotlights. I'll keep by the phone here in the hall and you stay by that one—the minute one of us knows something we'll phone the other. Now, make yourself a cup of tea, girl. Mark my words, he'll be found before dark!"

But it is already dark. Has been dark for some time. I make myself a cup of tea, then pull a kitchen chair over to the phone—as if the seconds it would take me to cross the room might make a difference. I sit in the dark, holding the tea, waiting, telling myself that children stray away all the time, telling myself they turn up—always.

Not always.

Near the end of that summer when we were twelve, the boys came back to Dugan Street. To me and Doreen they seemed larger, rougher than they had in July. They had grown careless with their bikes, left them leaning against fences, lying in a tangle of wheels while they played ball, or joined the young fellows who smoked outside Chittel's Grocery, wolf-whistling at girls. Ben and his friends swooped down on the clubhouse, grabbing me and Doreen, giving us Chinese burns, rubbing their knuckles into the soft underside of our arms.

"Bugger off, Ben Pendergast!" Doreen had screamed as we were expelled, pushed blinking and crying into the sunlight.

I don't remember much about the next few days. We drifted, doing nothing, fitting nowhere, becoming aware that a street party was being planned for the last Saturday before school. This idea, new to everyone, seemed to have originated with the baby-borrowing girls. Maybe it was what they had been waiting for all summer. There were to be fireworks, ice cream, games, go-cart races and a dance. Doreen's grandfather had offered to take people for rides on his motorcycle.

"Bo-or-ing!" Doreen drawled, and I tried to imitate her. Secretly I was astonished. During the summer Doreen had changed, become someone totally unlike the person I'd known ever since we shared a playpen. To hide my bewilderment, I tried to copy my mother's shrug, learned to stare cool-eyed at people without saying anything.

When the new, bold Doreen suggested we not go to their stupid street party—"Let's snitch two bikes and ride out to Fairfield Park on our own!"— it seemed like a wonderful plan. I imagined us riding across a vast expanse of green, swooping down grassy hills, almost flying.

On the day of the street party we waited until they began to raise a canvas awning between King's Meat Market and Chittel's Grocery. Men and boys hanging from second storey windows caught ropes and pulled the flapping canvas across the empty lot. Women and children watched, everyone holding something: folding tables, boxes of streamers and balloons, pots of fried chicken, salads set down in buckets of crushed ice. Not a soul noticed us when we picked up two bikes and wheeled them quietly away.

At the last moment I hadn't wanted to go, "We don't even know the way to Fairfield Park," I whined, suddenly wanting very much to be part of the party, to hear Mr. Pendergast's harmonica, to see the cart-race, the fireworks. We were already around the corner, pulled into a narrow alleyway beside St. Kevin's.

"I'm going anyway," Doreen took off, rode halfway down the block before coming back. "Look!" she said, "What's the worst thing that can happen?" She seemed confident, grown-up. Although we were both wearing the same cotton skirts and old school blouses, Doreen's looking crisply new, while mine were limp and wrinkled because my mother never ironed.

The worst thing that can happen.... It was a question Doreen and I had asked ourselves for years—the question that gave us courage to sneak the doctor's book out of Mrs. Pendergast's bureau, to steal the boys' comics, to smoke, to ask Father Mac if I could join the Children of Mary. That day, though, I didn't want to think what the worst thing might be—maybe what happened to those dead children in old Life magazines, maybe things Doreen and I had whispered about in the shed: bleeding, having babies.

I shrugged, "What?"

"We'll get lost. We'll have to phone home and they'll come and get us."

"What if they don't?" I knew even as I asked that would be the worst thing—to be abandoned, left behind, forgotten.

Doreen thought I was joking. "Stupid! Of course they'd come!" She wheeled off towards Gladstone Avenue and I followed.

Even now, all these years later, memory of that moment brings, fleetingly, the sense that I can go back, reverse time, change events. If only I had known the formula. Surely I could have distracted Doreen. Children do—I've watched Todd divert Matthew from some toy or game. Children can lead each other on, too: dare one another to tease the sea, to test the harbour ice, climb hydro poles. I imagine Matthew stepping tentatively onto black ice, hear a voice egging him on. I make myself stop. I must not invent, invite, the future.

Back then I needed only to shout something foolish to Doreen and the two of us would have gone racing around the block, whizzing past the women holding salads, past the girls with their arms full of balloons. We would have skidded to a stop in front of the boys, jumped off the bikes, yelled some taunt, then sauntered away to buy ice cream or try the ring toss. If we had, would I be here now, staring out at Velda's frozen garden, waiting for the phone to ring?

Useless speculation. Doreen and I went to the park. Slowly. The streets were unfamiliar and the bikes were hard to pedal. We had chosen badly, they were too big and the steel crossbars made our skirts hike up over our thighs.

We came into the park at a corner playground, a place too young for us but we chased each other up and down the climber and pushed the merry-go-round for little kids. My feeling of apprehension had dissolved. When we came upon a bandstand we went inside, lay on our backs and shouted up at the arched roof.

"Doreen Pendergast!"

"Margo Stein!"

"Doreen Pendergast!"

"Margo Stein!"

Dizzy with sunshine and power, we staggered out of the bandstand, found the swimming pool and splashed around in the low end for an hour. When we came out of the pool there was a stall selling hot dogs, cotton candy and pop. With the last of our money, we bought a hot dog each, laid the bikes on the grass and sat eating under a tree in which we'd hung our wet towels and swimsuits.

"Bingo-bango-bongo, I don't wanna leave the Congo, no, nono, nono, no..." Doreen hummed. We smiled at each other, grown-up, in control, well pleased to have planned such a perfect day, to have even remembered to bring the sweaters we pulled on because it was beginning to cool off. It was then the three boys came, and the good part of that day was over.

I don't want to remember those boys. I stand up, walk back to the window and look out at Turks' Bight, a scattering of houses nestled between pillows of moonlit snow. It feels like midnight but the red clock on the stove says 5:15—less than half an hour since Velda phoned.

They looked like ordinary boys. At a distance, they might have been mistaken for Ben and his buddies. They arranged their bikes in a kind of fence around Doreen and me, then they leaned on their handlebars and stared down, watching us eat.

The biggest boy took a comb out of his pocket and ran it through his wet hair. "Saw you in the pool," he said, smiling at Doreen.

"Nice bike you got there Foxy," one boy said. He had the largest ears I'd ever seen. Looking up at him I could not see his face, just the dark outline of his head and his ears glowing red and transparent. His boot nudged at my bike. I wanted to tell him that I was not foxy, that, like his ears, my hair was made red by the sunset. I kept silent, concentrated on my hot dog, breaking off little pieces, making it last. While it lasted I was invisible.

The boys dropped questions down on us, quick and fast, never waiting for answers: "They your bikes?" "What street do you live on?" "What school do you go to?" "Come here often?" "What are your names?" "Do you have names?"

Neither of us answered. By sliding my eyes sideways, I could see that Doreen had finished eating, could see her leaning against the tree, smiling. I knew that any minute she would begin to talk.

"I'm Doreen and she's Margo," Doreen said, although we'd long ago made a plan to tell boys our names were Rita and Paulette. She told them she had noticed them in the pool, explained that we'd never been to Fairfield Park before, that we were thirsty, that we'd spent our last quarter. She lied, said we were both fourteen and that the bikes were ours.

The one who liked Doreen was the leader, said his name was Nick, that he was seventeen and finished with school. He bought all of us lemon drinks from the stall. When we got back on our bikes Doreen and the boys rode ahead, swerving around each other, stirring up puffs of dust, tipping the bikes back on their rear wheels, yelling "Hands Up!" and "Stick em up!" as if they were children.

It was almost dark when we left the park. Still
they dawdled. The streets had gone quiet; in the
houses, lights were being switched on, blinds pulled
down. Men in white shirts picked toys off lawns,
rolled up hoses. Women called from doorways and
the children playing around street lights went one
by one into the houses. The uneasy feeling I'd had
in the morning came back, and I yelled over my
shoulder to Doreen, "Hurry!" I waited. "Ben and
his crowd'll be looking for their bikes," I said when
she and the others caught up.

"Let them look—what do we care?" Doreen had
taken her sweater off, knotted it around her shoulders; above the red wool her face was flushed and
pretty.

The boy who had called me Foxy said,
"Spoilsport!"

"Shut up, Big Ears!" I said, and turned to
Doreen, "I don't care—I'm going straight on
home!" I told her.

"You can't! You don't know the way.
Remember?" Doreen leaned forward, one leg
hooked over the bike, her sandalled foot dangling.
Her hair had fallen forward and, in a gesture I'd
never seen before, she reached up and swept it back
so that it slid like silk between her fingers. Nick was
watching; Doreen looked into his face and laughed.
"Margo is afraid of a lot of things," she said.

It was true—true then, true now. Near tears, I
turned and pedalled away. One of the boys called
after me, but I didn't look back. The streets were
dark. For a time I was afraid, but three blocks on I

saw the lit spire of St. Kevin's and pedalled towards it.

In a surprisingly short time I turned into Dugan Street. People still loitered around the remains of the street party—adults sitting on doorsteps and folding chairs, standing in little groups talking, children running about with sparklers. There was music. At first I thought it was Doreen's father playing his harmonica, but no, someone had propped a record player on an orange crate in the grocery story doorway. In the dimness beneath the canvas, couples moved slowly about in each other's arms.

Nothing bad had happened. I was so happy—so happy riding down my own street. I circled twice, weaving through the well-known lanes, swooping around corners, skirting behind houses, forgetting I was on a stolen bike until I almost ran over Kev and Shirley lying on the narrow patch of grass behind the book shop. The shadow untangled; Kev swore and grabbed at the bike, but I had time to jump off and run for home.

In the shop my mother was stacking books back on shelves. "Had supper, did you?" she said, not even looking up from the boxes she'd put out on the sidewalk that morning.

I nodded, went upstairs and crawled into bed. I was exhausted and still angry at Doreen—but not as angry as I had been. I fell asleep thinking I'd probably acted dumb, wondering if Doreen would still be friends with me.

Sometime in the night my mother came into the room, woke me, leaned over whispering that I must get up, must put on my dressing gown and come down to the shop.

Downstairs, Kev Pendergast and his mother stood just inside the bookstore door. No one had turned any lights on but the moon was so bright that I could see Mrs. Pendergast had been crying. One hand, fat and pale blue, gripped the edge of the counter as if she might fall if she let go. She said that Doreen was not in her room, that no one had seen her all day. They had been searching the neighbourhood for hours.

I could hardly hear Mrs. Pendergast. All I could think of was how I must look standing in front of Kev in my ugly plaid dressing gown with the frayed hem, my hair all bushed out around my head the way it gets when I sleep. I told them about taking the bikes, about going to Fairfield Park, but all they wanted to know was where Doreen was now. Kev spoke sharply, sounding like his father those times he warned Doreen and me not to do something. I explained how I'd come on ahead, left Doreen with Nick and his two friends. I was drowsy, half asleep, but Kev kept prodding me, asking questions I couldn't answer. Finally they let me go back to bed.

In the morning, though, Doreen was still missing. I was taken in a police car to find the place where I'd left her. It was Sunday morning, barely light. They drove slowly up and down the quiet, identical streets, but I could not be sure, couldn't help. It seemed impossible that these were the same ominous streets I'd ridden through the night before.

By nine everyone was searching. All the Pendergast relatives had gathered. My mother went to sit with Mrs. Pendergast and Doreen's aunts. My father went looking with the men. All the fathers, uncles and brothers, even grandfathers were out searching through school playgrounds and empty lots, stopping passers-by, asking if anyone had seen a blond twelve year old girl on a boy's bike. Over and over again I was asked to describe Nick and his friends, asked what I could remember about their bikes, their clothing. I answered without really thinking. I didn't want to think about the boys, or about Doreen. They were out there somewhere, I was sure of it, all four of them having fun, whirling around the park, hiding, laughing at everyone for being worried.

I decided I'd hide too. It was barely noon but I considered going back to bed. Then I thought of the clubhouse. I would go there, have a nap—Doreen would come back when she felt like it. I half expected to find her waiting inside the clubhouse, but it was empty. I laid down, stretched out on one of the box-benches and dozed off.

I woke, thinking it must be night. Only when I reached out, pushed the door open a crack and a bright strip of sun cut across my face that I remembered where I was. I got up slowly; my neck was stiff, my mouth dry and I was hungry. I hadn't eaten for hours, not since the hot dog in the park. But I didn't want to go home. Thinking the boys might have something to eat or drink hidden there, I lifted the cover of the bench I'd been sleeping on.

"Doreen!" Anger and a sense of betrayal—always my first reaction. She was curled onto her side, knees folded below her chin, the red sweater under her head.

"What nerve—hiding in here all the time!" I reached down to grab her shoulder. But I didn't. Doreen's shoulder was bare—still, yellowish. So was her face. Coldness was rising up from her. My throat closed over; I wanted to call out, wanted someone to come, but I could only make short gasping noises. I backed into the sunshine, fell over the steps, got up and crossed the small yard. It seemed to take hours until I got to the Pendergast kitchen where the women were.

A bad thing to be thinking about right now, those women in that kitchen, their eyes turning to me as I came through the door—Doreen's mother, about whom I can remember nothing, my own mother, who grabbed my shoulders and shook me until I stopped whimpering.

The tea is cold. I cannot stand another moment in this kitchen, cannot stand this waiting for someone to come and tell me what has happened to my son. I get up and rush outside, leave the door wide open. The freezing cold stings my face. Did I put an extra sweater on Matthew this morning? I cannot remember. I walk down the white lane; there is a full moon, the snowbank covering my car shimmers like the back of a blue whale. On the far side of the harbour I can see lights: cars or snowmobiles. Over here, nothing, not a sound, not a light, only moon and snow.

Realizing I will not hear the phone from where I am, I run back to the house, return to the kitchen, to the shattered teacup and spilled tea. I sweep up the broken china. Then I get a bucket of water and begin to scrub the floor.

In the weeks after Doreen's death I would sometimes wake forgetting, thinking she was still alive. I would begin planning what we would do after school. Then I'd remember. This happened over and over, Doreen dying each morning. I wanted desperately to skip that moment, to wake remembering Doreen was dead—or better still, to wake not remembering her at all.

Late in September, when I came home from school one day and my father was not in the store, a policeman was there, over beside Papa's desk talking to my mother. His voice was low, urgent; my mother was shaking her head. I went over to stand beside her. He stopped talking, and I saw that he was one of the men who had driven me around that Sunday morning, searching the streets for Doreen.

My mother told me to go down to the sewing shop, "Lena needs to measure you for a new school skirt," she said in that dismissive voice I remember so well.

I didn't move. The policeman studied me. "Mrs. Stein, I think you should tell the child," he said.

My mother said nothing; she wiped the desk with a cloth.

The policeman just waited, watching my mother line up the receipt book, the pen, the picture of Papa's other family. Then he told me that my father had been taken down to the police station for ques-

tioning. It was because of a cigarette—one of the
Gauloises only Papa smokes. It had been found
underneath Doreen's body, the policeman said,
"near the victim."

I couldn't look at my mother's face, only at her
hand, her index finger peeling a spot of glue off
Papa's desk. It was quiet inside the shop—silent. I
remember the feeling that everything in the world
had stopped; everything—the cars on the street, all
the cash registers in the stores, Lena's sewing
machine—all frozen in mid-stroke. Only my mother's fingernail moved, urgently scraping at that
small blob of bookbinding glue.

I had to confess—to tell them how I'd taken cigarettes from Papa's desk, how Doreen and I used to
smoke in the clubhouse.

The policeman took us down to the station
where I was led into an office and directed to tell a
different policeman everything I had ever stolen.
He wrote it all down; comic books, candy and coke
from the clubhouse, nail polish from Doreen's Aunt
Angela, the doctor's book from Mrs. Pendergast's
bureau drawer, Papa's cigarettes...it was a long list.
The policeman read it all back to me and made me
sign at the bottom.

After that he took me into a room where there
was a wire cage no bigger than a cupboard. The
policeman told me this was where they put little
girls who stole. Sick with fear, I promised if he let
me go I would never, never steal again. I had forgotten all about Papa—all I could think of was getting out of that building, saving myself.

When the policeman finally led me to the door, my parents were waiting outside in a police car. My father's face was grey; he didn't speak. I thought they must have put him into the wire cage. I should have told him I was sorry, but the thought did not occur to me until much later. When we got back to the house my mother and one of the policemen had to help Papa out of the car and lead him upstairs.

My father stayed in his bedroom for weeks. When he came down again he seemed smaller, as if he had shrivelled. He hardly ever spoke, spent hours sitting in a rocker near the back, staring towards the store window. My mother now did all the store work. Papa no longer went outside, not even to Mr. Worbel's newsstand for conversation and morning coffee.

I missed Papa even more than I missed Doreen. I wanted to hold the folding bone in my hands again, wanted to watch his hands, hear his voice, to be back in that safe place we'd made. But my father no longer took in books to bind; his hands were not steady enough, he told my mother. Sometimes I tried to talk to him. Once I even got up the courage to ask what was wrong.

He studied my face, as if we'd met long ago and he was trying to remember where. "This is no country for old men," he said, but by then he was looking towards the window again—although all you could see from where he sat was the top half of the wire factory across the street.

The Pendergast family moved to Timmins. They sold their house, left quietly. Everything changed. The people who bought the house were young, had no children. They pulled the clubhouse down, paved over the yard, put up a pink neon sign and opened a record store in Mrs. Pendergast's living room. The Pendergasts were never mentioned. It was as if they had never existed, as if Doreen had simply moved away with the rest of her family. After a while I began to imagine her in Timmins, in a new school with a new best friend. So clear was this picture that one day in history class, the teacher's voice droning in the background, I found myself writing a letter. "Dear Doreen," I wrote, "Everything is so changed since you left...."

Only my mother continued as if nothing had changed, as if the three of us were like other people. She still went to Saturday night movies, now with Lena the sewing lady. She still sent me around to neighbourhood shops, still stood in the doorway on warm evenings nodding, but never speaking, to people who passed the store.

I began to think differently about my mother, started to wonder if what I'd taken for sophistication, for aloofness, might be stupidity, or a kind of deliberate innocence which, in my estimation, amounted to the same thing. How else could she not see that it was only our friendship with the Pendergast family that made us ordinary? Without Doreen and her family all the peculiarities of my parents—worse still, all my peculiarities—were revealed, exposed to the world.

I am still scrubbing the floor, scrubbing unnecessarily, when the phone in Velda's kitchen rings. I scrabble towards it, tripping, almost upsetting the bucket.

As soon as I hear Velda's voice I know the worst thing has not happened. "Found! He's been found—Found, Found, Found!", she screeches, repeating the word until I order her to shut up. I ask if my son is all right.

"He's fine, fine—just a bit cold. He was hiding all the time in the back of the teacher's van, under an old jacket. Right there in the van, all the time they were driving around looking for him! The little nuisance!" she says with admiration. "Apparently he heard Mr. Richards promise the youngsters he'd take them for pizza before the concert—not the best idea if you ask me—still, Matthew wanted to go too." Velda babbles on, describing where each searcher had gone, what each one said when they came in. It is ten minutes before I can interrupt, ask her to put Matthew on the phone.

"Oh, he's not here, girl! Gone off happy as a lark with the rest of em. Three or four parents, Ruby and Dunc, most of the teachers and all them youngsters—traipsin all the way up to Greenspond for pizza. They've decided to set the concert back an hour." She paused, "I told Ruby we'd meet her over at the Lodge." The triumph in Velda's voice makes me wonder for a minute if she could have arranged all this in order to get us together, to devise a celebration we are all part of.

It is almost nine when we get to the hall. The room is filled to capacity. For this night the pub must be deserted, television sets abandoned. Ruby has managed to save only two seats so I take Matthew up on my lap. A dozen or so young people, most of whom I've never seen before, stand near the back, sons and daughters home from St. John's, from Lab City and Goose Bay, from Toronto, from Fort McMurray. Home for Christmas. Ruby reaches behind Velda to tap my shoulder, points out her three good-looking boys around whom a bevy of girls have clustered.

As the hall becomes hotter, more overcrowded, a briny smell seeps up from the planked floor, the spirits of salt cod once stacked by the thousands in this room. The smell is euphoric—it reminds me of my father's binding glue. I glance at Velda, hoping to convey the happiness I feel sitting here with my son safely in my arms. But she is focused on the opening curtains, on Jesus, Mary and Joseph who occupy centre stage. They sit rather uncomfortably, this holy family, arranged atop a blue plastic fish crate onto which evergreen boughs have been stapled. This year there are not enough student voices, so the church choir has been brought in, adults arranged in a semicircle behind the children. To one side Nurse Johanssen stands by the piano, peering down into the audience, waiting sternly for the pointing and whispering to stop.

Nurse Johanssen is a large woman, not fat but tall, with breasts that have become a single unit. At the clinic she wears white blouses and firm gabardine skirts, but tonight she is flamboyant in red velvet, long and flared and embroidered with green and gold. When the audience is quiet, she moves regally to the piano, sits and begins to play "Silent Night."

Scene follows scene: meek sheep and dancing stars, shuffling angels, self-conscious shepherds and kings mime their parts. Older students stand to one side, reading appropriate sections of the Christmas story. In between, choir members are efficiently herded on and off stage by Nurse Johanssen who seems to be in charge.

I watch in a daze of tiredness, leaning into the pungent dark, my lips brushing Matthew's hair. His hair is still wispy soft, angels' hair, but with a musty smell—probably from the jacket he'd covered himself with in the van. The worst thing about not believing in God is not that you cannot ask him for help, but that you cannot thank him for happiness.

Near the end, when every performer is on stage for the grand finale, Nurse Johanssen comes to the front again. Holding her hand above her eyes she peers down into the audience.

"Looks like a Christmas rooster, her Ladyship do," Velda whispers.

It is true. Ruby and I start to giggle. Then we realize that Nurse Johanssen is looking at us, see that she is beckoning to Matthew, inviting him to come forward, to join in the last carol. "Bless her heart!" Velda says, repentant now, though I know that tomorrow she will again refer to the nurse as a CFA. She takes my son's hand and, all smiles, leads him to the front, lifts him onto the stage.

Nurse Johanssen sits down at the piano and, with great relish, ripples out a few notes. She points a commanding finger towards the fifty or so people on stage.... "Star of the East/Thou hope of the soul/Guiding us on while dark billows roll..." they sing, the music rolling out, filling the small room.

It is the Star Song Matthew talked so much about. He is standing next to Todd, fair and square in front, singing with all his might. He is flushed with happiness; any moment he might burst into tears or throw up, as he often does when excited.

I will lose him. I know I will lose him. But not now, not yet. For the moment he is mine, for the moment he stands before me safe—safe and loudly happy. "Gladly we follow/In thy holy light/Pilgrims of Earth so wide," he sings.

The words remind me of my father, of Matthias Stein the wanderer—of my mother, too—of myself—perhaps of everyone—pilgrims moving across a vast spinning planet. Pilgrims of earth so wide.

Enclosed by the smell of salt cod, sitting in an over-warm room on the edge of nowhere, I watch my son's face. I let myself sink into happiness— wrap myself in it, as I might wrap myself in a good dream, knowing it is a dream, giving myself up to its temporary safety.

Part Two

Imaginary Doorways

Vain Deceit

$\mathcal{K}$ate is sitting on the edge of the hospital bed when the blood trolley rattles in. She doesn't speak or look up. Slowly, carefully, she folds back the sleeve of her silk shirt and holds out her arm. The lab technician is impervious to charm; she's given up on him, calls him the Vampire, though not to his face. She is a little afraid of him.

His fingers slide under her palm, lifting her hand as if about to kiss it, he reads her wrist band— Catherine Foley, born August 3, 1924—followed by coded information Kate cannot make head-nor-tail of. She hopes it's more accurate than her name and age, neither of which they will take her word for. The man touches the loose skin of her underarm. She has learned not to watch his well manicured fingers move between the green and purple bruises. Each day it takes longer to find a good vein, but Vampire doesn't fill the time with chit-chat. "I've met coat racks with more personality," Kate has told the nurses.

Then he mutters something, and she realizes someone else is standing on the other side of the trolley—a youngish man she hasn't seen before.

"S.V.D.," or "S.V.T.," Vampire says—then two words. "Vain deceit," is what Kate hears, though she knows it is not what he said. "Vein deterioration," he repeats loudly, accusingly, as if he can read her runaway mind.

"Deceit, not deterioration," she says, but neither Vampire nor his handsome young assistant pay any heed.

Vain deceit was what Mamma used to say when I started using lipstick, Kate thinks. She had been almost sixteen, in town a week and desperate to look like other girls. Ten cents, the tube of Tangee Fuschia had cost, a lovely orange colour. She remembers the sweet creamy smell of the lipstick, wonders where she could have gotten the dime. Not from her mother, that's for sure.

It wasn't just lipstick that Mamma was against. Lydia Davis had hated everything about St. John's. "Sodom and Gomorrah," she called it. Godless. A place with more taverns and movie theatres—"dens of iniquity"—than churches. A place where candy shops and ice cream parlours stayed open on Sunday, where youngsters were disrespectful, and women, who should have been home teaching their children manners, traipsed the streets day and night.

Even had Mamma been so inclined, there would have been no money for such frivolities as lipstick. Kate remembers their last morning on the Cape, that sepia coloured world where she had been called

Catherine, remembers watching her mother count the money saved from a lifetime of fishing.

They had gotten up at five on that last morning, packed their night things away and made a breakfast of bread and tea before Brose Vincent came for their trunk. The room was almost empty, mats gone from the scrubbed floor; pictures, dishes, even her father's books given away. As soon as Brose left, hauling the wooden trunk by its rope handles, Mamma shut the door and pulled the inside latch. Then, to Kate's amazement, Lydia Davis set about destroying her husband's notebooks. There had been twenty-six of them, one for each year of her parents' married life—twenty-six small black covered books like the ones schoolchildren wrote spelling in.

Mamma had picked each book up, shook and ruffled it until a few bank notes fluttered onto the table. When she was satisfied nothing else was hidden between the leaves, she had torn the books apart, dropping pages into the fire a few at a time. Kate stood beside the stove watching the notebooks burn, her father's neat script lifting off the ash— words ("shadows on water," "dear perpetual place") appearing for an instant, then gone.

When the last pages were burnt, Mamma had doused the fire with a dipper of water, muttering some Bible verse. Kate caught the words "sojourned" and "strange country." Her mother gathered up the bills from the table and counted the money carefully, three times. Sixty-eight dollars. To Kate it had seemed a huge amount. She remem-

158   The Topography of Love

bers feeling safe and quite rich watching her mother fold the bills over and pin them inside her purse.

Her final household task performed, Lydia Davis had taken her apron off, rolled it up and tucked it into the paper bag containing a bottle of tea and the last of the bread and butter. She stood in the middle of her bare kitchen, turning slowly, looking around the room she had worked in all her life, the room where she had raised seven children, where her husband's body had been laid out ten days ago. "Get thee out of thy country, and from thy kindred and from thy father's house," she said, and let out a great sigh. Without another word her mother walked out of the house, and, with Kate hurrying behind, marched down through the garden, along the landwash and up the gangplank to the Glencoe.

"Vain deceit!" her mother had proclaimed a few weeks later, watching her youngest daughter paint her lips with Tangee Fuschia. "Vanity of vanities; all is vanity," and "Dear Lord and Father of mankind, forgive our foolish ways!"

Are you pleased, Mamma? After sixty churchless years I still remember those old hymns, can still call up Bible verses, still hear you chanting, still see you pacing the floor in poor Jean's kitchen on Cook Street! Silent pacing and soft chanting that could continue for hours—a quiet woman, Kate's mother had been, but persistent.

For all that, her nagging never stopped me from wearing lipstick, or from being vain, or from doing anything else I wanted to do, Kate thinks. She smiles.

The young assistant, clearly vulnerable to charm, imagines she is smiling at him and smiles back. Kate knows he is wondering where he's seen her before. People in the hospital often do that, people on buses and in stores too; they give her that quizzical look. Sometimes they come right out, asking if they've met her somewhere.

All she has to say is "Jackman and Greene's," and they remember. In the twenty-eight years she stood behind the grocery store counter, she must have served every person in St. John's at least once.

But sometimes, especially if it's a good looking man who's asking, Kate's imagination will suggest more exotic possibilities: isn't he the one she bumped into at the corner of Hollywood and Vine, met on safari, sat with in that tiny cafe around the corner from the Louvre or smiled at in a street market outside Morocco? Kate has an eye for detail. Beyond the shoulders of movie stars she has observed the world: seen Mongolian horses roped and milked, watched bombs fall on London, listened as Tibetan monks chanted from hilltop shrines and heard vendors sing their wares on Jamaican streets. She has had some interesting conversations, enlivened many a long bus ride with talk of faraway places.

She is beginning to see St. Clare's Mercy Hospital as a faraway place. The idea came to her a few nights ago when she was again wakened by odd noises outside her hospital room door. In a faraway place one might hear such shufflings, might lie awake considering the wisdom of moving to a better hotel in the morning. She'd drifted through the

night considering other similarities between the
hospital and faraway places—she might, in a foreign country strain to understand words, try to convince herself that the food was edible, wish that the
natives—the Vampire for example—were more
friendly.

It is, Kate knows, quite different in the teaching
hospital across town, the hospital where they
installed her valve ten years ago. Although that hospital is bigger, less personal, she hadn't felt so side-
tracked there, so alone as she does here in St.
Clare's.

It's your age, you were only sixty-five last time,
Sweet Reason says. As always, Kate tells Sweet
Reason to frig off. Her age has nothing to do with
it. Anyway, that's not her age. No minister set foot
on the Cape for years after she was born, and the
one that finally did come was some old, senile
preacher who recorded the date wrong. She's only
seventy.

It's the age of St. Clare's—this mouldering old
hospital in the middle of town, this place where traffic noises interrupt sleep, where echoing hallways
and shut-down wards whisper of closure and demo-
lition, this place where convent smells, perfume of
holy water and incense, have seeped into the
cracked plaster—that gives Kate the feeling of
being becalmed in a country she's never visited or
even imagined.

There are other things, too. Averting her eyes
from almost-purple liquid being sucked into plastic
tubing, she ponders on black symbols stencilled
onto the wall beside her bed, on dawn visits from a

retired nun, on sentences that drift off into incomprehensible sounds, on combinations of letters that have no significance. All very peculiar if looked at in a certain way—and Kate does.

Not that she's complaining. This sense of being somewhere else, somewhere foreign and strange, has cleared a space, made an emptiness inside her, a space where she can move around and think. Not an unpleasant place to be, this in-between country, though others seem to find it so. Each day, when the doctors make their rounds, she can hear patients along the corridor begging to go home.

Kate makes no such requests. Once home—back in familiar spaces, in rooms where every inch of flooring, ever corner, crack and creak in the woodwork is known—she will be expected to get Frank's meals, to accompany him on countless errands, to wash and clean, to babysit one or another of her great-grandchildren whenever the need arises. Once home, worries about her three sons, about their wives, their ex-wives, their children and grandchildren, will flow in, will fill every inch of her—the way a bucket is filled when you lower it into water.

Here in St. Clare's her family seems far off. Frank seems far off. It's as if their marriage might not have happened—as if she had imagined him, imagined their sons, imagined all those years. In the empty hours between x-rays, CAT scans and blood tests, the thought of family hardly crosses Kate's mind. What, after all, can she do about the lives of her grandchildren and great-grandchildren? Tara's thug-like boyfriend, Shawn's slowness at school, her son Gary's inability to keep a wife, Frank's surliness and indigestion, are all one. "One with Babylon and Rome, One with Ninevah and Tyre," as Mamma used to say.

In here she doesn't even worry about her own ageing body. In here it's not her problem; she has placed her body in the hands of others. The defective valve in her chest, the blood percolating too slowly through her thinning veins—these things are now the concerns of paid professionals.

It pleases Kate to imagine that she's returned to what she was the day her feet (she remembers them clearly, shod in ugly laced-up clodhoppers passed down from her two older sisters) first stepped onto the cobblestones of Water Street. Agog, she'd been, beside herself, bug-eyed with delight at this technicolour world where shops stood side by side, lined up along sidewalks—shops with big windows in which statues posed, wearing dresses she would have killed to own. And streets—streets with lights, streets with horses and carts, with cars and streetcars. And people, people everywhere, people with places to go, things to do—parks and parades, concerts and movies, dance halls and ice cream parlours where, for a ten cent dish of ice cream, you could sit at a glass topped table and watch it all. Lying in her hospital bed at night Kate recalls those things, things that had so horrified Mamma and so delighted her. Ah, long ago—long ago and far away—just down the stairs and out onto LeMarchant Road.

"Your first day on the job is it, Rodney?" Kate asks.

The young lab technician looks up, surprised, forgetting the plastic name tag clipped onto the pocket of his white coat. "Rod," he says, "everyone calls me Rod." He asks if they've met somewhere.

They haven't, but Kate nods, "I think I know your mother—didn't she use to work in the cafeteria down at Woolworths?"

"No, no Mom never worked—well, she used to mind this little store my grandfather once had near the top of Barter's Hill—but that was eons ago, before I was born...."

So amazed is Kate that she forgets the rules of tongue-pulling, "Your mother was Floss Hayward?!"

"Her married name was Florence LaFosse—my father died years ago," the boy falls silent, turns and begins searching for something on the blood trolley.

Strange way of putting it, Kate thinks, wishing she had not interrupted what he'd been about to say. Does he mean his mother has remarried? Or maybe she's shacked up with someone, someone he doesn't like? That's probably it. So this is Florence's son, she who was Floss Hayward. Plain, Floss had been. A nice enough girl, but plain, plain as a turnip—for all that she got herself a good looking son.

"You must be called after your grandfather, got his looks too!" Kate has come alive, as if the blood flowing out of her body had suddenly reversed itself. "Haywards' Grocery! How many times was I in and out of that store!" She studies the young man with delight. "Your grandfather used to serve me—handsome a man as ever walked on leather. So were your uncles. I went out with your Uncle Steve before he left for overseas. Make no wonder you're so good looking!"

Rod LaFosse is embarrassed. He fumbles, almost drops the vial of blood he is labelling. The Vampire scowls at both of them. "Mr. LaFosse is just a student, he has to concentrate on what he's doing, Mrs. Foley. Don't want your blood mixed up with someone else's, do we?"

Kate doesn't answer. She winks at Rod, she smiles: "Come and see me later—come later and I promise you a good time," the smile says. Unlike her ageing skin and unhealthy blood, unlike the rusting valve implanted in her chest, Kate's come-hither smile has not changed with the years.

Oh the things I could tell this boy! Kate thinks. She won't, of course, she is far more discreet than people imagine. Still, tomorrow or the next day she will manage to get Rod LaFosse aside, manage to have a good talk. She'll ask about Floss, about his poor, mad Grandmother Celie—without, of course, saying she was mad. She'll find out who his dead father was, and what became of his grandfather—though he must be dead too by now. Impossible to think of Rod Hayward dead. He has to be, of course. He must have been almost fifty the last time Kate saw him, and that was years ago, the night the war ended.

Kate had never imagined anything like St. John's that night, the whole town filled with firelight, with electric light, with searchlights sweeping back and forth across the sky. After years of pitch blackness to have so much light at night! Light and music and the war over and everyone in the streets, singing and dancing, wishing they had fireworks but making do with car horns and ships' whistles, with street lights and shop lights, with bonfires and flashlights and small sparklers people had been saving for this day.

The radio announcer said the police were not letting any more cars onto Water Street. He said half the street had been blocked off, taken over by the Navy. Sailors had flung hundreds of pounds of Lux Flakes onto the street, slipped and skated on the waxy surface until it became a polished dance floor.

Kate, stuck in a tiny bed-sitter way in Rabbittown, didn't need the announcer to describe it. She could picture it. This very moment, barely a mile from where she stood ironing Frank's blue work shirts, streets glittered like diamonds, an orchestra played. No, two or three orchestras, all crowded onto the Court House steps along with cowboy singers, jazz bands, Mr. Hatcher's violin group, the C.L.B. boys and even a few Salvation Army bandsmen, all joined in one joyous, wild cacophony. Kate imagined music splashing like a river down the stone steps, down onto the shiny black street, down onto the jubilant soldiers and sailors, onto the swirls of men and women and shouting children and dogs and cats and gawky boys and laughing, half-sad girls who know there will never again be a night like this.

And Kate Foley was not there. Tears sizzling onto the hot iron, her three month old son finally asleep in the borrowed crib, the house around her silent as a grave, no footsteps, no voices, no plumbing noises, no cooking smells, not a sound in the house she and Frank shared with the Coady family. She felt completely alone. Very young, Kate had been back then, ironing and crying, knowing Frank wouldn't be back for hours and, when he did come home, he wouldn't want to take her out. Young, married barely a year, but already she knows her husband is suspicious of happiness, especially hers. Especially if he's had a drink or two.

What could Kate do but cry? Here she is, the only person in all St. John's left at home, left with a baby and a radio for company, with recorded congratulations from Mayor Carnell, from Churchill and the King saying how proud they are of the common people, with Bob MacLeod describing what is happening in the streets and playing old war songs on the studio piano one last time ("...there'll be love and laughter and peace ever after...") What else could she do but cry? Twenty-one and missing the party of a lifetime!

She had considered waking the baby, bundling him up and taking him down to Duckworth Street. But what fun could she have, carting a baby to a dance? Besides, he'd probably cry. He's been crying most of the time since he was born, both of them have. Poor little Gary, poor little mite—it's not his fault he's got a sad mother and a gloomy father, not his fault he's awake most of the night. But he's asleep now, sound asleep. She could lock the room door, leave the house and he would be perfectly safe. He seems to have a pattern, dropping off around four in the afternoon, sleeping soundly till midnight or one, then crying all night.

"Conceived in sin, shapen in iniquity, and born to sorrow. Born to sorrow as the sparks fly upward," Mamma had said, standing over the infant, shaking her head the one time she deigned to darken the door of their bed-sitter.

The words sounded to Kate like the curses made in children's stories by a wicked godmother, the godmother not invited to the wedding. And it was true, Mamma had not been invited to Kate and Frank's wedding, had not even been told of it.

Only Doris and Dolph had been there, standing dumb with fright beside her and Frank in the empty, unheated church, with the minister looking through them, past them, as good as telling them he found no joy in marrying a girl named Catherine Davis to a man named Francis Xavier Foley.

Kate did not really decide she would go out that night the war ended. What she did decide was to get ready. At least I can have the fun of getting ready, she thought. She'd pulled off the limp house-dress, brushed her shoulder length hair and, in her slip, skiddered down the hall to the shared bathroom where she washed and dabbed Mrs. Coady's perfume behind her ears. Back in the bed-sitter she patted colour onto her cheekbones, lightened the dark circles under her eyes, applied bright red lipstick. Her best summer dress hadn't been worn for a year and was tight around the waist. Kate had trouble getting the back zipped up, but when it finally closed the bias-cut material fell smoothly over her hips and flared out nicely around her legs.

Once dressed, she'd danced around the room, swinging to the radio music, avoiding the table and crib, the line of soggy diapers hung over the daybed. There was only the tiny wall mirror, but Kate could see herself full length, imagine herself from above, as if a camera had been mounted in the ceiling. Lovely, she'd been, a lovely girl in a smoke-blue frock and strapped sandals, dancing by herself in a shabby little room.

She doesn't remember going through the door, only being outside, the warm night dropping like lace around her shoulders, pulling her down the lane towards the street.

Even now Kate is not sure if she would really have gone and left little Gary alone. She might have. Different times back then. Mothers left infants outside shops. On nice days sidewalks beside stores would be lined off with baby carriages.

But she hadn't left him alone—never had—so you can't trace Gary's problems back to that. She hadn't left him alone because when she got to the gate, there was Sarah, her dead sister's girl, slouching up the road towards her.

What relief she'd felt when she saw Sarah, relief mixed with that twitch of annoyance the sight of her niece always provoked. Imagine, on a night like this, coming to visit a married aunt. The girl was clutching some book against her chest as if it was all she owned. Read, and visit relatives—you'd think someone Sarah's age could find more interesting things to do! And she should know better than to wear that awful wine coloured sweater—a lumpy, ugly thing Mamma had knitted—the sweater made Sarah look like one of those displaced persons you saw on newsreels.

At that moment, watching her niece walk towards her, it occurred to Kate that there was something wrong with Sarah, something she would never get over. The girl had started visiting once or twice a week, dropping in to see the baby on her way home from school. Kate supposed she should be thankful. Sarah was her only visitor now that Doris and Anna had stopped coming. Sarah'd been reading a book aloud, a story about Catherine the Great. The movie, with Garbo as Catherine, was better, Kate thought. Books never were as good as movies. This book was especially boring, and Sarah refuses to skip, reads descriptions of people freezing and starving to death over and over. Kate, who tries to forget unpleasant things, often interrupted the reading to tell her own stories.

Mostly, Kate's stories were recountings of movies she'd seen. "First, you see..." Kate would say, and continue on scene by scene to the happy ending. They all had happy endings: the flawed, sorrowful hero, having saved the lovely (but loveless) heroine, is in turn saved (from sorrow and flaws) by her goodness, her charm, her beauty. Wedding bells ring out, credits roll up. While Kate retold movie plots, she and Sarah would make each other up—paint eyebrows, lips, cheeks, arrange hair, copying the Veronica Lake or Paulette Goddard look from movie magazines.

No matter what they were doing, around five-thirty Kate would become edgy, her attention would waver. She and Sarah would stop talking. Makeup

would be scrubbed off, hair unpinned, movie magazines tossed into a box, pushed under the daybed.
Kate would dart back and forth from table to window, keeping a lookout for Frank. The minute he
turned into the lane she would run down the hall to
Coady's kitchen and snatch his supper from the
warming oven so it would be on the table when he
came through the door.

He would stop just inside the door, pulling off
his work boots and overalls, leaving them in a heap
on the floor. If Sarah was still there he'd stare at her.
"What are you here for? What do you want?" he'd
ask.

"Nothing," Sarah always said. "Nothing."

Frank would sit down to his supper, pick up a
fork and point it at the door, "Then take nothing
and go," he would say, and Sarah would scurry away.

Still the girl came. Kate was glad she came, yet
it bothered her. By rights, Sarah should be hanging
around with youngsters her own age. There were
women—men too, sometimes—back on the Cape
who had gone strange. "Low-mindedness" was what
people called it. When a young cousin of her
father's died suddenly, low-mindedness was what
the minister wrote in the church record as the cause
of death. It sounded horrible, something to be
avoided at all costs. Kate had asked Mamma what
low-mindedness was.

"No gumption!" Lydia Davis told her daughter.
She'd quoted a verse of scripture that Kate hadn't
understood, about the sins of the fathers being visited upon their children unto the third and fourth
generation. After that, Kate always connected low-

mindedness with her father, with his writing, his book reading. Maybe young Sarah wasn't just grieving over her mother, maybe she took after her grandfather.

Sarah had stopped beside the gate that evening, studying her aunt up and down, "You're all dolled up."

"Frank won't be home for hours and hours—I thought if you came I'd run down and see Doris." Kate had expected a nod, but the girl continued to stare as if trying to figure something out.

"I won't be long," Kate said. She was desperate to escape, "I won't be long and I'll give you fifty cents." She'd pressed the room key into her niece's hand. "Here, if Frank does come in you can go on home. Tell him I'm gone down to Hogans' Drug Store to get gripe-water for the baby. Don't mention Doris. Say I'll only be a few minutes."

When Sarah nodded, Kate went dizzy with relief. She hadn't waited a second, had turned, run down the street as if she was trying to catch someone. Breathless and uncomfortably warm, she'd kept on running until she reached LeMarchant Road where the sidewalks were so crowded she had to slow down.

Everyone was out in the street. Everyone who could walk and some who couldn't, small children being trundled along in wicker carriages, old men, veterans of other wars, some in wheel chairs, others held upright by comrades. The lame and the foolish, people who hadn't been through the door in years—wandering, stumbling, pushing and being pushed through the soft night. People waving small

Union Jacks, smiling at each other as if in a dream, congregating in parks and empty lots, standing around street corners where houses were draped in banners and flags, where radios propped on window ledges provided music that drifted from street to street. People were singing along with the music, singing, dancing, laughing, simply being happy.

Kate had never seen anything like it. She made her way along LeMarchant Road soaking up the excitement, yet feeling alone, somehow apart from it all. A young sailor waved to her, brandishing a bottle, inviting her to join the cluster of men and girls sprawled off in someone's front yard. She waved back but kept on walking, hoping to see someone she knew. Just a few months ago it would have been so easy. Back then she couldn't have walked fifty feet along LeMarchant Road without running into Doris or Wes, or Dolph, or Anna, if it was her night off. Someone was always around— Canadians from Buckmaster's Field, Americans she'd met at the roller rink, Irene and Tom hanging out at Rice's chip-shop or sitting on the stone wall in front of Tooton's.

People seemed to be moving one way, Kate realized, moving in a kind of festive camaraderie towards the huge bonfire that was lighting up the sky behind the houses. When she saw that the fire must be in Martin's Meadow, she'd turned, cut down a side lane, and came out right beside Haywards' Store.

In the shadow of the store she stopped to count the money in her coin purse. She'd promised Sarah fifty cents and would have to buy gripe-water as proof to Frank that she'd come out for a reason. Although the Haywards were friends, Kate felt awkward going into their store without buying something. She decided she could afford one Coke. She would go in and chat; if Floss Hayward was around maybe they could go over to the bonfire together.

It was the Hayward boys Kate had been friends with, not Floss who was only about thirteen. Still, they'd gotten along well enough when Kate and Steve were going out together. Sometimes, when she and Steve had been out so late she didn't dare face Mamma, Mrs. Hayward, Steve's mother, would shoo Kate in to sleep with Floss: "Don't worry about it—I'll phone your Mamma, tell her I made you stay over," Celie Hayward would say.

The Haywards were different from the Davises, different from any family Kate had ever known. Unguarded, happy-go-lucky people, their flat above the store always full of neighbours, smoke and talk. Mr. Hayward worked part-time at Fort Pepperrell and all the family helped with serving in the store. Mrs. Hayward, who liked to be called Celie, treated her sons' girlfriends as if she and they were the same age. And indeed, the Haywards did seem impossibly young to be the parents of Steve and Ken, or even of Floss. Kate had once seen Mr. and Mrs. Hayward coming out of the Paramount. It was snowing, big white flakes catching in Mrs. Hayward's hair and on the fur collar of her coat. They had stopped on the sidewalk, right under the movie lights, and kissed. It was the most romantic thing Kate had ever seen real people do.

The night before Steve went overseas the Haywards had a party. Everyone on the street came, so many that the flat and store overflowed. Kate and Steve ended the night asleep in each other's arms, lying on an old sofa, on the veranda out back of the store. It's a pure wonder, Kate reflects, that we didn't go all the way.

They hadn't, though. Next morning, at dawn, Steve's mother had gently prodded them awake, gotten breakfast for everyone, and even called Mamma. "We're all so charmed with your daughter, such a lovely girl—what beautiful babies she and my Steve will have when he comes back!" she'd been horrified to hear Celie say into the phone.

After breakfast, Kate, along with the Haywards and half-a-dozen neighbours, had walked Steve down over the hill to the ship he'd been ordered to report to. The ship had not actually sailed, of course. In those days no one would be told when a ship would sail. "Under cover of darkness," Steve's father said, "some night when all the convoy is ready and the U-boats offshore are otherwise occupied."

Nevertheless, Kate has a picture in her mind of the ship sailing. Tall, blond Steve in his tight navy jumper, waves to her from the upper deck as the grey ship pulls away from the wharf and she, in a white dress trimmed with red and blue rick-rack, weeps, voices sing "Now is the hour...."

In fact, Steve had been wearing his good serge suit with a navy-blue armband that said RN (uniforms would be issued in England). And he had simply gone aboard, and Kate had walked back up

the steep hill to home, still pure as the driven snow
for all Mamma met her at the door demanding to
know where she had slept last night and why Mrs.
Hayward was talking about babies. Kate had not
had sex with any man before Frank. Standing in
front of Haywards' store—thinking about Steve—
she regretted that.

Steve Hayward had joined up early in the war
when it still seemed like a great game, before any
boys she knew had been killed. The news that Steve
was missing had shaken Kate. For weeks she had
nightmares in which she saw bits of his body floating in the ocean, bits of him tangled up with twist-
ed grey metal. She remained friends with the
Haywards, dropping by once or twice a week. Later,
she even considered going out with Steve's brother
Kenny, then thought better of it. Both Doris and
Cass said it didn't look right, going out with the
younger son when his brother had been killed.
Besides, Kenny turned out to be a real Mommie's
boy, not a bit like Steve who'd had a way of teasing
Celie but ignoring her cajoling.

Celie Hayward had raged and bawled when her
second son announced he was going to join up. She
pleaded with her husband to stop Kenny, told the
boy she would break his legs if he dared go near the
recruiting office. When he persisted, she promised
him a car. The Haywards had never had a car, yet
Kenny knew the make and model of every car ever
built. He'd been pasting pictures of cars into scrap-
books since he was six. Celie promised that if he
stayed on at Memorial College she would get him a
car of his own. She did, too. Although you couldn't

buy tires, and parts were scarce, Celie found a lovely little Plymouth some old guy had bought and
stowed away in his garage before the war.

Money for gas had been scarce, yet Kenny somehow got enough to take all the crowd for rides.
Every night they'd be in Bowring Park or out by the
lake, five or six of them squashed in tight, arms
around each other, parking for hours beside country lanes. In the pitch blackness with the windows
rolled down they would talk quietly and smoke,
watch the stars, tell each other what they were going
to do when the war was over, say things they would
never have said in broad daylight.

Kenny gave everyone rides, even people he did-
n't know. "What's mine is yours, sweetheart!" he'd
say, slowing down beside some pretty girl.

He didn't have the car three months before he
went off a cliff down by Logy Bay. Killed himself
and crippled a girl named Diane Mac-something
who was with him.

Kate had tried the door of Haywards' store, rat-
tled it. Strange, to be closed when the streets were
crowded and the field out back full of customers.
She pressed her face against the glass. There was no
light inside, but at the far end of the long, narrow
room she could see someone. It was Mr. Hayward.
He had opened the back door of the store and was
standing there, leaning against the door frame,
looking out into the field. Maybe earlier in the
evening he'd been selling beer and ice cream to the
revellers out back. Now, though, he was just standing in the doorway staring out.

Watching the black form outlined by the red glow, Kate wondered why she was so sure the man was Rod Hayward. It was something about the way he stood, all his weight on one foot, one long arm holding onto the door frame above his head. It was how Steve used to stand, but the father was taller, thicker than either of his sons had been.

As if sensing her scrutiny, Mr. Hayward had turned and come slowly through the store towards her, had unlocked the door and peered out. He looked into Kate's face and didn't know who she was. She had been surprised, a little hurt. She'd enjoyed flirting with Steve's father, and Mr. Hayward had flirted right back, but nicely; he wasn't one of those grabby old men. He used to tease her about her Bonavista Bay accent. Once he'd shown her how to make a cat's cradle, transferring a web of white string from his fingers to hers without dropping one loop. She remembered noticing his hands.

"It's Kate—I was wondering if Floss is in," she'd said. She had been shocked at the dullness of his eyes, the deep lines around his mouth. He looked old.

"Oh yes, so it is—Kate—Sweet Kate from the Cape," Mr. Hayward sighed, shook his head as if he was just waking up. "Come on in. Half St. John's is out back," he gestured for her to step inside. "Floss's not here, gone up to her friend's house— they're having a party. But you're welcome to cut through to the field—there's sure to be some of your crowd out there." He reached past her and relocked the front door.

Kate followed him in through the store, sawdust on the floor muffling their footsteps. She still remembers the sawdust, the springy feel of it underfoot, its damp familiar smell. She liked the store very much: the wide wooden counter, the white enamelled shelves holding artfully arranged tins and packages, the ornate balance scale with its shiny brass weights, the smells—she always loved shop smells—of cheese and tea and vegetables, of apples and sweet biscuits—and of something else, something she'd never been able to identify, mice perhaps. The house was old, joined onto other houses on either side; generations of mice must have lived between its walls, built nests under its floorboards. For some reason the thought of those mice had made Kate's eyes sting.

If she'd married Steve—even if they hadn't married, if she'd been having his baby—she could have come to live above the store. Celie and Mr. Hayward would have insisted, welcomed her, made room for her, tucked her into a bed somewhere. Perhaps she could have helped in the store, Kate thought. She'd have liked working in the store. She had swallowed, concentrating on Mr. Hayward's back. He looked unkempt, was in need of a haircut. His hair, which had turned quite grey, curled down to touch the collar of his shirt, a blue shirt, clean but unironed—for a moment the thought of Frank's shirts crossed her mind; she hoped Sarah would finish ironing them.

Mr. Hayward had paused beside the Brookfield Ice Cream cooler. He pulled two cones from the cardboard container and scooped up double deckers for each of them, maple-walnut and orange-pineapple. He handed one to Kate, and without a word they walked onto the veranda and sat down on the sofa. The sofa was old, the leather peeling; the Haywards had put it outside long ago, when their children were little. She knew this because Mrs. Hayward—Celie—had told Kate that on warm nights she used to come out on the veranda to nurse her babies. Celie Hayward said things like that, nothing vulgar but things you never heard other women talk about. Later, when Steve and Kenny got bigger, Celie would have sat on the sofa watching her husband and sons play ball in the field. Kate remembered herself and Steve sleeping on the old sofa that last night he was home. She wondered if the Haywards had ever made love out here.

"How is Celie?" Kate had not intended to ask this and was immediately sorry.

She had not visited the Haywards after Kenny died, had kept putting it off, couldn't stand the thought of how it must be for the boy's parents. After a month passed it was too late. Someone told her that Celie didn't come downstairs anymore, that after her second son's death she had stopped washing herself, stopped combing her hair, stopped talking. No doubt Celie was in the flat overhead right now. The thought of Steve's mother up above her, perhaps crouching beside an open window listening to people in the field celebrate the end of the war, sent a chill down Kate's spine.

"She'll never get over it," Mr. Hayward said. He didn't look at Kate, but patted her shoulder: "None of us will ever be over it—nothing will ever be the same again."

He was right, Kate knew he was right. Nothing would ever be the same. Not ever. Kate could feel sadness seep out of Mr. Hayward's hand into her shoulder. Horrified by his hopeless misery, she fought to hold back tears. Never the same again— Kate could not bear such despair.

She concentrated on herself, on her own living body, the cool sweetness of ice cream on her tongue, the green holiday smell of crushed grass, on the cracked, slightly damp leather of the sofa she could feel through her thin dress, on the look of her own long legs, the shapeliness of her ankles, the neat prettiness of feet in cross-strapped sandals.

The girl sitting on the veranda finishes every bit of ice cream, lifting the cone, biting off the point and sucking out the last melting mouthful before tossing it over the railing.

Then she lowers her head and touches the back of Mr. Hayward's hand with her cold tongue.

The man gasps, a wrenching intake of breath, before turning to give her a startled, questioning look. Even when she smiles—smiles deliberately, invitingly into his eyes—he waits a long moment before pulling her towards him, over him, sliding down with her into the soft, sagging sofa.

For a time she is on top, her mouth on his, her hands unbuckling his belt, his hands tugging at the long zipper of her dress, unpeeling cloth from her shoulders, uncupping her breasts. Then she is below and he is inside her, and they are together, both of them urgent, alive—relentlessly, uncaringly, selfishly alive.

Quite suddenly, the need is gone. He pulls back; night air, cool air, rushes in filling the space between their damp bodies. Beyond his shoulder Kate can again see red sky, smell grass, hear music, hear people laughing.

Mr. Hayward stands, pulls on his pants and shirt; he buttons and buckles. She watches, phrases fill her mind: "engulfed by passion," "overcome with desire," "swept away." None of the words fit. Later, she promises herself, she will find the right words, will make them fit.

He picks up her dress, shakes it, spreads the smoke coloured cloth carefully over her naked body. "I'm going upstairs to check—I'll be back in a few minutes," he says, and goes inside.

Kate has been lying there some time before it occurs to her that he has not really gone to check on his demented wife, but to give her a chance to compose herself. To leave.

And in a minute she will leave. Kate the dreamer will dress, cross the field and join the dancers. Kate the mother will go home, will walk through the soft blue night with what has happened folded inside like a secret message, will remember to buy the gripe-water at Hogans' Drug Store, will return to the smelly room, she will feed her baby, will finish ironing Frank's shirts.

For now, though, she is content to lie watching shadow-figures cross the sky—shadows meeting shadows, meeting and merging, changing direction. Giants circling a giant fire, moving with the ebb and flow of light and music. Occasionally someone flings boxes or blasty boughs onto the flames and a great burst of sparks leap into the night.

"As the sparks fly upward—born to sin as the sparks fly upward..." Kate muses on the words. They no longer seem accusing but liquid smooth, words someone in a movie might say.

The woman sitting on the edge of the hospital bed remembers everything. Everything. She smiles and presses the cotton wool against her deceitful veins, holding on to everything she has ever tasted, imagined, touched—every face, every piss-a-bed, every song, sermon, story, every Bible verse, every movie, every sunrise, every party dress, every tube of lipstick, hair ribbon or pair of high heels she's ever owned—everything she's ever seen, smelled, heard. And still Kate wants more, always more—will spend the night imagining what Rod LaFosse may tell her tomorrow.

Poems in a
Cold Climate

$\mathscr{A}$ woman stands in a window, smoothing the sleeves of her red wool dress. Through the double glass she watches the first snow of winter swirl into drifts around her car.

A passerby, glancing at the lighted window, would think her young, happy, a woman waiting for her lover, would imagine an open fire, wine glasses on a tray in the room behind her. The passerby would shiver and trudge on feeling deprived.

Sarah Norris is in fact neither young, nor, at the moment, happy. She is the recently deserted (she can think of no other word, although this one seems dramatic, replete with soap opera overtones) wife of Ted Norris, who is, by the grace of God, Sarah's typing ability, and years of summer courses, now a Ph.D., professor of cultural anthropology and author of the just-published book *Patterns of Settlement and Folklore in Newfoundland Outports*.

The room behind Sarah is as comfortable as the passerby would wish. It has soft chairs, soft lighting, many books, and pictures that do not scream for attention. It is, a friend has told Sarah, a civilized room. The idea pleases Sarah who pretends to be a civilized person. Really, the room gives nothing away. It is a room that could, and does, exist anywhere in the world where American magazines and American furniture can be shipped.

Half-a-mile from this civilized room the continent of North America ends, slashed-off black cliffs knife into the North Atlantic. Sarah Norris is thinking about these cliffs as she stands looking out at the snow and stroking her wool-covered arms. How easy it would be to gun the car up that last steep hill. To shoot out over the ocean for a second before plunging down into the icy darkness. She shivers. It would be a cold going and Sarah loves her comfort.

Stupid, really, to even think this way. Self-indulgent and pointless, her grandmother would have said. Over the years Sarah has replaced God with a group of women, her grandmother and great-aunts, who gaze down with stern disapproval from some Protestant heaven Sarah refuses to believe in. Having spent their lives fighting the sea, moving slowly inland, these women have no sympathy for thoughts of easy death.

Sarah cannot assess how serious these thoughts of death are. Is it possible that she is really considering such a thing? She thinks not. Yet the picture of that last, minute-long flight fascinates her—the car arcing through swirling snow into a frozen sea. She suspects she would change her mind halfway through that final plunge; reverting to type she would try to climb out, claw her way back onto the cliffs.

It is Sunday, the fourth since Ted left. Having deliberately rejected her parents' Sunday rituals of church, roast beef and afternoon drives, Sarah thought she had no rituals of her own. She now knows better. Memories of late breakfasts, of toasted muffins and marmalade, of the untidy living-room strewn with newspapers and coffee cups, of long walks and sometimes, when the boys were gone, of afternoon love-making, all depress her.

I'll just have to make new rituals, she tells herself, reviewing a catalogue of ways a single woman can spend Sundays. The muffins and marmalade, newspapers and coffee, and even the long walks—she could borrow the neighbours' dog—can all be enjoyed alone. What about sex though?

She thinks about the men she knows: those at the office, all firmly married and totally unattractive; her dentist is half her age, besides he has long limp fingers, quite revolting. The only other man Sarah can think of is Mike. The thought of going to bed with plump, rumpled Mike makes her smile.

Maybe she could go down to the waterfront and shanghai a Spanish or Portuguese seaman—she's always thought they looked sexy and quite harmless, if one of them could be cut off from the pack. Into bed, sex and a few murmured phrases neither could understand, out of bed and back to the waterfront. It would be efficient and quite satisfactory. It's an idea worth thinking about—altogether as fascinating as the car going over the cliffs at Cape Spear.

When the phone rings she is still smiling, adding convincing detail to the scene with the Portuguese. Will she ask him to take a bath first? No, better not, he might be insulted. Maybe she can turn it into a game, they will take a shower together. He might think this is the usual prelude to sex in Canada.

"Well, you certainly sound happy. What have you been up to?" It's Beth, of course, making sure no one has forgotten tonight's poetry reading. "...you know the last time we had a reader in—that art gallery reading—there were only twelve of us."

Sarah knows. She often wonders why The Poets' Guild sponsors these readings when so few people seem interested. Well, it puts some badly needed government money into the hands of a few writers, and sometimes the visiting poets are quite nice, willing not just to read their own work but to do workshops with the Guild. And for the poets it's almost irresistible, every author in Canada seems eager to visit Newfoundland at least once. Sarah cannot understand this sudden popularity of the place she has lived in all her life. In the last few years it has become exotic rather than quaint, culturally rich rather than backward, an impressive addition to any writer's curriculum vitae.

She assures Beth she will be at the reading. Yes, she remembers it's been moved to a downtown pub. No, she doesn't need a lift, she can clear the snow off her car in a minute. As she hangs up Sarah wonders what Ted is doing tonight.

It would be awkward if her husband turned up at the Ship Inn with his girl. But it seems unlikely.

Leah (a young anthropology student whom Sarah has not seen but who she has a very clear picture of, having forced Ted to describe her in detail) would surely prefer a more upscale place. Anyway, if Ted saw the sign Poets' Guild Reading on the door (Sarah knows they are there, having made the signs herself) he will never go in. Now a published author, Ted has no patience with people he refers to as hobby writers, a term that infuriates Sarah. It is so unfair. Useless, of course, to point out that at least three of the group have had books published and that every one of them gets an occasional poem in one of the little magazines that spring up and die continually across Canada. Ted has selective hearing.

Everyone has a special thing, Ted once told her, something that becomes a logo of identity. It can be almost anything, a distinctive eye coloration, a talent for fortune telling, for making good fudge, winning at card games or taking diesel engines apart. Whatever it is, it becomes in each person's mind the thing that defines them, that makes them separate, better than anyone else. Hers, Ted said, was the idea of herself as a poet.

Sarah does not recall what had gone before this conversation. They had never mentioned it again but she thinks of it often. Maybe it is so. Occasionally, Ted said things to remind her of it, like, "The poet at forty..." (looking at family pictures taken on her birthday) or, more coldly, "The poet is temperamental," (this when she'd refused to attend a faculty Christmas party). He made these remarks in a charming teasing way that many women found endearing.

For the first time Sarah wonders what Ted's special thing is. Surprising, really, that she hasn't pondered this question before. It might, as the magazines say, have saved her marriage.

Sarah has not told her sons that their father is gone. In a few weeks they will be home for Christmas, Peter from the University of Toronto and Jesse from whatever god-awful job he is now doing in Alberta. She will explain to them then—or maybe it will all be over by then.

She decides to go out to clear snow away and make sure her car will start. It hasn't moved since Friday. Quickly she pulls on an old jacket Ted has left hanging in the back porch. It smells of him. Sarah can remember him wearing it years ago when they'd taken the boys skating on Burton's Pond. The bitter cold had driven the grownups back into the car where they sipped cocoa from a thermos and listened to CBC music. She remembers cuddling into the furry collar of the coat. He'd put his arm around her and hummed along with the radio, all the songs from Showboat— "Old Man River" and "Only Make Believe," as they watched their sons swoop across the blue and white ice.

The Hollywood snow, so different from the real stuff that will come later, sweeps away easily. By the time Sarah stomps back into the house she is feeling cheerful and competent. The living room looks so inviting and tidy that she quickly lays a fire. After the reading she will ask a few people back.

Just as she is about to leave, the phone rings again. This time it is Mike, the token male in the poets' group. He is looking for a lift. Other men come and go (Beth says this is because Ruth and Marcie are feminists and scare them off) but Mike, chaser of dreams, joiner of good causes, sometimes teacher and always bum, remains. He attends all the workshops and even takes his turn at entertaining the women in his grubby basement flat. The Guild has been together for sixteen years. Sarah knows this because it began the year that Peter, her youngest son, started school. After so long no one hesitates about asking small favours, visiting each other during sickness, or confiding to each other griefs they cannot write poems about. Once every two or three years a new person comes and gets absorbed into the circle, or someone moves away, often writing to the group for years afterwards.

Ted had all the tribal customs of The Poets' Guild worked out. He once joked that he was going to produce a paper on the subject for some anthropological journal.

On the streets leading downtown the snow has turned to ice. Sarah parks near a church several blocks from the waterfront pub she's never been in. Mike tells them insiders refer to it simply as The Ship. It turns out to be a comfortable place, apparently subjected to a burst of decorator's fever that passed before the project was finished. An artificial log burns happily inside an open Scandinavian wood stove, oak church pews are pushed up to red arborite tables. One corner of the room is raised and covered in orange carpet. This platform holds an untidy collection of sound equipment, cords, loudspeakers and a mike, along with an old fashioned parlour piano painted shiny black.

Sarah and Mike are half an hour early but Beth is already there, sitting alone in a pew jammed tight against the orange platform. She waves and they zig-zag between the empty chairs to join her. Two regulars, no doubt having read the sign on the door, sit as far away from the platform as possible, drinking steadily and silently.

The only visible employee is a woman of about forty with black curly hair and very red lips. She has a pleasant motherly face but keeps it firm and businesslike. She is getting through a Sunday night shift as painlessly as possible.

Neither Sarah nor Beth is used to pubs; Mike is too poor, so no one offers to buy a round. Instead, awkwardly, they each order and each pay for one drink. The waitress is very conscientious, counting out three piles of change, but she doesn't come back to their table. She has resigned herself to a low-drink, low-tip night. Watching her, Sarah thinks they have already been catalogued. She can see the woman pulling off her tight boots, hear her telling her daughter about the terrible slow night, poetry reading bunch—Newfoundlanders, but not a lively crowd, and terrible tippers.

Beth, who is small, dark and nervous, keeps counting the empty chairs, willing them to fill. "We did everything we could, sent out a press release— of course no one printed it—put signs up all over the university, at the health food stores—what about the bookstores? Did anyone put posters in the book-stores?"

Sarah nods. She doesn't share this sense of responsibility and is afraid that any minute Beth is going to insist that the three of them take some action—call Guild members, make a larger sign for the door, go out into the alleyway and force passers-by to come in.

Mike will have none of this. He pats Beth's hand in his absent-minded way, tells her to hush, relax, people will turn up. He tells them that a copy of *Pottersfield Portfolio* containing his new poem arrived today. He's pleased; the editors gave it a full page and a nice layout, but he is a bit mystified; for some reason the last verse is missing.

"I don't know if it was an accident or intention-al. Maybe the poem is better without the last verse. Look, what do you think?" Mike pulls the magazine and a crumpled notebook from his knapsack which, like Mike, is a relic of the wonderful sixties, still showing the stains of wine spilled at Woodstock. Mike has written a poem about the knapsack.

They talk, Beth stops counting people. Mike eventually catches the eye of the waitress and they each order another drink.

Slowly, the room begins to fill: Mary and her husband Andrew, Ruth and Marcie and, at another table, Pat with her new boyfriend and an unknown couple. A local printer cum publisher arrives with two people from the university's English Department.

Beth counts twenty-seven people. "Not too bad a showing. Of course some of them are just here to drink. Still, you can never be sure. I think one of those guys in the corner is a Telegram reporter; he might be interested in poetry."

Then Cora and Margaret arrive with the poet. He is young, tall, thin, good looking. They've driven around the bay, given him the obligatory view of real Newfoundland that St. John's presumably cannot offer. He's been lucky; Margaret has an aunt in Bareneed and they were invited to dinner.

Margaret brings him over to their table.

His name is Julian Grant. Is this possible? Sarah wonders, or is he one of those writers who make up a name for themselves? He is aglow with spillover from the experience of an outport Sunday dinner complete with fourteen assorted relatives of Aunt Grete's and, he tells them, roast beef, salt meat and cabbage, three other vegetables and Yorkshire pudding, topped off with trifle and strong tea, and a large drink in the living room while the women were in the kitchen cleaning up, and stories—he calls them yarns, and has written several down in his little notebook during the drive back to town.

Sarah nods and smiles and nods, willing herself to flow with the brimming goodwill. But honestly, she is thinking, do people believe these events are real? If he arrives at Aunt Grete's door next Sunday the relatives may well be in the middle of a bitter argument. And without doubt, unless he is accompanied by Margaret, Aunt Grete, whom he now thinks of as his closest relative, will not remember ever having seen the sky over him.

Sarah is probably being unjust; she often is.

She estimates Julian Grant to be only a little older than Jesse. Jesse would admire him. Admire the soft worn cords, the faded L.L.Bean shirt that sells for $150. Sarah has become an expert at estimating how much the casual look for men costs.

The poet jumps onto the platform, begins arranging material on the piano stool—his file folder, three magazines and his published collection of poems. All have little markers of coloured paper. In a conversational tone he tells them that the coloured markers are his wife's idea. Different colours indicate poems for different moods, so that he can suit his reading to the audience. But, he says, looking up with a happy smile, he will not tell them what the colours indicate. He also has extra copies of his book, which he hopes they will buy later. He takes his time, moving the sound equipment back, tapping the mike with the tips of his fingers. He asks the waitress to please turn off the music and, if possible, dim the lights. The woman, Sarah notes, obliges with the first kindly look of the night.

Eventually he begins to read. He has a confident, pleasant voice. Even the regulars sitting at the bar seem to listen.

The readers are always good-looking, either handsome young men or handsome older women. Sarah mulls over this phenomenon. Where are the plain young women, the ugly old men poets?

Julian Grant is good. He gestures a lot. Sarah, who notices hands, likes his. They are tanned and long fingered. Between poems he talks about how he gets ideas, about his place in Nova Scotia—an old farm house overlooking the river—about his wife Teresa and his five year old daughter Amanda, about the pets they shelter in the winters and free in the springs. Sarah suspects this easy involvement. He and Teresa do not seem to get stuck with dogs in the early stages of prolonged death or neurotic cats who want to live on top of the fridge. She resents this ability, which she totally lacks, to garner all the blessings of caring without any of the messiness. Is it just very good luck, or are some people more selective in their loving?

Or maybe the secret is Teresa. Sarah imagines a beautiful Irish woman with dark red hair and pale, pale skin that gives her a fragile look. But Teresa is not fragile. She drowns the cats, dogs and birds when Julian is in town talking to his publisher. He doesn't know this of course, and continues to write poems about them foraging through the summer countryside.

He tells the audience he has just put in a flush toilet, a real sign of success, he says, for an Atlantic Canadian poet. Then he reads a wonderful poem about this acquisition. Leaning back, his hips jut out, the muscles at the back of his legs make a long strong line in the grey cord. He is the only person in the room with hip bones.

"If I had a daughter I would lock her up," Sarah thinks.

She turns her head slightly to study the faces around her. As always, the audience is made up of middle-aged women and a smattering of men, one or two obliging lovers and husbands who have grown to accept the eccentric activities of their partners. Sarah once heard Andrew, Mary's husband, tell Ted, "Well, it's better than Valium...."

In the dim, blue light the ageing faces tilt upward, moon-like, adoring, held captive by the beautiful young man, by the words that flow down, so neatly, so cleverly contrived, so charmingly delivered.

Sarah thinks she might be ill. She can feel bile rising at the back of her throat. She hates Julian Grant. She hates him more than she has ever hated anyone. She begrudges him his apple tree, his Teresa, his Amanda, his view of the river, even his flush toilet.

There is a lot of applause when he finishes. People get up, mill about looking happy and relieved; happy for the audience that the poet was so good, happy for the poet that the audience was so good. They chat, buy more drinks, buy the poet drinks.

"He was great—even Andrew enjoyed it!" Mary whispers to Sarah.

Beth and Mike go up to talk to him, and Beth buys one of his books which she brings over to show Sarah. He has written, "To Beth of Newfoundland, fellow poet. From your friend Julian."

Sarah decides she will not, after all, ask anyone back to the house tonight.

Mike, Beth and Sarah walk up the hill together. Mike recites a few of the poet's lines. There is a long pause. Then Mike says, "You know, the likelihood of anyone publishing a first book of poetry after the age of forty is one in 600,000."

They are all quiet.

The night has turned clear and still. Snow scrunches underfoot. Inside their clothing their bones are ever so fragile, thin as the shells of sea creatures bleaching on rocks. They move closer together, the heavy cloth of their winter jackets touching, so aware of the cold flesh underneath, that had they been another race, they would have embraced and cried in each others' arms.

Cautionary Tales

The Empress and her daughter Olga each tried to make the sign of the cross but did not have time. After the first round of shots young Prince Alexis, three of the sisters, Tatiana, Marie and seventeen year old Anastasia remained alive, as did the maid Demidova. Bullets fired at the princesses' chests seem to bounce off, ricocheting around the tiny room. Later, when the bodies were stripped, it was discovered that the Tsar's daughters wore corsets into which diamonds had been sewn so closely that they acted as armour. Terrified and almost hysterical, the twelve executioners continued firing.

I stand beside a magazine kiosk in the lobby of St. Clare's Mercy Hospital reading and rereading this magazine article, a secret report written before I was born, written by Yokov Yurovsky, Chief Executioner of the Russian royal family. Despite all the horrors that have taken place since, the

Executioner's words still have the power to chill. Seven Romanovs, after months of imprisonment, are led down to a small cellar room. Arranged, they think, for a group picture, the family find them- selves looking into the barrels of twelve pistols. The maid, who stands to one side, doesn't count; she can be killed later.

The magazine is for my Aunt Kate who will be fascinated by the beautiful and tragic young princesses. But it is the maid Demidova who inter- ests me. Why is she there?

> *...at the end only the maid remained upright, screaming, running back and forth along the wall, clawing at the wallpaper. Even when the soldiers pursued her with bayonets she tried to fight them off. When she finally collapsed, the enraged men pierced her body more than thirty times.*

I justify my interest in this long ago slaughter, tell myself that having a son in Russia makes my curiosity natural. But contemplation of the unpleas- ant, the dreadful, has long been a pastime of mine—a rather commonplace one, judging by the magazine covers displayed before me on the hospi- tal newsstand.

Since my son Jesse went to Saint Petersburg, information about Russia seems to find me, swim- ming like tadpoles beneath my life, leaping into view, surfacing like the magazine in my hands. Russia, it appears, has descended on Newfoundland: Russians by the hundreds leaving Aeroflot flights in Gander, Russian paintings in gal-

leries, Russian dancers at the Arts and Culture
Centre, Astrakhan hats and Russian sailor caps in
second-hand shops.

The horror of what I am reading holds at bay
the horror of what might be going on upstairs in my
aunt's hospital room. Screaming, bleeding
Demidova keeps me from thinking about Kate, my
chameleon aunt who once fancied being Russian.
For a time, when Anastasia surfaced, Kate began
calling herself Katrina. Since then she's compro-
mised on Katya, though I am the only person who
ever calls her Katya now, and that rarely.

My aunt is slated for open-heart surgery in the
university hospital to replace a valve installed ten
years ago. A valve that is, much to her doctor's surprise I gather, wearing out faster than she is. Kate
has been here at St. Clare's for over a month. The
big hospital across town is overloaded; doctors,
operating rooms and anaesthetists are double
booked. Even were space available, the nurses tell
me that Kate is too fragile, too thin, to undergo
surgery right now. She needs rest, needs to eat
more, to be built up. Today I have been turned away
from her room, told to wait. Experts are with her,
doctors or blood specialists I suppose, poking and
prodding at her poor veins.

I have known Kate all my life. She is the only
surviving Davis girl, the youngest sister of my long
dead mother. Christened Catherine, she renamed
herself Kate when she arrived in St. John's. I have
known her forever, have asked her questions, talked
to her, listened to her talk, for countless hours. Still
I am enthralled: I know all about her, I know noth-

ing about her. She is a mystery wrapped in an enigma. Who said that? Churchill, I think—about Russia.

"Of course you must go," I said when my son first mentioned the possibility of teaching English in Saint Petersburg. In theory I've always believed in taking chances, opening new doors. "A decent job, a chance to see all those wonderful art galleries? I'm delighted!" I told him.

I lied. Half the thirty-somethings in Canada are teaching English in foreign countries—or so Ted, my ex-husband, says. "The new colonizers," Ted calls them. He thinks it's wonderful: good for free trade, good for banks. Ted still professes faith in the old religion, the trickle-down theory of economics—a religion the Russian royal family seems not to have subscribed to.

I re-read the bit about corsets into which diamonds had been sewn so closely that the bullets bounced off. Those diamonds, who had they trickled down to? According to the magazine, Chief Executioner Yurovsky remained poor. "He did not profit from the procedure," his grandson is quoted as saying.

My ex-husband and Leah, his almost-new wife, profit from all procedures. They work as consultants, advising on social trends that can be translated into business opportunities. I still find myself amazed that a Ph.D. in patterns of Newfoundland settlement can be parleyed into a lucrative occupation. Apparently it can. Ted and Leah have lived in Saint Petersburg for two years now; before that it was Saudi Arabia, before that Mali. They spread prosperity. I hope some of it trickles down to Jesse. God knows our son can use it. Jesse, who used to call himself an artist, has been drifting from one awful job to another for years now, never staying in one place, never painting.

When Ted left me and moved in with Leah, Jesse and Peter refused to have anything to do with him. For more than a year our sons would walk out of any room their father came into. They returned his letters unopened, hung up when he telephoned. Their fierce loyalty pleased me, although I could see that some of it was rooted in fear that I might collapse, become one of those sad, helpless old women who cling to their grown children.

In the end, of course, I had to put a stop to it. "Look," I told them, "if I can be civil to your father and herself so can you two." I did not mention the awful words I'd spit into Ted's face when I found out about Leah, the curses I'd called down on both of them, the wine bottle I'd hurled at his head that last moment as he walked through the door.

Now Jesse is with them, sharing their flat in Saint Petersburg, studying part-time at the Repin— something Leah arranged through one of her artist friends. He speaks glowingly of Leah, of what she has done to the tiny rooms, how she entertains, of the friends she and his father have made in the arts community. In thirty years of marriage I could never drag Ted to a dance performance, art gallery or poetry reading.

Kate, the dreamer, says I should go to Russia myself. My aunt believes in romantic endings, is sure Ted and I will remarry. Dismissing the absurdity of such an undertaking, she urges me to go and visit Jesse. "I don't know what makes you so slow, Sarah! Take a chance, girl! Go when Ted and that other one are off somewhere. I'll come with you. We could buy beautiful fur over there—white fur coats, long, with hoods like in *Dr. Zhivago*."

Kate has always encouraged me to take more chances: "Stop reading so much, go out more! Meet people, take life less seriously!" She cautions me against brooding. Brooding, she tells me, is a family trait, one she's managed to shuck off, but only with a huge effort. Kate speaks of her mother, my Grandmother Davis, a great brooder who courted unhappiness, who walked the floor, quoted scripture, hurled Bible verses sharp as spears at Kate when she married a Catholic.

"Wait til I tell you!" my aunt says when I finally get into her hospital room. It turns out not to have been doctors who were with her but reporters—well, one reporter and one photographer. They are doing a story on the old hospital.

She shows little interest in the magazine article I've been reading. Other, more immediate things occupy her mind. I am persistent. I want to talk about the Russian royal family, about Demidova. I want Kate's opinion on why the maid would follow the Romanovs down those cellar stairs to her death.

I press the magazine on her, point out the cover photo of the doomed family—Tsar Nicholas and the Tsarina, their delicate son and beautiful daughters posed in the gardens of the Winter Palace. The father and son stand stiffly in sailor suits. But Alexandra and her daughters, Olga, Tatiana, Marie and Anastasia, are dressed in white organza. They recline on striped lawn chairs. The curve of the princesses' young bodies, their long languid arms, copies the listlessness of their mother, the Empress. But the girls' faces are filled with repressed joy, with a kind of impish delight, mocking this arrangement of limbs the photographer has imposed upon them.

Behind the royal family are grassy lawns, a marble fountain, high enclosing hedges. No sigh of Demidova, or any servant. Still, I imagine her there, hovering in the shadows, holding a tea tray, perhaps, or a parasol. Standing just out of camera range waiting to be called. I could stare at the picture for hours; each detail seems laden with significance.

"That would be Anastasia," Kate points to the youngest face, the girl whose dark eyes, high cheekbones and full, slightly pouting lips seem very modern. It's a lovely face, what I think of as a European face. The kind of face my husband's new wife has.

"The same age as your poor mother, Anastasia was—she didn't look a bit like that in the movie. Older, more like a queen—I think she was Ingrid Bergman." Kate flicks through the glossy pages, grimacing at pictures of shattered skulls, close-ups of the ploughed over burial pit, the massacre room with its ripped, blood-spattered wallpaper.

"I never could abide history," she says. This is not true. Kate has told me whole plots of a hundred movies—those she loved best were always about historical figures, about wars and intrigue, betrayed kings and beheaded queens. "First, you see..." she would say, then describe the opening scene, every detail of every ballgown, every military uniform, each moat and drawbridge, every arched eyebrow, curled lip, every dropped glove.

Today, though, she dismisses history, dismisses the Romanovs. "Never mind that old stuff," she tosses the magazine aside. "Wait til I tell you what happened to me just now!"

Though pale and painfully thin, my aunt seems quicker, more happy than she's been in weeks. Kate never wears hospital clothes but gets up each morning, dresses and makes up her face as carefully as if she were on holiday. Today she has on stylish grey slacks, a fluffy yellow sweater, yellow sandals. Pewter earrings that look like wind chimes dangle from her ears. The earrings tinkle as she gets down from the hospital bed to go and push the door shut.

"There's not another person I know things happen to the way they happen to me!" she says, marvelling at the adventures life has delivered up to her. She hops back onto the bed, kicks off her shoes and sits, backside on heels, like a child, smiling at me—promising me a story, the best story I've ever heard.

Before settling into the room's only chair, I pass her a small tub of blueberries I picked this morning.

"This reporter—her name's Laura—asked me about something she called the Catholic presence here at St. Clare's. Didn't ask if I was Catholic—just went by my name I s'pose—Kate Foley's a real Mick name. Anyway, Laura came over, sat herself down right here with her tape recorder between us. She had on this beautiful green skirt—woven....." Kate pats the place where the skirt had fallen and I can see the soft green cloth on the white hospital sheet.

"Catholic presence! And what did you tell her?" I'm smiling. To the best of my knowledge Kate hasn't been inside any church since the night she got married—but I have no doubt that the young reporter got a good story.

"Oh I told her all about that nun—the one who comes to see me every morning, says that in her day there used to be holy pictures in all the rooms and little shrines built into alcoves in the hallway walls. Red candles burned in the shrines, a candle for each saint, Saint Theresa, Saint Anne, Saint Joseph—and, of course, Saint Clare and the Blessed Virgin. It was a comfort at night, the nun says, making your rounds in the dark, moving from saint to saint. Laura was real interested. This nun—she's a hundred if she's a day—came to Newfoundland when she was seventeen, from County Cork. An Irish peasant she calls herself...."

According to the magazine, Demidova was a peasant, sister of a stable hand at the palace. She came to Saint Petersburg from a village in the Urals. Had she lived—if she had abandoned the Romanovs, not followed them down those cellar stairs—she would now be the same age as Kate's nun.

"The article is about hospital closings—for some big mainland paper. I told her how Protestants wouldn't go near St. Clare's when I first came to town, told her that story about Cass Vincent ...." Kate is saying.

For the first time her stories do not hold me.
Today she has misjudged my interest as I have hers.
My aunt, who grew up in a outport on the northeast
coast of Newfoundland, would understand the
maid Demidova, would know how it feels to come
into a new place, a new time. To come into a time of
lights and theatres, shops and streets and soldiers, a
time of parties and pretty dresses—to leave behind
old time, earth and fire time, sea and rock time. Oh
yes, Kate would understand that.

I imagine Demidova escaping from some hidden village, from dark forest and evil woodsmen,
from Baba Yaga the curse-carrying old woman, the
eater of souls. I see her walking away from a hut
with dirt floors, one room, shared with her parents
and five other children, the cow in one corner on
cold nights. Imagine such a girl coming into the
great chambers of the royal palace, the security of
sleeping in a place protected by Rasputin the mys-
tic, the miracle worker. Protected, as well, by a thousand Imperial Guards, tall men in high hats, wearing bright blouses, rattling sabres, drilling their
horses in paved courtyards. I picture Demidova in
such a place, scrubbing floors, cleaning commodes,
changing beds—watching.

She would have fallen in love, of course. With
Rasputin, with one of the Imperial Guards—but
mostly with the Romanovs. Would have made cheap
copies of dresses worn by the young princesses,
learned to curl and coil her hair, leaned to nod, to
curtsey, to say "Yes, your Majesty."

Long ago Kate did the same. She has told me
about it many times—how she taught herself to sew

flared skirts, to trip along hilly St. John's streets on high heels, to curl her hair and rinse it with lemon juice so that it turned blonde in the summer, to tilt her head and smile up at soldiers, just the way Rita Hayward did in the movies.

Demidova was bright too, eager. She learns quickly, is promoted to serve at table, to bring morning tea to the Tsarina, to fetch books and gloves and wide brimmed hats that protect the delicate complexions of the beautiful Romanov daughters.

"...and all the while me and Laura were talking—sat here just like I am now," my aunt is saying. She leans forward. "All that time this photographer—gorgeous looking, like Robert Redford in *Out of Africa*—was racing around this room. Jumping onto that chair you're sitting on, standing on the window ledge—click, click, click!" Kate moves her head slowly, a flower following the sun, a model following the camera's eye. "Click, click, click—he must have taken five rolls of pictures. When he was leaving he said, 'Oh Mrs. Foley, if only everyone was as photogenic as you!' "

The story is over. Kate sits back on her heels, beaming down at me from the hospital bed, basking in the attention she's received. "Now!" she exclaims. "What do you think of that?"

I am about to tell her it is remarkable—which it is—although I am not surprised. It is the kind of thing that happens to my aunt, the kind of thing that has always happened to her. Before I have a chance to say this, the door is pushed open.

Kate's husband Frank, and Gary, the oldest of their three sons, come in. How much weight my cousin has put on! A dozen years younger than me, he looks as old as his father. It's been a long time since I've seen either of them. Kate and I usually meet in restaurants or at movies. Occasionally she comes to my house; I never visit her.

"Still here—Jesus, it's been a month—and the government talks about savin money!" My uncle tosses a plastic bag filled with mail onto the hospital bed. "More of your junk!" Every word Frank directs at his wife sounds like an accusation.

"Twenty-eight days. It's not my fault. I don't ask them to keep me in here...have you seen Tara?" Kate's voice is so low I can hardly hear the question. She seems to have shrunk, curled into herself. She is looking down, picking through the pile of bills and advertising, setting aside the get-well cards.

"Tara! Tara! That's the only one you ever thinks about—spoiled from the day she was born! No I haven't seen Tara. Six grandchildren and I haven't seen one of em!" Frank turns to me, shakes his head, "They don't come near me—never crosses the door!" He seems proud of this neglect.

His hair has turned white, he wears glasses, is fuller of face and figure but not fat. Kate has told me that he's given up drink since he retired, started eating whole grain bread, walking around the block twenty times each day. He is still handsome.

"Gary comes to see you," I say, nodding to my cousin who has gone to fiddle with the small TV that swings on an arm beside Kate's bed.

Frank snorts. "Oh yes, he comes!" Something is implied, some insult to Gary. I see Kate glance at her son, but neither of them speaks. Frank ignores them, he is talking to me, "...but not the rest—and when they do come to see me it's because they're lookin for somethin. I tells em right off—soon as they walks through the door—tells em they're not gettin a thing!"

"Maybe they'd come more often if you said something nice," I say in a joking voice.

He smiles, a canny, satisfied smile, "Oh, I don't care if they never comes—I got the old cat."

I too have a cat. We exchange stories about cats, about their intelligence, their loyalty and wit. I can tell my uncle is pleased that we can talk like this, so pleasantly, about something we both understand. I am pleased, too—and surprised that I'm pleased, surprised that I can banter with this man knowing all I know of his small and big meannesses, knowing that Kate had to have her much-loved dog put down last winter because the animal was old and sick and Frank wouldn't let him into the house, not even on bitterly cold nights.

I know how they met. It is one of Kate's stories: she arrives at a party, comes through the door, looks up and sees this man standing halfway up the stairs on a little landing, one arm resting on the window ledge. Kate has described every detail, as if it were a movie: the love song playing in the background, the man's tweed jacket, his leather riding boots she'd never seen the like of, the handsome unhappy face—Clark Gable's face—outlined against the sky. "An azure sky" Kate says—a distant azure sky in

those last moments of a summer's day, a wartime
summer in 1944.

"...she's a scrawny old thing—hates youngsters," Frank is still talking about his cat, telling me
how she was once lost for three weeks.

I imagine him that night, young Frank Foley
standing on the narrow landing. He's been standing
there for some time, the position has gotten uncomfortable. He is embarrassed, becoming angry, he's
made a fool of himself. Those strangers downstairs
are probably laughing at him, wondering who he is,
why he would come to a party and not speak to anyone, wondering why he hovers on the stairs, looking
out the little window, looking down at a dirty back-
yard.

Everyone else in the house seems to know one
another. Five girls have grouped around the gramo-
phone to sing. Others are dancing. They are all
showing off, making up variations on the song,
whirling each other in and out of the living room,
sweeping down the narrow hall, the men bending
their partners backwards nose to nose, the women
flipping their legs up so you can see their underpants. They are the kind of people Frank cannot
stand. Townies—foolish, giddy girls with made up
faces, soft, silly men, people who laugh about nothing, whisper in each others' ears, tease each other as
if they were children. They probably think he's a
thief—lately there's been a rash of houses ransacked
by unknown guests. He can feel their eyes on him,
watching to make sure he doesn't hook anything.

Frank curses the boarding house crowd who
persuaded him to come. Most of all he curses Mr.

Kippens, the bloody black Englishman who lent him this outfit he's wearing, who convinced him it was just the thing for a party in a house at the top of Brazil Square.

"Now if it was the bottom of the Square," Tony Kippens said, "if it was the bottom, wouldn't matter a damn what you wear—but up near the top, oh no, dear boy, up near the top you're in the Higher Levels, in toff country, must wear toff duds. You'll come to appreciate these distinctions after you're in town a while longer." Kippens had given the tweed jacket a good shake, pulled the silk shirt off the hanger. "Go on, try them on. I'll not need them till the Walwyns get back."

"I'll kick the shit out of Kippens when I gets outta here—no matter that he is sixty, no matter that he teaches the Governor's kids how to ride. I don't care if they sends for the Black Maria, I'll break the frigger's neck for makin' a fool outta me." Even as he thinks this, Frank Foley knows he has only himself to blame. Kippens is just the kind of snot his grandfather warned him about.

"St. John's is chock-a-block with shit-headed shaggers thinks they knows it all," was what the old man had said.

They were just outside Harbour Main, Frank sitting on his canvas sack, wet and cold in his thin jacket, the fog so thick he could barely see his grandfather standing a yard or so away with one foot on the iron track. They had been waiting alongside the railbed almost an hour, and these were the first words either of them had spoken. Frank heard the train, as she came around the bend, doing no more than ten miles an hour. He got up and went to stand beside his grandfather.

"Keep yourself to yourself—don't expect nuttin from none of em and don't give em nuttin and you'll be all right!" The old man let three cars pass before he gave the boy a shove and shouted, "Now get the fuck outta here—and don't come back!"

Frank had lunged blindly forward, grabbed at something and jerked himself up between the moving cars. By the time he steadied himself and turned around there was no sign of the old man. A cold hearted bugger, his grandfather. Still, he'd managed to feed the two of them for fifteen years without help from church or charity. Frank, who never will go back, never see the old man again, stands at the top of the stairs vowing to remember his advice in future.

It is a warm evening. The house is small and overcrowded. Heat, pulsating music, loud laughter and a smell of something like burning candy rises from the rooms below. Above it all, Frank can smell his own sweat, mixed with the horsey smell of Kippen's hounds-tooth jacket. He counts the number of steps below him, estimates how long it would take to get through the mob in the hall. Would any of them notice him leaving? Stop him, perhaps, before he reaches the door? They might want to talk, be friendly. The very thought causes him to sweat even more.

And outside, on the front steps of the house, a young woman, a girl really, is standing. Her name is Kate Davis; she is beautiful and knows it. Pausing there in her borrowed dress of apricot coloured crepe, Kate glows with life, with expectation, with longing.

She has not been invited to this party, but in wartime St. John's boys and girls gather nightly to say goodbye to friends and everyone is welcome. You're sure to meet people you know—boys bring Coke and beer, girls bring a cake and twenty-five cents. Kate has been to three such parties already this week. She's alone tonight because her current boyfriend is fed up with parties, and her girl friend has been called back to work at the last minute.

"You go, anyway," Doris said, "take my cake— you can even wear the dress I bought Saturday, if you like."

Kate has come because she hates to stay home, because she cannot resist a party, because she loves music and dancing and kissing, loves the excitement of saying goodbye to boys who are going away, going to England, to France, going to war, perhaps going to die.

The young woman standing on the front step knows just how she will look when she walks through the door, is aware of how the soft material accentuates her tiny waist and smooth hips, how the spike heel shoes lengthen her already long, painted legs. She knows how her blonde hair looks caught up in the black snood, how the jet mesh lets soft curls escape around her ears and at the back of her neck. Kate Davis licks her bottom lip, smiles. She doesn't knock but simply reaches forward to let herself in.

The man standing halfway up the stairs is someone she has never seen before. He is dressed in a way she's never seen any man dress in real life. He's wearing a tweed jacket and riding breeches, tight, knee-high riding boots and a cream-coloured shirt, no tie.

The girl stands in the hallway, oblivious to the merrymakers around her, deaf to their laughter, to the squeals of girls, to some boy's voice crooning *Auf Wiedersehen*—"With love that's true, I'll wait for you. I'll veder same sweetheart," he sings.

Everything has stilled. Kate looks up, smiles her come hither smile and slowly climbs the stairs. Detached from sound, detached from earth, she floats upwards—moving towards the soft brown sheen of riding boots, towards the rough tweed of the jacket, the fold of cloth where the shirt has fallen open at his throat, towards his face, his mouth....

Frank's voice has stopped. I realize that he is looking at me, expecting some response to his story. I nod, smile. Neither Gary nor Kate have spoken for an age. Gary seems lost in the soundless football game. My aunt has picked up the blueberries I brought, screwing and unscrewing the cover of the little container.

There is an awkward silence. I stand, pat Kate's shoulder, "I have to go, have to find a present for Jesse," I tell them. "His birthday's next month. I might get him a jacket—young men always need jackets."

Something is happening, suddenly my voice is thick with tears, but no one speaks and I plunge on, "I have to get it sent—it takes weeks for mail to get to Russia. Weeks!" the last word is half croak, half sob.

While I get control of myself, my cousin and uncle begin talking hurriedly, not just to distract me but, it seems, to keep me in the room. They are full of advice about where I can buy the best made jackets, with suggestions for other gifts. They ask about Jesse, about Peter, want to know if Russia is a safe place.

Frank says he cannot understand why people always want to be off someplace else, "Never content—all you Davis crowd are the same!" He jerks his head towards Kate. "Her there'd be gone tomorrow if someone was foolish enough to give her a ticket. Don't know where ye're well off!"

But Gary admits he would like to go to Russia some day, says he's talked to some Russian immigrants around town and read a lot about the Russian revolution. I suggest he take the magazine lying on his mother's bed.

Kate is eating the blueberries, studying each berry before she puts it into her mouth. I tell her I'll be over again tomorrow, ask if there is anything she'd like me to bring. She shakes her head. Although we seldom make such gestures, I kiss her cheek, wink at her, say, "Goodnight Katya."

The day the Bolsheviks came, Demidova the maid was with the royal family, holding a cream coloured shawl in her outstretched hands, reaching towards the youngest Romanov daughter. She is about to drape the silk square over Anastasia's shoulders when they hear shouting and shots, hear boots hit marble, hear men marching towards them down the long corridor.

In that last moment there would have been time. Still time to escape—a servants' exit, a back stairway down to the kitchens, to the stableyard, to her brother who has already made friends with the Bolshevik guards.

The maid Demidova leans forward. (Does she consider escape? Perhaps not.) She folds gossamer cloth around the Princess's shoulders. "Your Highness," she says, and the door splinters.

To The Promised Land

I'd been tossing Lisa's records out into the street for a good while. All her Noel Redding and Mitch Mitchell records were gone before I had the idea of matching titles up with whatever I was aiming at. About six in the morning I got creative, sent "Electric Ladyland" winging at the back of a B.C. Hydro van, "Axis" at a truck that was towing illegally parked cars off the street. "Purple Haze" was the one I hit the convertible with. After that Harry and Gino broke into my room, dragged me downstairs and dumped me down on one of Gino's sidewalk chairs.

Gino keeps bringing me those creamy-white coffees, lowering the cup down on the marble top table so there's no click. Across the street Harry Wu is standing in the door of his fruit store, watching in case I go berserk again. Wasn't for Gino and Harry, I'd probably be in court this morning charged with lopping someone's head off with an old vinyl record. Top   story   on   the   National:

"Newfoundlander beheads passerby with Jimi Hendrix record." Mom would be some ticked.

I'm not much of a talker, but right now I'd like to tell someone about Lisa. I want to say her name out loud. I suppose I could call Mom, or even Winse. Only thing is, I know just what they'd say. Old buddy Winse'd tell me to get a life. "It's Monday morning, Rod boy! It's the 1990s for God's sake! Get your arse in gear! Forget her!" Mom's message would be the same, only in different words.

They're right, and later I'll do what they say. Later. For now I just want to sit here holding onto my cup, feeling the sun on my shoulders, remembering the first time I set eyes on Lisa, that night in the new library.

I hadn't been in Vancouver long before I got to appreciate dry quiet places where I could be alone without looking conspicuous. Which meant I was spending most of my time in art galleries or in the downtown library. For hours on end I'd stare at paintings and wish I'd studied art. Then I'd go to the library, checking every newspaper in Canada for jobs, wishing I'd finished that lab tech course, wishing I'd studied anything except architecture.

That night the library lights had already blinked. I was on my way out when I glanced into one of those study rooms with a door that's half window. Inside, a man about my age sat hunched over a computer. A second man, tall, black and handsome, stood beside the table leafing through a pile of books, marking pages with slips of yellow paper. In the foreground, between the men and the window, a girl paced back and forth, back and forth.

She was raking her fingers through her hair. By the look of her hair she'd been doing this for some time.

I often wonder why I stopped, why I stood in the dark hallway watching the pacing girl, the strangely lit faces of the men. Perhaps, as Lisa once suggested, it had something to do with paintings I'd been looking at—an exhibition then on at the Vancouver Art Gallery. "To The Promised Land" it was called. Large biblical pictures dominated by darkly bearded brooding men wrapped in layers and layers of cloth, billowing cloth that made them seem huge and powerful as mountains. Cowering in the corners of these paintings were naked, pale-fleshed women. Women, and sometimes children, hiding themselves in the shadows of rocks, stumbling into deserts.

Lisa says that such pictures reflect deeply repressed sadism—or did she say masochism? She told me this one summer's night when we were walking home from a similar exhibition. We'd stopped outside some sex shop, laughing at the window display, comparing it to the pictures we'd just seen. In the window a male dummy, armoured in chains and black leather, sat astride a motorcycle. Posed on either side of him were two female mannequins wearing ragged scraps of lace. They seemed to be attached to the handlebars of his Harley-Davidson by chains welded into their nipples. This display, Lisa said, was today's equivalent of the Victorian art we'd just seen. She has that kind of mind; it leaps, makes connections, zooms off, leaving plodders like me blinking in the dust.

I don't think it was masochism or sadism—or
even eroticism—I felt that night in the library as I
watched Lisa pace. It was more curiosity—curiosity
and pity. Right then I abandoned my search for the
kind of job I'd come to Vancouver to find. I stopped
reading want ads, stopped sending out applications.
Thinking about the girl with the cream coloured
hair, wondering why she seemed so unhappy, occupied most of my time.

I never actually followed Lisa. What I did was
search through galleries and art shops for her. I
stood next to her at book signings, watched as she
bought fruit in Granville Market, sat in on public
lectures and hung around outside The Emily Carr
Institute where she was a student. Within a week I
knew her name was Melissa Jordan, that her friends
called her Lisa and that she was from somewhere
near Toronto.

Once, at a poetry reading, I sat right behind her
and two tall guys who looked like twins. I couldn't
decide which geek she was with. She sat between
them, kept turning from one to the other, touching,
laying the pads of her fingers on the sleeves of their
jackets—a gesture that sounds impersonal but to me
seemed overtly, embarrassingly, sexual. Lisa's hair
was soft, silky smooth that night, not a bit like the
electric tangle it had been in the library.

After the poetry reading I didn't see her for
days. I worried, thinking she might have left town
with one of the twins, gone back to Ontario to get
married, taken off to Japan to teach English. Even
then I knew she was the kind of girl who could disappear. Although Lisa filled my thoughts I never

spoke her name. Even when I ran into Winse, with whom I share a hundred Famous Firsts, I didn't mention Lisa. I remember wanting to, but I didn't.

Winse and I were friends even before we started school, since the year Council condemned our house and moved us into Housing. I still own the land our old house was on. Pop left it to me, the family estate, a twenty-five foot square of rock and rubble on a hill in downtown St. John's. In Housing we were attached on one side to Winse's family, the MacLeods. We had identical houses, for all there were seven MacLeods on their side and only my grandfather, who I always called Pop, my mother and me on our side.

One day, when we were teenagers, Winse and I found his baby book. It had a pale blue cover with "Famous Firsts" written on it in pink. Mrs. MacLeod had filled four pages with Winse's achievements before she lost heart: his first word, his first step, a curl from his first haircut and his first tooth, sealed under plastic. The last entry was a picture of Winse as Tiny Tim in a school play when he was nine, the year he got suspended for evacuating the school by imitating the Principal on the intercom.

We left the book where we found it, in a box behind the hot water tank in the MacLeods' base-ment. It's probably still there. After that, Winse and I started using the words "Famous Firsts" as a kind of code for things that would never have made it into his mother's book: our first cigarette, first drink, first joint.

Winse's mother phoned me long-distance just after I came out here. Mom was over there visiting and I daresay she suggested it. Winse was in Vancouver, Mrs. MacLeod told me, and she hadn't heard from him for months. "I'm afraid to turn on the news," she said, "afraid I'll see him begging in the streets, or with that squeegee crowd what runs out in front of cars. I do wish you'd keep a eye out for him, Rod."

When I didn't jump at the job of finding Winse, Mrs. MacLeod put Mom on. I started to tell Mom that Winse and I hadn't seen one another for years, not since he took off as PR man for a group called Trouters' Special, the year before I left for Dal. Then I remembered that I had seen him once in Halifax. He'd waved to me across a bar one night, pointed to the stage where a perky singer was wiggling herself around a mike cord, and mouthed "Famous First." I gave him the old thumbs up sign, but neither of us bothered to fight our way through the crowd. There wasn't much for us to talk about any more.

"Look," I said, "I haven't set eyes on Winse for years."

Cut no ice. Mom, who takes obligations seriously, started layin it on me. Hadn't the MacLeods always been good neighbours? Didn't I remember how Mr. MacLeod used to take Pop up to Mahers? And that time I broke my leg, didn't Art MacLeod drive us down to the Janeway in his truck? In the end I promised to keep an eye out for Winse.

I hadn't. I'd had enough to do looking out for myself, looking for a place to live, keeping my feet dry, looking for work, buying food, watching out for

Lisa. All such an effort that I didn't see how I'd have the energy for a real job, even if I found one.

Then, one morning when I'd been walking for hours, way the hell over past King's hoping to catch sight of Lisa, I spotted Winse.

My first thought, like always when I see someone from home, is "What'll I say I'm doing?" It's not the best thing to be thinking as you stick your hand out. I have two stories. I tell people I knew at university that I'm looking for work related to my degree, which sounds snooty, but by then I've usually been listening to their onwards and upwards stories for an hour. To people I really know, I admit that I'm working part time in a coffee shop and getting the odd maintenance job with the city. Which was what I told Winse.

"What the fuck you mean, maintenance job?" Winse asked. He looked good, well fed, and a lot better dressed that I was.

We went into a sports bar, one of those places with hockey gear hung everywhere and about twenty television sets going, each one tuned in to a different sport. Horses raced across the screen above our table. "Friggin nice shots," Winse said, "see how they got two cameras right down low on the ground?"

"It means I'm picking up trash in parks and scrubbing vomit out of bus shelters—maintenance jobs like that," I said.

"Jesus! What you're tellin me is you're a garbage collector, just like my old man—and you with two university degrees!"

I said it was hardly a fair comparison. "Your father had a full time job. For over forty years he supported your mother and five kids. I get odd jobs that last a few days. I barely support myself."

"What's your mother say?" Just like Winse to think of that. And to ask.

"She doesn't know. Two months ago she was so worried she got after me to go home, wanted me to finish a lab technician's course I started between degrees. So I told her I had a job. A permanent job, drafting with Leewood Stone," I said, and Winse, who I figured must be dealin drugs, looked shocked.

"I told her the job was not important—just entry level," I said, trying to justify myself like I always do with Winse. Really, though, the job I told Mom I had was the kind I'd pictured myself getting when I came to Vancouver. I told her I was working in a big airy office, sitting at a drafting table with my shirt sleeves rolled back, making black lines on white paper.

I always enjoyed making straight lines, neat designs. When we were little kids Winse and I would sit at our kitchen table for hours drawing on brown wrapping paper Pop had left over from when he owned a store. Winse drew rockets and I drew buildings, mostly houses because Pop liked houses. I remember wet snow hitting the window, Pop watching television or peeling vegetables for supper. Each time one of us finished a drawing we'd take it to Pop for inspection. He would consider each picture carefully, sometimes nodding, sometimes making a comment. Once he pointed out that two flags on my building were flying in opposite directions, "Wind changed, did it?" he asked. He was often gruff with me, but I could tell he liked my pictures best, especially the houses. After a while that was all I drew, clapboard houses. It was the only thing I did better than Winse.

"Look," I told Winse, "I'm never going to get a decent job with a good architect. I've given up, haven't even looked for anything for weeks." It was the first time I had said such a thing. The first time I'd admitted, even to myself, that I've tossed away years of my life learning something I'm never going to use.

"Fuck!" Winse said. We didn't look at each other, just sipped beer and stared at the TV screen, hooves pounding into turf, grass so green it hurt your eyes. Winse started telling me something else about the cameras, how they're mounted on motorized dollies out in front of the horses—something like that.

"Firms like Leewood Stone don't hire the likes of me—fresh out of university, no connections, no experience, wrong schools, wrong accent," I said.

Winse gave me this long sober look, like he could see inside my skull and what he saw there disappointed him. He drained his glass; "All I can say, old cock, is ya best get a good story ready for when your Mudder finds out. And find out she will. This place is crawlin with Newfoundlanders. As for me, I allows Newfie talk's a real asset!" He stood up and proclaimed this in an outport accent he had never spoken in his life. People at the next table swivelled around, smiling expectantly, until he snarled, "Piss Off!"

We left then, me apologizing, Winse swearing loudly he would never tell a living soul Rod LaFosse is a failure. Outside, he gave my shoulder a punch, "Early days yet, old man, lots of Famous Firsts yet!"

We parted ways, him still laughing, not even exchanging phone numbers. Halfway down the block I saw a girl with creamy hair. She disappeared into a bakery. I went and stood by the window, staring at bread shaped like dinosaurs and crocodiles. When the girl came out she was not Lisa, just an ordinary girl with pouty lips.

It was like that whenever I missed seeing Lisa for a day or two. I would roam around Vancouver like someone demented, searching for her, raging at myself for not having spoken to her the last time. It's a wonder I wasn't arrested.

The day I finally spoke to Lisa I hadn't seen her for a week, was sure she'd gone for good. Then I looked up—and there she was walking right towards me. I was working that day, cleaning the fountain outside the Art Gallery of Vancouver. They'd turned the water off, but I was wearing a black plastic cap and slicker and scrubbing madly at slimy rocks. I knew from a block away it was her. She was wearing her blazing red shawl below which you could see nothing but legs, long black-stockinged legs. She was carrying an art portfolio. She stopped, not three yards from me, lodged the portfolio against one leg and stared up and down the street.

It was the closest I'd been to her since the poetry reading and the first time I'd seen her alone. I was so relieved. Without giving myself time to think, I clambered out of the fountain, scuffed across the

grass in my rubber boots. Smiling like the village
idiot, I threw a lifetime's caution to the winds.

"I've seen you around the Emily Carr," I said.
Then, realizing I still held the hose in one hand and
the wire brush in the other, I tossed both to the
ground. "I'm an artist," I said, I don't know why—
well, I do really, I was frantic to get her attention.
She threw it up to me later as an example of what a
liar I am.

At the time I was not sure she heard me. Her
glance flicked my way, ricocheted off my headgear,
came to rest on the hose gushing into the grass near
her feet. She was not impressed, and why should
she be? The guy who takes tickets inside the gallery
is a published poet, Old Herb by the transit booth
paints flowers on driftwood while he's begging, and
the woman who sleeps in Gino's alley is a novelist.
That's the kind of place Vancouver is—the
promised land.

Sighing, as if she was tired of being accosted by
strangely dressed men, she stepped smartly away
from the muddy water. Her portfolio fell over and
expensive paper fanned onto the wet sidewalk. We
squatted together, scrambling to pick up the drawings before they got wet. I realized that Lisa was
sniffing, swallowing, like a youngster about to bawl.
I couldn't think of a thing to say.

"My friend is supposed to be here," she said.
She straightened up and began flicking at a spot of
mud on her shawl, "We're supposed to make a presentation in ten minutes." Lisa has this gentle,
beautifully pitched voice mainland women have,

never angry or accusing, just sorrowful. It made me
feel I was the one who'd let her down.

I carefully slid her drawings back into the portfolio. They were not pictures but diagrams, nice
clean plans. Layouts for a display the gallery might
mount, she said.

"Interior spaces—it's our major project. If the
gallery likes our design they'll build it to display a
ceramic show they plan for next spring. My friend
and I are working on it together—if he ever gets
here."

It was like I'd been struck dumb—perhaps I
had. For lying. I passed her the retied portfolio and
she took it without even a thank you.

You know how sometimes you get tired, fed up
halfway though something? It happened to me a lot
back then, in lineups at those employment centre
machines, or when I'd be put on hold by some telephone robot, or even when I was getting myself
something to eat. I was always finding food I'd lost
interest in around my room: open tins of soup, half-
made sandwiches, boiled eggs I'd forgotten to eat.
That was how I felt at that moment, standing there
on the sidewalk beside Lisa. I'd been half-mad over
this girl for months, worn myself out trying to catch
a glimpse of her—but what was the point? To hell
with it! I picked up my brush and started to turn
away.

Then she touched my shoulder. "You're the
Newfoundlander," she said. Like someone might
say, "You're the Mona Lisa"—as if I was the only
Newfoundlander on earth. I turned around and
there she was, looking at me, really looking at me.

Winse might find being a Newfoundlander an asset. Up to that moment I had never considered it anything but a liability. Turned out this girl had recently discovered David Blackwood. She now understood the tortured soul of Newfoundland. I assured her I love Blackwood's work. I do. His stuff makes me depressed as hell but I think it's great. We talked about towering icebergs and burning ships, which she seemed to think is some primitive Newfoundland ritual. Then Lisa gave herself a little shake and said she guessed she would just have to go in and make the presentation alone.

She seemed resigned, stoic, as if she expected to be let down. It occurred to me that I should offer to go in with her, but I was hardly dressed for making presentations. She did ask me to watch out for her friend, "He looks like a young Ovide Mercredi," she said, "black braid down his back, an attitude—the whole bit." She smiled, "Only he's Italian, not Native. If you see him, tell him I've gone on in. Chances are he'll park right here under the No Parking sign—a protest."

She looked so brave and fragile marching off with her oversized portfolio, I wanted to protect her from whatever was on the other side of those doors. I think I'd have punched buddy out, attitude or no, if he'd turned up.

I went back to work, keeping an eye on the street but mostly watching the gallery door. She was in there more than an hour. When she finally came out she didn't go off like I expected, but made herself comfortable on a bench and began sketching. I waved to her once, but kept on cleaning the foun-

tain, doing some serious thinking at the same time.
I decided, if she was still there at five, I'd make
myself ask her out.

After the city truck picked up my work stuff, I
splashed water over my face and hands, put on my
own shoes, walked over and asked her if she'd like
to go get something to eat.

She gave my face long, serious consideration, as
if she was trying to decide something much more
important than if we should have a hamburger
together. While she was making up her mind, I got
to look at the drawing she'd been working on. I
could see the Blackwood influence; she'd drawn me,
made me into a troll-like fisherman growing out of
the rock. When she saw me looking, she snapped
the sketch book shut and dropped it into her portfolio, which she then passed to me to carry. It was a
queen-like gesture. I loved it—the way she handed
the thing over, and the way I took it. Anyone watching would have thought we were lovers who met
beside the fountain every evening.

When I woke next morning it was warm, sticky,
like it often is out here in the fall. I lay in bed—well,
on the mattress, I don't have a bed—reviewing past
relationships: from Sherry Dawe in high school, to
Jan who I had this sort-of affair with last year when
we were planting trees up near Williams Lake. I was
trying to reconcile the circuitous courtships I
remembered with what had happened between Lisa
and me the night before.

I was not really sure what had happened the
night before. Maybe nothing. We just talked, sat for
hours in a restaurant discussing her project, talking

about interior spaces and art, about the terrible cost of living in Vancouver. She told me her parents ran a market garden near Kingston. I gathered they were not very well off. Lisa called Kingston "Dick, Jane and Sallyland," said she was never going to go back there. I told her my family was poor, too. I didn't say how poor, didn't tell her Mom scrubbed floors in a funeral home. I explained that Gino let me have this room for half price in exchange for working five mornings a week in his coffee shop.

That was when Lisa told me the place where she lived was really sad. That's what she said, really sad. I could see her in some dank, dingy room with a naked light bulb, a nasty landlady who probably bullied her. Around midnight I heard myself asking her to move in with me. "Any time you want," I said. And Lisa, dead serious, or so I thought, said, "Would tomorrow be too soon?"

I lay in bed until nine, reviewing our conversation, remembering her accent, her voice, her words. "Tomorrow I'll be by with my stuff," she'd said. Maybe she had just meant she was coming to show me some of her art work.

I decided that I'd probably misunderstood her, jumped to conclusions. Still, I made myself get up, put mugs in the sink, stack books in a corner. I do jump to conclusions a lot about people out here, though not so much as I did. First when I came out West I kept thinking people were going to actually do things when they were really just tossing ideas around, making conversation, changing the air in their mouths. I've learned to slow down, not assume

I've fallen in with the world's most original thinkers just because everyone around me is talking smart.

I took a shower and dumped all my dirty laundry into a pile in the middle of the mattress, planning to tie the sheet around it later and lug it down to the laundromat. Gino calls this place a studio apartment, but it's just one long, narrow room with one window that looks down on the street. In the gloomy back half of the room there's a closet-size-bathroom with a sink and shower. I'd gotten to like the room's barn-like emptiness, but I thought Lisa would probably leave as soon as she saw the rusty sink, the cracked plaster, the wooden floor black from age and ground-in dirt.

Across the hall two gays rent a huge space that really is an apartment. I feed Juno, their dog, when they go out of town, so I often have the key to their place. It used to be a small, smart restaurant, it still has a stainless steel kitchen and floor-to-ceiling windows with louvred shutters. Dave and Martin had their floors stripped and polished so the Scandinavian furniture seems to float. I was wishing I had the key that morning, I would have gone across the hall, told Lisa their apartment was mine.

I was trying to get my window open, to clear out some of the dust, when an old Volkswagen van rolled up. Tied onto the roof with bungee cords was this piece of brown furniture the size of two coffins. Lisa and three men jumped out. They began unloading the van, Lisa supervising, the men stacking stuff on the sidewalk.

Two of these guys were strangers to me, but one was the good-looking black man I'd seen in the

library. Turned out he's a Jamaican named Kalli,
doing graduate work at UBC and teaching a few
first year courses. Months after she moved in, Lisa
made some casual remark about having left sheets
over at Kalli's place in Victoria. It was only then I
realized she'd been living with him when we met.

He seemed cheerful enough that day. "Oh, it's
you," he said. The same way Lisa had said, "You're
the Newfoundlander." Right then I guessed that
everyone she knew had seen me skulking around
like a sick dog—not a pleasant thought.

I watched my almost empty room fill up. In
came chairs and lamps, wicker baskets and bookcas-
es. In came art supplies and potted plants, posters
and pictures, a microwave, a drafting table, boxes of
records—but no record player that I could see,
though of course it could have been in one of the
twenty or so boxes that never did get unpacked. In
came a large umbrella stand, stacks of cushions, a
food processor, an African mask, bureau drawers
full of clothing, two black on black oil paintings,
each the size of a sheet of plywood.

I was in shock. Not just by Lisa's arrival, but by
the profusion of belongings this girl I had imagined
possessionless conjured out of the van and into my
room. She flitted before us up and down the stairs,
directing our labours with smiles and chirps of
encouragement, never touching anything herself.

"Lisa is a remarkable person," Kalli said, smiling, shaking his head. We stood side by side at the
window watching her talk to Steve and Cory on the
sidewalk below. All three of them were staring at the

remaining piece of furniture, the big highboy, which, having been hoisted down from the roof of the van, looked as if it had taken root in the concrete.

It was nearly noon, late October but sweltering. Lisa wore shorts—shorts and some kind of white shirt. You'd have thought she was the most tidy, organized person on earth. When Lisa is happy she wears white and keeps her hands out of her hair. That morning it hung neat and smooth around her neck—like Eve the first morning after creation.

Kalli and I watched as she bent down, pointing to the squat legs of the highboy, giving Cory and Steve instructions on how to lift it. Her hair fell forward, exposing her neck. I lost track of what Kalli was saying. I was thinking how right the Japanese are to consider the back of a woman's neck erotic.

"Looking down from above like this, she looks like a Japanese woodcut, even the angle is right," I said, showing off, letting this guy know I'm not a complete hick. I hate it when I catch myself doing stuff like that.

"Except the hair would be black," he said, "ink black." He sighed, and I had the feeling he was going to tell me something important, indeed might have already told me something important that I'd missed. Instead, he asked if I was studying art.

"Sort of—I thought I should broaden my education." I would probably have gotten in deeper, but just then Lisa looked up, smiled, and gestured that we should come down and help uproot the highboy.

When her belongings were all in the room—
though not in place, never in place—the five of us
sat on the floor with our backs to the wall staring at
the mess we'd created. I went out and bought a
dozen beer which we finished off, talking quietly
with long tired silences in between. Everything was
relaxed, as if we'd known each other forever, though
it turned out that the men had just met. Lisa's being
there generated camaraderie between us. We might
have been cousins, even brothers, helping some
female relative move house. How simple life is, I
thought, how simple when you go with the flow.

The others left, pounding down the stairs, calling best wishes over their shoulders like wedding
guests. Silence dropped down between us. "You did-
n't really expect me did you?" Lisa said. She leaned
against the door, looking at me, waiting for an
answer.

I was afraid to answer. If I said yes, she would
think me cocky, smart-assed. If I said no, she might
get angry, call the others back, reload the van and
go away. I waited until the downstairs door
slammed, until I heard the Volkswagen start up,
then I said, "No—no, I didn't dare to expect you."
She laughed and everything was all right. Then we
made love, rolling around in my pile of dirty laundry like children in hay.

Having a woman beside you is like a seal of
approval—like getting one of those signs you see on
elevators: "Inspected and Guaranteed Safe." Lisa
moved me from the edge, pulled me into the crowd.
With her I was indistinguishable, part of a couple.
We went out almost every night, dropping in on

readings, gallery openings, book launches that Lisa
got invited to. Often we just walked, I began to see
how beautiful Vancouver is. Once or twice we rented bikes and rode around the sea wall. We rarely saw
any of her old crowd, but in a few weeks we did
become part of a group—not friends, exactly, but
people we could drift along to a bar with after a play
or a reading.

The semester at Emily Carr ended, but Lisa still
had work to do and went over to the school two or
three afternoons a week. I never met the young
Ovide Mercredi. According to Lisa, he was buckling
down, working day and night now that she'd gotten
acceptance from the gallery for their joint project.

I still had my five morning shifts at CapoGinos,
but city work dropped off as it got colder. People
don't seem to litter in winter. I paid for our rent and
food—which was fine with me. I never mentioned
money to Lisa. I didn't want her to think I was
mean.

I worry about money. I want to be able to see to
the end of the month, would like to be able to see to
the end of the year. It's the way my grandfather was,
too. I remember Pop sitting at supper, doing sums
beside his dinner plate, marking PAID on the cloth,
drawing a little box around the word. "Greatest
word in the world," he'd say.

For years and years, right back to Mom's grandfather, the Haywards kept a store in a row house on
Barter's Hill. The family lived above the store,
something like my place over CapoGinos, only with
Dave's and Martin's rooms added in. There were
enough rooms for Pop and Nan and their three

children, my mother and her older brothers. Besides the usual stock of tinned goods, barrel apples and sliced bologna, the shop sold Nan Celie's homemade candy and spruce beer along with windows and storm sashes Pop made on the side.

Must have been a nice place to grow up. Mom used to tell me about it, about how the store smelled, about characters who used to come in. Usually Mom would say it wasn't really much of a business: "A little bulls-eye shop that never took in more than ten dollars a day." Other times she'd talk as if the family was on the way to becoming Eatons or Bronfmans until, all of a sudden, corner stores were displaced by supermarkets, and wooden windows by aluminum ones, the kind in Housing, with sliders that leak.

"The Haywards have come down in the world," Mom said at such times. My mother is not a proud woman, or a greedy one. I don't think it's the loss of money she was thinking of but the loss of hope. The day I got my second degree she was gleeful. "We got our toe in the door again," she told me. And I thought she was right.

Lisa and I never talked about our families. Sometimes she got letters from Ontario and once, just after our phone was taken out, she went across to Dave's and Martin's apartment to call home. She came back crying. When I asked what was wrong she told me to mind my own business. I figured she'd been asking her folks for money.

Before the money situation got altogether desperate, Winse came along and, in a way, saved us.

We met at the Cinematheque. Lisa and I had gone
to see a series of old black and white movies—and
there was Winse. He left the crowd he was with and
came over to sit with us, sizing Lisa up, giving me a
look that suggested approval and surprise.

Winse and Lisa hit it off right away, fell to talking about Italian movies, only they called them
films. Winse knew all the right names; Antonini,
Fellini, Visconti slipped off his tongue like candy.
He'd lost his Newfoundland accent completely and
picked up one I couldn't place. I was dumbfounded.
During the movie I kept nodding wisely whenever
he pointed out some special lighting technique or
camera angle. Afterwards we joined up with his
friends and went for a drink. One of them asked me
if I'd ever done work as an extra. He said it was simple, a good way to make a bit of money and learn
something about "the business."

"They're looking for bodies down at West Jasper
Productions right now," he told me. "Apparently
they need hordes of peasants for this TV series
about a Scottish superhero."

That night I suggested to Lisa that we both try
for jobs as extras. She wasn't keen on the idea, not
even when I mentioned that we were low on cash.
"You're such a stick about money—something
always turns up," she said. But she let me convince
her that the extra business would be a bit of fun.

Next morning the two of us walked over to the
production office buddy had told me about, an old
school building down on Logan Street. I half
expected to see Winse and his crowd but none of
them were there. The woman who hired us said no

acting ability was required. Peasants, it seems, have a limited range. She spoke as if random words were capitalized: "You'll be TOLD how to look—ADMIR-ING, FESTIVE OR ANGRY. Just DON'T look at the fucking CAMERA!"

After taking our names and social security numbers, she directed us to the gym where we dressed in dirty plaid blankets. Lisa and I put our own clothing into lockers and, with a bus load of other peasants, were driven to a field way out in Lynn Valley where the filming was going on.

Working as an extra consisted of displaying the appropriate facial expression while running over hill and dale behind a camera mounted on the back of a jeep. Mostly, though, we huddled around under a tarp, waiting and drinking free coffee.

Our second morning on the job this suit came around the corner of the coffee trailer, spotted Lisa, made a beeline over and stopped in front of us. White shirt sparkling, smile beaming good will, he bent forward, staring intently into Lisa's face. "Did everything work out for you?" he asked in an urgent half whisper. He looked for all the world like the knight who, having rescued a damsel in distress, comes back years later to claim his laurel wreath, or whatever the hell it is knights get.

Lisa barely glanced at him. Clutching the bit of ragged plaid around her shoulders, she nodded. "Yes, yes, everything's fine now," she said. Her tone was cool, her eyes swept past Sir Lancelot to something of great interest beyond his left shoulder. The goose girl, having become a princess, was not inclined to chat.

"Oh!" You could almost see buddy deflate. "Oh—that's good," he said, and sort of melted into the crowd.

"What the fuck was that all about?" I said. I wanted to hit her. The worst of it was I wasn't even sure why I was so angry.

Lisa just shrugged.

A little while later, after one more run behind the jeep, she said she couldn't stand this another minute. She began to cry, tears making paths down her dirty cheeks. She was sunburned, covered in fly bites, and there was a cut on one of her bare feet. She stood in the mud, crying like a child, until I took her hand and led her to the shower stalls. I told her to strip and wash while I went off to steal a towel from one of the trailers used by the actors and production crew.

Trying to look as if I'd been sent on an errand, I walked over to the little enclave of ten or twelve trailers. Back-on to the churned up meadow, the trailers were arranged in a neat circle like settlers' wagons in old cowboy movies. The bus driver had pointed to this area when we arrived, told us it was out of bounds for extras. "Actors want to keep to themselves between takes—you crowd got orders to stay around here," he'd said, pointing to the huge tarp that covered two portable toilets, four picnic tables and a coffee trailer.

The location was full of confusion, equipment and noise, people and movement. All I had to do was keep cool, step into a trailer, pick up a towel, and slip back to Lisa. But when I walked into the circle, disorder vanished, I was in a small, enclosed suburb. The trailers had little paths; stencilled above the doors of some trailers were the owners' names. I already had my hand on the doorhandle of the nearest unmarked trailer when the door of the one next to it swung open and Winse stepped out.

"Hi," he said, as if it was the most natural thing in the world—as if we were youngsters again, coming out of adjoining houses, ready to start off to school.

I backed down the steps. "Someone told me you were here," I said, pleased with myself for being so quick.

Winse took one look at my face and started to laugh. "Jesus, Rod, you should never try to lie! What are you looking for?"

"A towel." I told him about Lisa not feeling well, wanting to go home.

He stuck his head back in the trailer. "Got a big towel there Dena?" Right away a pretty woman wearing a long cotton dress and sandals came to the door and handed him a towel. "Dena this is Rod. Dena's the chief seamstress. We share trailer space."

The young woman waved and went back inside, I recognized her as one of the people we'd met at the Cinematheque.

Winse wasn't going to pass me the towel. He was grinning to himself, walking beside me back towards the shower stalls. "What do you do here?" I asked him.

"I'm a consultant—I work here. Well, most days I work here; sometimes I have things to do downtown," he said.

"And what do you consult about?" Suddenly I was feeling relaxed and happy—like I was home safe, like I knew the rules.

"Scottish plaids and tartans, Scottish folklore. Meet Russell MacLeod." Winse bowed, flicking the towel out like a cloak. "Scottish lore consultant is what the credits will say—it'll be a Famous First." He was laughing like a nut case. "Russell's my middle name. Didn't know that, did ya?"

"What the frig do you know about plaids and tartans—or anything Scottish, comes to that?" I asked, but just then we got up to the showers. I called out to Lisa and, when she answered, grabbed the towel and tossed it over the stall door. "Winse is here—we'll be outside waiting," I told her.

Along one side of the shower stalls a tin roof overhung a line of wooden benches. We went over and sat down. "Nice place, what," Winse waved at the muddy fields and plastic rolling stock. I just gave him a blank look.

"You know yourself that Granddad MacLeod was from Scotland," Winse said. I didn't think it was true, but he maintained it was, said he'd spent summers with the old man out in the Codroy Valley—which I knew was a lie. Until he was eighteen, Winse was never farther than Bowring Park, and the only grandfather I ever heard him mention was mine.

"What can you do, boy?" Winse asked. "Ya gotta make a life. 'Make a life for yourself laddie'—that's what Granddad MacLeod used to say."

"Didn't he say wee laddie?"

"Well, he hardly ever said wee—used the Gaelic you see—but you wouldnae credit how much he knew about plaids and tartans."

"Pays well, does it?"

Winse gave me a wink, "Yes, lad—gives me a nice bit of brass. Scottish is in—you can hardly walk over a hill without bumping inta a Rob Roy or Bonnie Prince Charlie. MacGregors or Stewarts, they're all one to us MacLeods."

Lisa came out just then. She looked cleaner and happier, though she'd had to put the dirty plaid on again. Winse said he was on his way down to Logan Street and suggested he give her a lift so she could get her own clothes. Then, noticing that she had nothing on her feet, he asked if she'd like to be carried to the parking lot. He was dead serious. Lisa looked at me; I could see she was tempted, but she shook her head.

"See ya, laddie," Winse grinned at me as they turned away. "And don't forget, next time you need something—the name's Russell." As the two of them walked off towards the parking lot Winse grabbed Lisa's hand and started singing that song from *Brigadoon* about going home with Bonnie Jean. He still has a pretty good voice.

When I got back to the room that night Lisa was in bed. She said Russell had waited at the school while she changed, then brought her right to the door. He told her she should go back the next day, ask for a job in properties or continuity; he would put in a good word for her. She wasn't going to go back, though—said she hated actors, they were a bunch of snobs, and the film crew was even worse.

But she liked Russell, wanted to know where I'd met him.

She looked pleased and eager sitting there in the middle of the bed in her yellow nightgown, like a child waiting for a story. She didn't seem to remember that Russell had changed his name since their first meeting. Having seen how tickled Winse was with his new identity, I decided to play along. "He was sent to relatives in Newfoundland when his parents died; that was after they lost their estate in Scotland," I said, and told her about his Gaelic speaking grandfather, his visits to that wonderful valley in Newfoundland. Winse would have been some proud of me.

I kept on working as an extra until they stopped filming—managed to get almost $600 in a savings account before the student loan people caught up with me. Winse was always around; sometimes he came over to the coffee trailer between takes, and I remembered to call him Russell. Lisa and I never ran into him, though. He asked after her only once, told me I was lucky, I should hold onto her. I said I hoped to.

I'd started to think that wasn't very likely. It was February, the room was damp, furry mould was growing around the window. I don't know why everyone goes on about how it doesn't snow in Vancouver. It's supposed to snow in winter. Lisa and I started having spats about small things like running out of milk, or big things like not having a bed. Lisa looks like a sprite, a being you cannot imagine encumbered with possessions. In fact, she has a deep attachment to mahogany. From the day she moved in she was after me to buy a bed. Sleeping on the floor was half my problem, she said. I didn't dare ask what the other half was.

"How can anyone feel settled in a place where they have to roll over onto their knees to get up every morning?" she asked more than once. According to Lisa, people without beds were uncommitted, not dependable. "Just look at Africa!" she said—and there I was, left behind again, shaking my head like a befuddled puppy.

We had our big fight the day her father came. Lisa was at school and I was in the hallway, rolling a ball to Juno the dog. The door to Dave's and Martin's apartment was open and anyone coming up the stairs would have thought that was where I lived.

"I'm looking for Miss Jordan, Miss Lisa Jordan," the man said. He was dressed in a suit, white shirt and tie, the entire bit. He was even carrying a black leather briefcase.

I didn't know who the shit he was, the Sheriff of Nottingham maybe. "Yes?" I said.

"I'm Lisa Jordan's father," he said. "This is her address, isn't it?"

"Yes," I said. "Yes." I could see he was getting irritated with me. "She's not in right now. I'm..." I stopped. I couldn't think what I was. "I'm taking care of the dog," I said. Then I added, "His name is Juno."

"Lisa has a dog!" The man stared at Juno as if the animal might speak, tell him where his daughter was. "I'm in town for a conference. Will you please see that Miss Jordan gets this?" He took an envelope out of his case and passed it over. I half expected him to tip me, but he just said, "Thank you," gave the dog another thoughtful look, turned and went downstairs.

The envelope had his name, Dr. Neil Jordan, and an address at Queen's University in Kingston printed on it. Below he'd written Lisa's name and "At Hotel Vancouver until Friday—Please call Room 406."

When Lisa came in I passed her the letter. "Well?" I said.

She looked at it, shrugged and, without opening the envelope, pushed it into her pocket.

"Well," I said again. And after a few minutes, "Some market gardener in a thousand dollar suit!"

"I don't understand why you're so upset," she said. "My parents do have a market garden as it happens. What's wrong with that?"

"I thought your folks were poor! You said they were poor!" I was trying to work out why I was yelling, why Lisa's being well off made any difference.

We argued for what seemed like hours, both of us incoherent, unyielding. "I can't believe you're giving me so much grief over a letter!' she shouted, and I shouted back that it wasn't over the friggin letter.

"This is all about money! You're so damned uptight about money—mean and uptight about money!" she finally yelled. Then she slammed out the door.

She didn't come back until two in the morning, dropped off from a taxi. I was frantic to know where she'd been, but I didn't ask. I pulled her down onto the bed, told her I was sorry, said I was unreasonable. She was right, I am unreasonable about money. I promised never to yell at her again. Then we made love.

Things seemed better after that. I didn't mention her father or the letter. We had five days of sunshine. Lisa became cheerful, she'd seen crocuses in someone's garden.

Then the art gallery decided they didn't want Lisa's layout after all. Sponsors of the exhibition wanted to use their own design team. The day she found out she came home and flung herself onto the mattress, sobbing that this was all the Italian guy's fault—the gallery board had sensed his lack of commitment, were afraid to count on him. I hovered as she raked her fingers through her hair and moaned.

That day Lisa reminded me of my Grandmother Celie. After spending years in a mental hospital, Celie still looked like a child those times Pop brought her home. He was always sure she'd been cured—and so it would seem for the first day or two. My grandmother would flit about the house in long flowery skirts, her grey hair wild and curly, rearranging Mom's dishes, kissing anyone who crossed her path, singing along with the radio, making taffy apples and candied popcorn for me and Winse. It was like having a good fairy in the house. Then, on the third or fourth day, Celie would go into a sulk, stop eating, start moaning, begin throwing things at Pop.

Lisa's sad arrangement of bones, her thin wrists, her sobbing, immobilized me. I stood over her, not daring to speak or even reach out. Everything would be lost, she wailed, all her work and study. How could she start a new project, even think of a new project, this late in the semester?

She made so much noise that Dave from across the hall came knocking at the door asking if there was anything he could do. Before I knew it he was sitting on the mattress, holding her hand, ordering me to make tea. He coaxed Lisa into telling him what the gallery project involved. When she simmered down enough to talk, he listened and then told her everything would be fine. He said he had an idea.

He did too. Dave is one of those calm, soft spoken gay men who have the ability to enthral people, especially women and children. Within an hour he had Lisa convinced that the project she'd designed for the gallery could be mounted in a different venue. "It's just the kind of thing we've been looking for to display a collection of gems Minerva is bringing in from Hong Kong," he told her. He called Martin over, made Lisa pull out her portfolio and show them her drawings.

The next day Lisa and I went over to Emily Carr and brought the original scale models home. There was no sign of the guy who'd worked with her on the project, and I didn't ask what had become of him. I congratulated myself; I was learning not to rock the boat.

We went down to the jewellery store where Dave and Martin work and measured the display space.

Then I drafted a new set of plans, from which we could build the scale model that Dave and Martin told us Minerva's management would want to see.

Every night for two weeks, Dave, Martin and I worked in our room. With three men hunched over her drafting table Lisa became subdued, unusually domestic, bringing coffee, holding glue sticks, passing us cards and bits of styrofoam.

When I woke Friday, Lisa was standing beside the bed dressed in her bright shawl, carrying the black portfolio, all ready to go off to meet the directors of Minerva. She looked just like she had that day beside the fountain. I wasn't sure I was awake. Despite her red and black outfit, there was something insubstantial about Lisa as she stood there looking down at me. For a moment I thought it was still that morning in October when I lay thinking, half hoping I'd misunderstood her promise to come. Maybe I had simply fallen asleep and dreamt the last six months.

She touched the edge of the mattress with her foot, "I'll send someone around for my stuff," she said. Then she left.

I waited all Saturday. Dave came by, stuck his head in the door to tell me the management at Minerva were delighted with the display. I nodded, and he went away. I woke Sunday expecting a van or truck, men who would come and make my room empty again. I spent the day sitting in her armchair, the one that tips over if you don't position your arse just right. Every now and then something I should do would cross my mind. I should shave, take a bath, go down to CapoGinos. I should check with

Dave and Martin, thank them. I should phone
Winse, phone Mom.

I did nothing. About four in the morning I
prised the fan out of the window, hauled Lisa's car-
ton of records across the floor, knelt up on the mattress and began tossing her records one by one into
the street. I would have liked to take them down to
the bridge, imagined them winging out over the
black water, but they were too heavy. I enjoyed it
anyway, watching old vinyls sail into the night, spinning across the street, twirling like Frisbees on the
sidewalk. Even after the guy in the convertible
braked and shouted at me, I kept at it. When Gino
and Harry Wu came, they had to call Dave and
Martin. It took all four of them to drag me, body
and bones away from the window and haul me down
here.

I'm pretty much mellowed out now, the record
throwing already receding, becoming a mildly
amusing memory. I sit at one of Gino's sidewalk
tables watching kids across the street horse around
on skateboards. I like skateboards, there's something innocent and old fashioned about them. The
skaters too, seem of another time, young boys
dressed in those sad baggy pants I associate with
photos my grandfather kept, cracked and faded
snapshots of my long dead uncles wearing their
father's cut down cast off pants.

The youngsters across the street have never seen
such pictures. They throw themselves along the
sidewalk, swim through air, through people, bounce
on and off the curb, veer dangerously towards an
old woman carrying two pots of yellow flowers,

towards the beggar who sits outside Shoppers. They speed past Harry Wu who shakes his fist at them.

There is a girl watching those boys. She is about their age. She laughs, taunting them, urging them on. The girl is beautiful, like pictures I've seen of Cleopatra—white skin, black hair, black nails and lips. She wears a kind of coverall—also black. The straps of the coverall keep slipping down. When she shrugs to reposition the straps on her thin shoulders her breasts are revealed, small and white, rising above her black garment. I am staring at the girl's breasts—not just me, either, the beggar and Harry are likewise transfixed.

We watch as she bends forward, her body palely visible inside the darkness of stiff cloth. She scoops one of the skateboards out from under a boy's feet. Her face is within inches of the spinning wheels. She slams the board onto the sunlit concrete, speeds away, crosses against the light, comes back on my side. She brushes past the table where I sit and my hands reach out to catch her, as one might reach to catch a snowflake or a butterfly. She whizzes by without a glance, pleased with herself, delighted with the power she has over the shouting boys who stream after her, little dogs panting after the Queen of Egypt.

A Commission
in Lunacy

When acute emotional stress finds expression in physical dysfunction, as in the case of Celia Sullivan, the resulting disability becomes a wall separating the self from reality.

– Dr. G.V. Thornhall, M.B., C.M.
Patient Review – Special Report to
The Commission In Lunacy
August 15, 1916.

May 12, 1967

It is almost ten on a weekday morning in a double unit room at The Hospital for Mental and Nervous Diseases. The room has two white beds, two closets, one chair and one window. The walls are painted a colour the patients call snot green. It is springtime but wind and cold rain pounds the window. Beside the window an old woman, narrow shouldered and with a fuzz of grey hair, crouches on the chair. Her name is Celia Hayward but everyone calls her Celie.

She is wrapped, rolled up really, in a grey hospital blanket. Her forehead is pressed against the glass as if she were studying the gutterspouts and slate roof, or perhaps the wet roadway four stories below.

The woman by the window is not alone. The room behind her throbs with gospel music, with the rattle of coat hangers, with the emotional vibrations of its other occupants: Gertie, the about to be discharged patient, and Sutton, the attendant, whose bad luck it is to be on floor duty this morning. Sutton is emptying Gertie's closet, flinging garments onto one of the beds, ignoring Gertie herself, who stands between the beds clutching her portable radio and muttering.

"...I wants someone called. I'm makin a complaint if someone's not called. People leavin are supposed to get a list of valuables—I never seen me list of valuables. Stuff I come in with's not here—me snaps, me bead purse. I'm tellin ya I'm not leavin without the things I come in with!" Gertie's voice is rising, "Mark my words I'm takin out a complaint against you—see if I don't!"

"Oh be quiet, for God's sake! You signed for all this months ago—way back in November when they processed your discharge papers." Sutton has been on duty for two hours and is already an hour behind schedule.

"Me bead purse is gone—and me shoes too, I always had nice shoes, I don't want to wear this pair of old scuffs out into the world! Besides, you got no right pawin through my stuff you haven't—I wants to go to the office!"

Sutton gets down on her hands and knees, pulls a suitcase from under the bed and plops it down beside the pile of polyester. She begins to roll Gertie's clothing into tight balls, cramming scarlet slips, fluorescent housecoats, lime green skirts and multicolored sweaters into the worn suitcase. "Why the hell didn't you leave everything the way I packed it yesterday?"

"I didn't get no breakfast!"

"You'd have gotten breakfast if you hadn't been so contrary." Sutton prays she will get Gertie out of the building without a complaint visit to the office. The office will require a written report, signatures—will use up her coffee break. Not that she's likely to get coffee, even if Gertie cooperates, not with the other one perched on her chair again.

"Mrs. Hayward's back to the gargoyle stage I see," Dr. Mac had commented when he did his rounds. He'd stared sadly down at the blanket-draped figure. "Too bad—she seemed to be making such progress lately." Before leaving he'd made a notation on his clipboard and promised to send the duty nurse up with medication, but Sutton knows that will take hours.

"I changed me mind. I don't want to go," Gertie says.

"Go on with ya! It's taken months for Social Services to find a nice place and now they got one—right in town like you wanted. You'll like it once you get settled." The attendant has seen this last minute resistance to leaving before; it's not unusual, especially in long term patients. "You'll do fine—sure

you've been tellin us for years you were well enough
to leave."

Gertie doesn't respond. Holding the radio
against her chest she shuffles over to the chair,
stands glowering down at the seated figure. "I
changed me mind. I wants to stay here with her,"
she says. Bending over until her lips are almost
touching the blanket, she shouts: "Celie! Celie
Hayward, come out of there this minute!"

"Jesus Christ himself couldn't get through to
that one once she's in one of her moods." Sutton
snaps the suitcase shut and sets it down on the floor,
"Anyway, you got to go. It's been all arranged. They
processed your discharge before Christmas. The
van's down by the door waitin." She smiles at
Gertie, wondering what sort of accommodation has
been found for this untidy, cantankerous creature.
Poor old bat! Rumour has it she used to be a street-
walker. No family, of course. Probably be put in
some place worse than here, some dirty welfare hole
you wouldn't leave a cat in. "Come on, maid,"
Sutton says; she links her arm into Gertie's and tries
to move her towards the hallway.

Gertie shakes her head, "No!" She makes as if to
sit on the floor beside her shrouded roommate.

"And that you will not!" Knowing once Gertie is
on the floor it will take hours and two strong men to
budge her, Sutton grabs her around the waist; holding her upright from behind she manages to propel
the old woman a few steps towards the door.

"Give me a minute," Gertie says. The whining
chant is gone from her voice, she is speaking quietly. "Just one minute. I wants to say goodbye to me

friend." She twists out of Sutton's grip but stays on her feet. Turning to face the attendant, she switches off the radio. "Please, Missis," she says, "please."

Sutton looks at Gertie. She doesn't look at the patients often. There's a rule about keeping your distance, not getting involved. A good rule it is, too, Sutton thinks, staring into the wrinkled face, realizing that Gertie is on the verge of tears. "All right— just one minute, though."

Praying she's not doing the wrong thing, the attendant lets go of Gertie's arm. "Just one minute. Mind now!" she says and leaves them alone.

❧❧❧

In a part of the hospital far below the room where Gertie is saying goodbye to Celie Hayward, there is a staff cafeteria to which Sutton will retire for her well deserved coffee—once she has Gertie safely stowed into the hospital van. Around the corner from the cafeteria, in the hospital's main corridor, there is a small canteen for patients.

Sharp at ten every morning, except Sundays, Miss Mugford unlocks the wooden shutters of the canteen and unfolds the plywood counter. Dozens of patients wait, crowding against the counter, clamouring to be served. In a British-tinged accent the almost blind woman orders everyone to queue up.

Word has it that Miss Mugford was once a mental patient herself, that she has connections, that even the doctors are afraid of her. Whatever the reason, her authority over this section of hall and the wooden benches on each side of her canteen is never questioned. She will exile any patient who bullies, fights or spits. She makes everyone pick up their litter, and insists that the ones who smoke must carry water in which to douse their cigarettes. For two cents she sells styrofoam cups half filled with tap water. Despite this, the patients like Miss Mugford. They trust her with messages; neither staff nor inmate, she is their link to the outside world. They make a game of trying to cheat her but never can. Even her milky eyes are able to distinguish nickels from quarters; she knows all their tricks and refuses to take paper money.

There is a nicely furnished common room on another floor, but most long-term patients prefer to spend what they call "rec time" hanging around near the canteen. It is their village pump, a free space where they can exchange information, grumble about rules and staff and tasteless food. Some cluster in little groups, others nervously pace the hall muttering to themselves, sometimes shouting. The more tranquil sit on benches, or when the benches are filled, on the floor with their backs to the wall: smoking, drinking Pepsi, reading newspapers and comic books, or just dozing.

If Gertie were down here this morning she would be sitting on the floor. For years she has sat in the hallway every day except Sundays when she goes to Mass in the Chapel. Even if there was room on the benches, Gertie would sit on the floor. Lately, she's been sitting for hours and hours in exactly the same spot, almost opposite the counter with her back to an unused door, her eyes shut, listening to Radio VOAR. Down here Gertie keeps her radio low because Miss Mugford doesn't like loud music even if it is religious.

When Celie Hayward is not in one of her black moods she is a pacer. If she were down here this morning she would pace and smoke, pace and smoke—then vanish. Celie is not one of the mutterers or shouters. In fact, she rarely speaks, though she sometimes hums, very low and nothing anyone would recognize even if they listened.

No one has noticed Celie's recent absences from the hall. No one but Gertie has seen her leave each morning just as Miss Mugford lowers her counter, just when everyone is pounding and shouting to be first to get their smokes. Just then the two women perform their daily ritual: a kind of quick dance, Celie unlocking the door, slipping through, easing the door shut, Gertie sliding down into place, back against the door, radio in lap.

On the other side of the door is a tunnel. It was originally built to connect newer sections of the hospital to the back wards. Though lit now, and given yearly coats of whitewash, the tunnel is ancient. It slopes downward, snaking under lawns and parking lots, between huge boulders, around the rotting roots of long dead trees. Indians once built fires beneath those trees, roasted animals in pits in the very space where Celie Hayward has lately been spending her days.

In the hospital's past these twenty four cells, twelve to a side along the tunnel, were used to confine unruly patients. Now they are used for storage. Each cell is the size of a dumpster; Celie has come to think of them as dumpsters, filled as they are with stained mattresses, rotting storm windows, dented pots and cracked dishes, rolls of wire, stacks of pipe, rusting bedsteads, with scrub boards and laundry tubs and old wooden mangles Celie recognizes from years ago when patients worked in the hospital laundry.

Since December Celie Hayward has been illegally in possession of a key, and therefore in possession of the abandoned tunnel. Through the dark days of January and February she has spent most of her waking hours in these small underground rooms. Surrounded by the detritus of madness, Celie's housewifely compulsions had been stirred to life, resurrected by piles of mildewed shoes and boots, abandoned satchels, saws and hammers, restraining devices of canvas, metal and leather, all mixed in with hay rakes and milk pails and crumbling brin bags from which mounds of unidentifiable grey matter spill—everything flung helter-skelter into small cells where disruptive patients were once kept, "retired," to spend nights, and sometimes days, alone with a bedpan, a sleeping pad and a blanket.

What this place needs is a good turn out, a good tidying, a long silent voice insisted. And Celie obeyed. She had started by sorting, stacking things in neat piles, separating mat frames from broken easels, typewriters and slide projectors from electric kettles and crystal sets, unravelling clotted string from candle stubs, untangling crepe paper from mouldy yarn. All this gave her immense pleasure—feelings of satisfaction that brought to mind other cleanings of small rooms, forgotten Saturday mornings in a house on Barter's Hill.

It was February before Celie got around to the back cells. In these she found the hospital's accumulated records. Stacked on wooden skids to separate paper from damp floors were yellowing piles of newspapers, government directives, medical journals: *Management of the Insane, Cure or Custodial Care, The British Lunacy Act, The Uses of Mechanical Restraint*. These paper artifacts are better organized, housekeeping is not needed, housekeeping is overtaken by curiosity.

As she roamed the back cells, poking and sampling, Celie began to see that nothing completely disappears, that underground everything is available. She could uncover the whole history of the mental hospital down here, perhaps the whole history of her own pliable, phantom life. Everything that has ever taken up space above her has been consigned to earth, everything now overhead will finally lie buried down here. Down here lies the rubble of Plak's Farm, broken hoes and bits of hay rakes from fields where the hospital's original patients worked, down here are restraining devices of canvas, mental and leather, instruments used in the 1940s to sever brain fibres, the reams of hemp from basketmaking therapy, tubes of clotted oil paint and the gory pictures made by a shell shocked soldier back from the Great War. Down here she might find hidden wine bottles and packs of cards and clay pipes from a time when guards were assigned to protect dead bodies from rats. She might even find the dead, stowed in dark corners during epidemics, small babies buried in crates, old women wrapped in crumbling shrouds. Yes, she could find anything in these back cells—if she had the time.

Celie Hayward has always known about time, how little of it there is. Things happen. She is, after all, in her sixties, certified as mad, restricted by hospital routine and using a key that might be taken from her at any minute.

Late in February, not without regret, Celie reined in her curiosity. She resolved to limit her investigation to written material, to the three cells where hospital records are stored, tried to ignore anything that originated before 1909, the year she has concluded she was first admitted to this place. Less than a week later her discipline was rewarded. Midway through a ledger with the words *'Committals and Discharges'* on its mouldy cover, she found one handwritten line: *September 30, 1909—Female child named Celia Florence Sullivan, committed by request of her grandfather.*

✕✕✕

September 26, 1909
It is a few hours after dawn in the graveyard of a Newfoundland outport. The sea is not far away— although it cannot be seen it can be heard, wave after wave slamming against rock; and smelled, too, a briny smell that makes cool air seem even cooler. This is an old place. Wild rose, nettles and rhodora bushes have overgrown some headstones; others have cracked with frost, crumbled or fallen. In all the graveyard only one plot has been cleared, a pillow of raw earth near the fence, a new grave into

which someone has plunged a temporary marker shaped like a small cross.

The graveyard seems empty, empty of living things, that is. But after a while you realize there are insects, worms and birds, dogs and cats too, and occasionally a goat wanders in. And there is the child. She huddles against the fence, half hidden by bush and deep shadow but within reach of the new grave—near enough to read the words on the marker: "Mary Florence Sullivan, 1883-1909."

The little girl's name is Celie. People have tried to keep her away from the graveyard. Father Fitzgerald has prayed with her more than once, and Mrs. Fowler next door has given her a good talking to. Twice her grandfather has tied her to the bed with a rope around her wrist, another night he nailed her bedroom door shut. Celie, who looks frail but is wiry as a cat, always gets away. She climbs out onto the porch roof and lets herself down the drain pipe.

Celie's grandfather has become resigned. These days he puts her to bed in heavy socks and her mother's old rabbit skin coat; tying a scarf around her waist to keep the coat in place, and hoping for the best. It has been her grandfather's experience that one way or another most things take care of themselves.

And so the child comes to the graveyard every night. She sleeps here—or maybe she doesn't sleep, Celie herself is not sure. Time passes. She watches the mound of earth that covers her mother, sees the white shape of the marker emerge from darkness, stares at the rough black letters that make her mother's name.

No one says her mother's name anymore. Not once since the funeral has the child heard Mary Sullivan's name spoken. But in her head Celie says the name over and over again, "Mary Florence Sullivan, Mary Florence Sullivan, Mary Florence Sullivan...." Each night she counts the days since her mother died, then she repeats the name in groups of months, weeks, days. The three names together become a chant, a kind of rosary that Celie intones over and over throughout the night. But not out loud, of course—the child has not spoken a word since the day back in June when her mother's body was taken out of the house.

The girl's silence upsets people, upsets them more than her sleeping in the graveyard. The silence has got to stop. Her grandfather must be made to see it's unnatural, even dangerous, for a seven year old to never utter a sound. The teacher has told her grandfather that Celie no longer pays attention, that she seems to have stopped hearing as well as speaking. Other children have grown bored with sympathy, boys have started teasing her. She's thrown stones at two boys who chased her home from school. Mrs. Fowler next door and Miss Minn on the other side say something has to be done before the ground freezes, before the child causes harm to herself or someone else.

Shortly after dawn on this September morning two old men come into the graveyard—Father Fitzgerald and a stranger, both wearing black overcoats and black hats. They are deep in conversation, walking slowly along the sunken paths between the headstones. Their shoes flatten the damp grass. They stop beside Mary Florence Sullivan's grave.

"The child is over there," the priest says, pointing to underbrush that lines the fence.

The men step carefully around the grave. They squat down, peering through the thicket. When Father Fitzgerald pushes low branches to one side the petals of wet, overblown roses fall onto his black sleeve. The men stare through shadow scented leaves at the little girl. She's slipped down into the oversized coat so that only her face can be seen, a small white face surrounded by brown fur. Celie and the two men watch each other for several moments.

"Has there been any sign of violence?" The stranger seems uneasy, as if the child were a wild animal or a cat who might scrob him.

The priest misunderstands: "Oh no! She has always been treated kindly. Her grandfather's a bit of a ne'er-do-well—still, he does his best, there being no woman in the house."

"Can no household in the community take the child?"

"We're a poor place, sir. People here have big families. For all that, if the child was normal someone would give her a home—but no one's satisfied to take on the burden of a youngster going out of her mind."

The men stand up, dark shapes unfolding against the morning sky.

"Chronic melancholia complicated by hysteria," the stranger says. He takes off his hat, scratches his head, stares out over the fence at the vast expanse of sky, rock and barren. "I suppose I'll have to take her into St. John's with me—though I doubt very much they'll do anything for her."

When the priest doesn't respond, the stranger jams his hat back on, "That's it, then," he sounds almost angry. "I'll have to get some kind of statement and her grandfather's signature. I'd be obliged, Father, if you could find a couple of women to haul the child out of there—separate her from that filthy garment and give her a good wash before we leave."

The little girl has not moved, has not blinked. The men turn and walk away. The brown fur becomes a shadow in the undergrowth, Celie Sullivan becomes part of the damp earth, the quiet graveyard.

※※※

One cell, Celie found, contained nothing but account books and memos and letters—hundreds of letters: official letters, letters from distraught patients and letters from their families, letters produced by electric typewriters and by old manual machines, letters written in pencil, in ball-point pen, in fountain pen and straight pen. Among these were many brittle ink-stained, often begging, epistles written by the hospital's founder, Dr. Stabb, in the 1840s, usually to government departments. These last had bogged Celie down. Dr. Stabb's need had drawn her in, wasted her time—time leaking away while she read about the doctor's concern for his patients, his grief for his half-mad wife and their dead children.

It had been a test of control, a test of sanity, Celie Hayward thought, with a tinge of pride, to put the poor man aside, to steadfastly search for her own name in this multitude of names, to move on to the third room with its stacks of patient reports and ward reports and bound books containing years of minutes from a committee called *The Commission in Lunacy*.

It was slow, close work and Celie's eyesight is not what it was. The long, echoing tunnel was well lit, bulbs encased in metal cages glare down on white walls. But the cells themselves were dark as caves. Celie had to take whatever item she was reading to the doorway of the tiny room, to sit for hours with her back wedged against a door frame examining reports to the Colonial Secretary, committal papers, registers of discharge and death. Worlds of grief and madness bubble up through the swirl of Victorian script. Sometimes she had to stop, to close her eyes, to hold onto her head, longing for the cigarette she dare not let herself smoke.

Weeks passed before Celie again came upon a name she recognized. In the third book of minutes for *The Commission in Lunacy*, halfway down the handwritten page, the commission's secretary for July 1912 recorded: *"This month, by appointment of Governor Sir Ralph Champneys Williams, The Commission welcomes Andrew Thornhall, M.B., C.M. as Superintendent of the Mental Hospital. A graduate of the University of Edinburgh, Dr. Thornhall brings wide experience of the greater London asylum system where he is considered an expert in diagnosis and classification of the insane."*

In the January 1913 minutes it was noted that: *"On December 21st Doctor Thornhall and his charming wife entertained Commission members at a dinner of exquisite sumptuousness in their home on Circular Road."*

A dinner of exquisite sumptuousness. Dr. Thornhall's charming wife would have enjoyed that. Eleanor—Ellie to almost everyone she knew, including her eight year old daughter Dorothea— had been an informal, modern woman; she smoked, played golf, shortened her skirts, went to moving pictures and pinned her hair up Gibson Girl fashion.

Celie could remember the dinner party—it may be her earliest memory—who knows what these other things rattling around in her head are? She might have been ten, or even eleven, that first Christmas after she went to live with the Thornhalls. There had been a tree with fifty tiny candles, gaslight and firelight, light and warmth, music and food—abundant food: roasted duck and sauce-covered vegetables, pastries and puddings and golden stuffing that smelled of cinnamon and apples. The wonder of it!

Celie and Dorothea wore tartan taffeta that Christmas. Her dress was deep green, Dorothea's bright red. Both girls had black velvet sashes around their waists and black velvet dancing slippers on their feet. They had not danced, of course, just sat in high-backed chairs in the drawing room, dangling their slippered feet, listening to Dr. Tait's string quartet playing carols. Before bed, Dr. Thornhall asked Celie and Dorothea if they would like to bring in sweets for the guests: Flemish creams, chocolate dipped cherries and crystallized apricots, all arranged like jewels, each in its own lacy paper cup, on small silver trays. Celie recalls the oohs and aahs as she and Dorothea walked into the room, the smiles, the hovering fingers.

Celie cannot recall being concerned that members of the Commission—those men standing around in dinner jackets, chatting with each others' wives, sipping Dr. Thornhall's port—might recognize the child in green taffeta as the half-starved idiot with hacked off hair they must have seen on inspection days at the Asylum. That place seemed so bleak, so remote from the firelit room that it might have been something made up to frighten children—like the ogre's dungeon in the fairy tales Ellie read to the girls each night.

The day she came across Dr. Thornhall's name, Celie overstayed her time in the tunnel. When she went to the door and gave her usual sign, scratching down low where Gertie would hear, there was no answering scratch. No sign to tell her it was safe to unlock the door and slip out. Celie tried again and again. Finally she eased the door open and stepped fearfully out into the hospital's main hallway. It was empty. The canteen shutters were closed, not a soul in sight—especially not Gertie, who promised every morning to watch, to sit with her back against the door until Celie was ready to come out of the tunnel.

The knowledge that she had been down in the tunnel with no one keeping watch frightened Celie. Panting, short of breath, she had scurried up and down the corridor, foolishly looking into closets and bathrooms, rattling the locked doors of offices and storage rooms. When it occurred to her that she should not be seen near the tunnel entrance she went upstairs to the empty common room, then to the patients' dining room where she found the kitchen staff clearing tables.

Only then did Celie realized how late it was. Day and night are one down in the tunnels, but here it was dark outside, not mid-afternoon, but night— she'd missed supper. Trying to control her breathing, she'd poured herself a glass of ice water. When one of the kitchen women asked if she'd had supper, Celie nodded, then quickly left. They were not looking for her! She hadn't even been missed.

She found Gertie listening to her radio, sitting on the floor of the room they have shared ever since Gertie got transferred from Ellis Wing.

These two women would not have chosen to be roommates, but patients have no say in such matters. Seven years ago Celie had come back from breakfast one morning to find the room she'd been alone in for months vibrating with gospel music. A woman with straw-like hair, wearing a not too clean pink housecoat, was sitting on the floor between the beds. Nearby two attendants stood yelling at this scarecrow; they had clearly been yelling at her for some time. The attendants, a man and a woman, kept ordering the patient to get up off the floor, to turn off her radio.

"Switch the thing off or we'll have to take it!" they shouted.

The woman's yellow head had stayed down, her arms had tightened around the small plastic radio in her lap.

The attendants tried reason: "Your chart says you're ready for an open ward—patients in open wards don't sit on floors." Then pleading: "Don't be foolish, woman, if this keeps up we'll have to take you right back to chronic care—and you know what trouble that's gonna cause."

Celie had stood in the doorway watching, wondering why staff bothered saying things anyone with a grain could see weren't true. She had gotten used to having her own room and didn't fancy the idea of sharing—certainly not with this gaudy gospel music lover. Still, she'd learned the futility of objecting to any arrangement the hospital wanted. Eventually she got sick of the racket, went over and squatted down close to the patient to see what she could do.

That was when she recognized Gertie. "Hello, Gertie Perkel," she said, almost shouting into the woman's ear.

Gertie's head had snapped up, her eyes made contact, angry, frightened eyes just inches from Celie's face. "Who told you that name?" she whispered. Then she pushed herself backwards, the heels of her laced shoes scribing black marks into the linoleum, the satin housecoat twisting up over her wrinkled stockings, "Who the frig gave you my name?"

"Turn that thing off and I'll tell you," Celie said.

Gertie did. The silence was amazing.

"She can't stay on the floor like that," the male attendant said.

"Why can't she?" Celie asked.

This had happened around 1960, fifteen years after Celie's 1945 admission—her second admission, but only she knows that—and sometimes even she's not sure.

By 1960 Celie had been treated with intravenous matrozol to induce epileptic-like convulsions, thus escaping one of Dr. Brownrigg's prefrontal lobotomies. She had been given something called block treatment, a hundred electroshocks at intervals of only a few days, had sporadically received psychiatry and, for six months, had been on a cocktail of newly discovered drugs.

By 1960 Celie Hayward was no longer bright, or pretty, nor as kind as she once had been. Still, at least in her own eyes, she had more seniority than the two young attendants. And so it seemed. When she said she would take care of the woman on the floor, they had simply shrugged and gone away.

Celie had watched Gertie. The woman didn't turn the radio back on, but neither did she look up or show any sign of getting off the floor.

"I suppose we can talk down here," Celie said. She'd pulled the pillow from her bed and sat on it. "Your name's Gertie Perkel—isn't it?"

The woman shook her head.

"That's what my boys called you."

"Who's your boys then?" the voice rasped, as if it hadn't been used much. Gertie cleared her throat, repeated: "What's their names?"

No one had asked Celie this for a long time— for years. It took a minute or so to straighten it all out in her mind. Not because she'd forgotten—not

all the electroshocks in the world could do that—
but because saying the names of her dead sons
required an unfolding of memory, a bracing against
pain.

"Kenny and Steve," she said. "My sons were
Kenny and Steve Hayward—Steve was the oldest."

"I remembers them! Little nuisances—particularly the smallest one. Kenny, you say his name is?"

"Was—was. They both died a long time ago."

"Was," Gertie said and became silent. Then,
"My boy is was, too," she said. After that she rested
her back against the wall, she closed her eyes and
turned her Christian music on again.

Celie got up and went to sit by the window. A
good thing the poor creature's not a talker, she
thought. I don't think I could stand being in a room
with one of them. Good thing she likes the floor,
too—the chair is important to Celie. From the chair
she can watch the road, watch a corner of Bowring
Park, see the path by the river where old people,
and sometimes families with young children, walk.
Over the years Celie has spent hours sitting at this
window.

Sometimes she sees her husband Rod walking
on the path. She is sure it is him though the doctors
say she's mistaken. Once she'd been almost positive
he'd been holding that girl's hand. Two of them,
bold as brass holding hands, never a thought for
her over here watching, never a thought for Celie—
but Celie has thoughts for them.

The night after her fright about staying in the
tunnel, Celie demanded of Gertie why she'd left the
door unguarded. Her roommate had just shrugged,

"It was suppertime," she said, refusing to take any blame, staring at Celie in that canny, brazen way of hers. "I don't see what use me bein there does. Year in, year out not a soul opens that door. All the time I been sittin in that hall I never seen it opened—not once."

Even after sharing a room for seven years, the two women were not great friends. By now Celie and Gertie have survived a dozen administrations, a hundred staff turnovers, government studies, policy changes and name changes, redefinitions of mental illness, rewrites of the Lunacy Act. They are old hands, familiar with words like regression, relapse, intractable; they know where such words lead. They get along because they have to. They observe boundaries: Gertie owns the space between the beds, Celie owns the chair by the window, Gertie ignores Celie's black silences, Celie ignores Gertie's non-stop gospel music.

But Celie had broken the pattern. Back in December she had asked Gertie to do something. Now she was insisting. Insisting that Gertie guard the tunnel. Celie could not explain why this was so important, only knew that she could not go down into the tunnel without someone protecting the door. And there was only Gertie to ask. "You've got to be there. Someone's got to know where I am," Celie repeated again and again.

She wasted days; days spent wandering up and down the hallway, days staring out the window; mindless, bereft days—like thousands Celie had survived before she found the tunnel key in a place where it should not have been. Finally, in her desperation to get back to the tunnel, she'd tried to barter. Patients were always trading—cigarettes, food, magazines, sometimes liquor or drugs. But Celie could not think of a thing to trade.

"I'll tell you everything I find out—maybe I'll find your file," she said one night when she'd been lying awake, brooding on the problem.

"Nothin I wants to know. No one I wants to know about," Gertie snapped into the darkness. But then, after ten minutes of silence, she suddenly conceded, "OK—OK—Ya got me tarmented half ta death—I'll keep guard for ya! Only on one condition though—I'm not sittin in that hallway after everyone's gone off to supper. We got to find some way to keep count of time when you're down there."

They have no clock or watch. Perhaps, Celie suggested, they could buy wrist watches. Patients get a small allowance for such things as soap and toothpaste, cigarettes, a daily coffee or Pepsi. Gertie spent hers on batteries for her radio and on the gaudy used-clothing she bought off racks the Salvation Army set up once a month in the common room.

"Watches cost a fortune—it'd take months to save enough for a watch," Gertie said—and that was that. Neither she nor Celie mentioned the small savings accounts the hospital held for both of them, money paid from times when they worked in the hospital laundry. A nest egg, they have been told, for when they're released, or to help bury them if they are never released—"headstone money" Celie once heard it called. Both women knew that getting money from their accounts would require the intercession of staff, questions, a trip to the office, more questions, forms. Bad luck to draw attention to their need, better to pretend the money isn't there.

"Maybe," Gertie said, "you could carry a reel of sewing cotton into the tunnel, one end tied around my wrist and one end around yours. I'd tug at the thread if something happened, you'd tug when you're coming out." She'd giggled like a child, clearly delighted with the idea.

A silly idea, Celie thought, but it might work. She had never seen her roommate so happy, never heard such glee as was in Gertie Perkel's voice when she elaborated on her plan—coarse sewing cotton they'd need, good and strong, the kind Gertie can steal from that Chinese woman who comes to repair the hospital's curtains and sheets.

Then Celie remembered a story Dr. Thornhall had read out loud once to her and Dorothea. Ellie read the girls fairy tales at bedtime, but the doctor read different stories, stories about gods and history. These, he said, would broaden the education they were supposed to be getting from Miss Frazer, who came to the house on weekday mornings.

After dinner on Sundays, while Ellie Thornhall took her afternoon nap, Celie, Dorothea and Dr. Thornhall would go into his study. The study was a small room that connected the greenhouse to the dining room. The doctor would sit on one side of the fireplace, smoking, sipping from a glass and reading out loud while the girls squashed together in the opposite armchair. Celie and Dorothea, happily sucking on peppermint knobs the doctor let them take from a jar on his desk, would be half asleep, hearing only bits of the story. It would be winter, the greenhouse would be empty except for a few hardy plants and the supply of wine the doctor kept beneath the potting bench. Once or twice during the afternoon Dorothea's father would go into the greenhouse to refill his glass. Whenever he did this a damp, earthy smell that bothered Celie would fill the study for a few minutes—then the fireplace smell and the smell of Dr. Thornhall's pipe would blot it out.

The story Celie remembered from that time was about a queen who took a ball of string and went down into a tunnel to slay a bull. The bull was called a Minotaur, a mad creature, half-man, half-beast. Celie has forgotten the details, only knows the story ended badly—the thread had broken, or been lost, the queen trampled, her body left in the tunnel, her bones discovered hundreds of years later.

Celie did not tell the story to Gertie. Gertie had by then gone to sleep, still muttering about thread and tunnels, things Celie also spent that night thinking of—imagining string unrolling into the tunnel, one end tied to her wrist. Near dawn she fell asleep, dreamt she had stopped breathing, woke gasping.

She woke Gertie, told her she cannot do it, cannot have string tied to her wrist. Her roommate, hurt and angry, still half-asleep, demanded to know why. Celie could not explain, "I can't, I just can't," she said, over and over.

Gertie ignored her.

But that night, long after Celie thought she was asleep, Gertie shouted blue murder into the darkness, "You're a stunned bitch, Celie Hayward—stunned as well as cracked!" She gulped air, listened, they both listened, half expecting the night nurse to come down the hallway, to rush into the room shining a flashlight into their faces.

Nothing happened, there was another long silence. Then, "I knows what you done, don't think I don't—tried to make away with a good, decent man," Gertie's voice was a malevolent whisper. "Should be in jail, you should—or in one of them back wards, chained onto a wall like in the old days!"

Celie could not speak. She lay quietly in bed, eyes closed, trying to forget, trying to remember. Most of the time she knows, even if she has no recollection of it, that what Gertie has just said is true. This was not the first time a patient had accused Celie Hayward of trying to murder her husband—though in recent times, there being many new acts of violence, people seem to have forgotten hers.

It must have been common knowledge back then, Celie thought, a respectable shopkeeper's wife going berserk, a wife and mother attacking her husband with a knife. A knife taken from the store, they said—one used for cutting cheese. Many even remembered the date, not too difficult a feat to recall a night when much of the world's population was celebrating the end of the Second World War. Doctors, too, have broached the subject of knives and blood to Celie—in different words of course, gentler, more clinical words—trying to agree on how to treat her black moods, on which legally required illness to affix to her case records.

The next morning Gertie would not go down to breakfast. She spent the day on the floor between the beds, listening to hymns—words about salvation and love and blood dripping sacrifice throbbing through the room all day until bedtime.

On the third night, after the radio was silent, after the lights were out, the two women lay in their beds, both of them awake and angry, listening to the hum of hall lights, the far-off sound of a fog horn, the nearby sound of an occasional car going in Waterford Bridge Road.

"Know how I knew your name was Gertie Perkel?" Celie asked.

"Tisn't!"

"Maybe not—but it's what my boys used to call you—they liked you," Celie said.

"No more'n they should! Wasn't I the one let em in me kitchen almost every night of the week?"

"You were—they told me about it," Celie lied— she'd never heard Gertie Perkel's name until the day her youngest boy was brought home by Hogan the druggist. Derm Hogan had caught Kenny stealing from his shop.

"Night after night your two and their buddies'd be in me house, smokin and playing cards—I always let em in."

"But not for nothing, Gertie, not for nothing," Celie is remembering Kenny squirming on the doorstep, Derm Hogan holding him by the collar.

"I only took a pack of Gertie Perkel," her son had said when she offered to pay Mr. Hogan for whatever he'd stolen. She'd thought then that Gertie Perkel was some kind of candy, or powdered

drink. But no, Kenny said, it was tooth stuff, "Stuff
Gertie puts in her mouth so's she can have teeth in
her head—so's she can go out with the men," he'd
added.

Celie doesn't tell Gertie this. She's afraid the
anger might return, Gertie might start yelling
again, might jump out of bed and turn her radio
on. Celie, who has seen the classifications on case
records, knows that Gertie was committed to the
Mental to get her off the streets. "Cleaning up the
town," the police chief used to call it. He did it reg-
ularly, every year or so, times like Regatta Day and
before Royal Visits. On Gertie's committal form the
diagnosis read Lues with neurosyphilitic written in
below.

"The man I was livin with—the one was Little
Doug's father—he knocked me teeth out, kept it up
till finally I only had the scattered tooth left in me
head. I was some sight!" Gertie's voice was matter of
fact. Then, to Celie's surprise, she'd chuckled: "I
got better teeth now than I ever had before in me
life—the one good thing I ever got out of the cursed
government."

Gertie began then to tell Celie about Little
Doug who had been born crippled. Probably from a
beating, Gertie said, a beating she got when she was
pregnant. Her son had never learned to speak, to
stand, or even to sit up. But he had a sweet nature,
always smiling. "I needed someone in the house you
see, to watch out for him when I was out workin
New Gower Street." She'd stopped talking while the
night nurse made her rounds.

Celie didn't say a word, and when the squeak of soft shoes receded down the hall Gertie continued: "They were always together—your two sleeveens along with three or four others, the Reddy youngster and the two O'Briens. Had a name for themselves I forgets now—Corner Boys or something like that. They made a clubhouse once—right in under the bridge goin into Pitts Memorial Hall. Shockin, and them Catholics! Wintertime it'd be too bitter—so they'd be all the time lookin for someplace warm."

"They could have come home," Celie said. She remembered telling her boys they should bring their friends home. But they never had, not until they started having girlfriends. She smiled into the darkness, imagining her sons in Gertie's house—on Deady's Lane she believed it was, a warren of rotting shanties, some without lights or running water, down below the hill from Haywards—people she and Rod gave credit to, people who kept them from ever making a go of the store.

"Boys never want to go home—boys, nor men either," Gertie was saying. "Likes their clubs and their bars—dark hidey-holes with no women around. I used to let em have the run of the house long as they'd take care of Little Doug. All I ever asked for was a few sticks of the stuff from Hogan's—so's I could go out, you understand. The youngsters called it Gertie Perkel—I doubt that was the right name of it," she said thoughtfully. "Maybe they made it up on account me Christian name's Gertie—though me last name's Power, not Perkel."

"What did you do with it?" Celie asked, although she already knew, having coaxed that much out of her son all those years ago. Celie was enjoying the novelty of having someone to talk to, the comfort of Gertie's gravelly voice in the darkness.

Gertie explained how she used to break the rubbery sticks into small pieces: "I'd roll bits of it between me fingers till it was soft like dough, make teeth. I was good at it. When I stuck em' in me mouth and put on a bit of lipstick—my dear, I wouldn't call the Queen me aunt!"

They lay in bed remembering how nice it had been to feel like that, remembering good times when they'd been young and hopeful. Celie listened to cars passing in Waterford Bridge Road and recalled the boy who came courting when she was in service with the Bradshaws, the boy who delivered groceries, pushed a handcart up to the back door. She remembered him kissing her while she hung clothes on the line, sunshine and white sheets all around. Celie could imagine such boys in the cars driving by on the road—boys and girls, driving out into the country, looking for a place where they can be alone, a place where they can kiss and cuddle, maybe more. She watched the pale sweep of headlights cross the ceiling and thought about flapping sheets and the boy's kisses and a red handcart shiny as the sun way over by the kitchen door.

Perhaps young people don't do those things nowadays—how would Celie Hayward know? All Celie knows, all she has known for over twenty years, is what she sees from her window in the

Mental. People on the other side of the road, people walking along paths, people with children, couples holding hands....

"That tunnel is down under ground," Celie said, trying to keep the desolation out of her voice. There was no answer. It was very late, Gertie must have fallen asleep.

But, "Never mind, girl—I'll keep sittin by yer friggin tunnel if it'll make ya happy." Gertie's bed creaked as she hove over. She gave a kind of snort, "I s'pose tis only fair and square considerin all them times Kenny and Steve watched over Little Doug for me."

For another month Celie went down into the tunnel every day. She grew used to the shiny brightness of the tunnel, the deep blackness of the tiny cells. She began to smoke down there, began to feel safe, almost at home in the enclosed underground place. She considered telling Gertie this, telling her roommate that she needn't guard the tunnel door any more—but she didn't want to lose Gertie's friendship, Gertie's talk.

For that month Celie and Gertie talked every night. They lay in the dark telling each other about their pasts, recalling old songs, neighbours, the names of shops along Water Street—almost happy, they were. The women never spoke of mothers or husbands, but of dead sons, of Floss, Celie's living daughter—a girl neither of them could remember clearly, though someone named Floss visits Celie at Christmas and Easter.

"What is it you're pokin around for in that tunnel, anyway?" Gertie asked one night.

"Missing bits," Celie said, "I've got holes—things missing inside my head." Searching for a way to explain her capricious memory, she told Gertie it was something like her missing teeth, "Something I can never go out without having."

"But I didn't go lookin for me old teeth—I knew they were rotted away and gone—I made pretend teeth," Gertie said.

The next day Celie found Dr. Thornhall's report. Things rotted away, she thought, looking at the yellowing paper. But not gone, never gone—and surely better than pretend.

She could easily have missed it: handwritten, titled "*Patient Review—Special Report to the Commission in Lunacy,*" it was not bound with the minutes, but slipped in at the back of the book for 1916. On two sheets of flimsy paper, Dr. Thornhall had submitted what he considered: "*A complete, though necessarily abbreviated, report on my research project related to patient Celia Sullivan. Diagnosed as mute and feeble-minded, this young female is typical of many inmates who push residency levels in asylums beyond capacity, making it impossible to admit new, possibly acute cases into such institutions.*"

With this in mind, the doctor reported he had administered tests to a select number of patients, choosing Celia Sullivan to be the subject of a small experiment by which he hoped to prove, through personal observation, "*that a patient, suffering from hysteria and impulsive insanity might be reconnected with the world, remade, so to speak, into a serviceable member of society.*"

Owing to external contingencies, the doctor was about to take leave of the Colony, and would, regretfully, have to cut short his three year observation of the patient in question. He noted that Miss Sullivan's condition had greatly improved, and that her muteness had completely disappeared. *"This young person now shows herself capable of undertaking various household tasks that will doubtless make her a valued servant,"* he wrote.

"Unless we pay adequate attention to the diagnosis of incoming patients we cannot possibly undertake a course of treatment that will ensure recovery of these unfortunates," Dr. Thornhall told the commission. He recommended that Celia Sullivan, having been considered a patient during the time she spent with his family, now be officially discharged from the asylum. He concluded by giving assurances that *"my experiment being an unqualified success, this patient has been completely cured and will never again be a drain on the public purse of the Colony."*

The report was dated August 15, 1916 and signed by Dr. Thornhall, M.B., C.M.

August 16, 1916
It is a well-proportioned two story house with five wide steps leading up to a door of leaded glass. There are two people in the picture, two servants. The grey haired woman standing firmly on the top step is wearing a long black dress and white apron. She stands stiffly, staring straight out, hands clasped across her apron, apparently unaware of the girl who seems to float halfway between her and the

pebbled path at the foot of the steps. The girl is a moving blur: long skirt, white apron, one white arm raised, moving through air, as if an eccentric whirlwind is sweeping her outward, spinning her away from the house, perhaps away from earth. The girl is young, she has not yet pinned up her long hair, which rises in a pale drift behind her head, one ringlet blowing across her face—a face that is alight with happiness and expectation.

The house behind the two servants seems empty, there are no drapes in the windows, no flowers in the small greenhouse that is attached to the south side. There are flower beds near the steps, vines that have been tied to a lattice, morning glory or spirea, it is impossible to say. There is no colour in the picture, which was taken only a second ago by Dorothea Thornhall. The first picture on her new camera. The camera is a gift from her parents. The Doctor has suggested to Dorothea that she record their voyage home: take pictures of the ship, of fellow passengers, of their arrival in England, of welcoming relatives she has not seen for four years.

"Crossings like this might end now there's a war on," he said, "taking pictures will teach you to observe." Dr. Thornhall and his wife feel that Dorothea is unusually talented, unusually intelligent. They have great plans for her. One of the reasons they are returning to England is to give their daughter what Eleanor Thornhall calls "A true English education."

The car had started down the driveway before Dorothea remembered the camera.

"I want a picture of the house," she said. And the chauffeur (sent around by the Governor to take his friends down to the harbour, to the Allan liner *Pomeranian* which is due to sail within the hour) had pulled the car around, gotten out and opened the door for the doctor's daughter.

As Dorothea Thornhall gets out of the car, the girl on the top step of the house raises her arm. Then—as if she's been expecting this, waiting for an invitation to join the departing family, her family— the girl leaps forward.

The camera clicks, the picture is taken. Dorothea, holding up the skirt of her pearl grey travelling suit, climbs back into the car. The chauffeur tugs once at a strap that holds a steamer trunk onto the back of the Daimler, then he gets in, pulls the door shut, they drive away.

The falling girl's feet hit the pebbled path, her legs buckle, her arm drops. For a minute she kneels watching the car drive majestically down Circular Road. Then she gets up. She turns and walks slowly up the steps to where the woman stands. Without speaking, the two servants go back into the house where they have been instructed to wait for the arrival of the new owner, Mr. Bradshaw, an English civil servant whose family will need a dependable cook and maid.

May 12, 1967

Neither soft words, pats nor curses move Celie Hayward. Resigned, Gertie at last takes leave of the room they have shared for seven years. "But mark

my words, I'll be back if they don't treat me good!"
she promises and dares to kiss the blanket-covered
head of the woman seated at the window.

By eleven-thirty, the rain having stopped and
Gertie's discharge having been completed, Sutton
stands with two other attendants on the hospital
steps enjoying a well deserved smoke. "That
woman's smarter that half the crowd in
Confederation Building," she says. She waves at
Gertie as the hospital van pulls out into Waterford
Bridge Road.

It is near noon and a brief stillness descends
upon the hospital. Morning rounds are over, beds
have been stripped, medication has been administered. Most staff people have returned to their
offices to fill out forms, to drink coffee, to grumble,
gossip, to read the morning paper. In hallways and
common rooms patients have settled into their
accustomed places, some have retired to bedrooms
to doze until lunch time.

In a now-silent room on the fourth floor the gargoyle stirs and then stands. The grey blanket slips
from her shoulders. Celie Hayward leaves the room,
she walks slowly down the long hallway, down the
stairway, down to the main corridor. No one notices,
no one sees. She unlocks the door, steps into the
tunnel, she silently eases the door shut behind her.

The tunnel seems empty but is not. Everything
is down here: this residue of madness is the archae-
ology of her life, everything she could ever want,
every moment she has ever lived. All recorded.
Inked words pressed into paper, paper filed in fold-

ers, bound into books, stowed safely away in shadowy corners.

"Hello" the grey haired apparition says. "Hello," she whispers into tiny cells where paper is piled ceiling high. "I'm back," she says, hovering in doorways, peering into the secret blackness. Then, settling amid innumerable leather-bound volumes, all titled *The Commission in Lunacy*, Celie Hayward lights a cigarette and leans forward. She squints at the fading words, "I'm here," she says.

Imaginary Doorways

In Floss's dream everything is just as it had been in life, Mrs. Cornish is bundling her into the back seat of a taxi, telling the driver, "It's all arranged—get the poor mortal over to the Grace right this minute!" And the gratefulness Floss feels for the woman's kindness is wiped away by being called a poor mortal.

Mrs. Cornish wears a hat, even though hats have recently gone out of style. Without the hat, without Mrs. Cornish's force of character, the taxi driver might not have let her into his car, and Rod would have been born on the sidewalk outside of Bowrings.

It has been years and years since Floss dreamt about that ride. But it all comes back, the driver's horrified face when he realized her condition, the car's jerking motion as the man changed gears and took off up Water Street. So real.

So real that on Friday morning she wakes with the plushy taxi smell in her nostrils, the warm stickiness of birth fluid between her legs. Sweet merciful God! she thinks, I've peed to bed! She feels between her thighs and, much to her relief, discovers she's dry. It would be bad luck to start bedwetting at her age—especially now, when she's about to begin sharing a bed with someone.

For all it's not light outside, Floss gets up. She strips the bed, tosses the sheets into the washer, makes one last check of the house. Her suitcase— new, Samsonite, an engagement gift, Bram says, though they are not engaged, of course—is already in the trunk of his car. After breakfast she has only to fold her new things into the cotton shopping bag she always takes to work: bra and underpants, a lacy slip, a washable fawn skirt and a cream coloured blouse—her going away outfit. She'll take her brown raincoat too; Bram says it's often cool on airplanes. She plans to have a shower and change after work. Floss is uneasy about that; she's never used the funeral home's staff shower before, but she's looking forward to stuffing her work outfit, black slacks and white cotton blouse, into the garbage.

Passing her house keys to Dora next door, Floss has the urge to tell her the dream. She cannot, of course. The only people who ever knew about that taxi ride were Mrs. Cornish and Pop. Now they're both dead and only she knows. Besides, Floss thinks, it was just Sunday past I told Dora about Bram—and that's caused enough trouble. Two revelations in one week might end their friendship altogether.

"Don't have no worries about the house. I'll take in the mail and keep an eye on things," Dora says.

They have lived in adjoining houses for more than twenty years. All that time they have been friends, their sons have been friends. Each woman thought she knew all the other's secrets. Floss can tell Dora is still hurt over not being told about Bram long ago, can tell by the way she stands, leaning backward holding a large white box against her chest. Still, Dora gives her a hug, then awkwardly pushes the box she is holding into Floss's arms. "A going away present," Dora says, smiling stiffly, humming some tune Floss can almost remember.

"Thank you—thank you for everything," Floss says. Then, quickly reminding Dora to switch the sheets to the dryer, she turns and hurries towards the bus that has just pulled in at the corner of Anderson and Empire. Floss knows the idea of a woman her age running off with a man—even a man she's been seeing secretly for twelve years—must seem insane, probably is insane, but she's not about to stand on the sidewalk justifying herself to Dora MacLeod.

Floss has never been one for conversation this time of day; she and the bus driver nod to each other as they do every morning. She's always his first passenger; he picks her up at six-fifteen. If she's not there, he thinks he's ahead of schedule and runs into All-Nite-Snacks for a Pepsi—which Floss takes to be an act of kindness. She wonders if he'll wait for her tomorrow, has half a mind to tell him this is her last ride on his bus.

After all these years, Floss still considers the bus ride a treat. She's told Bram this, how the driver waits for her, how she has her own seat well down

towards the back, how the whole empty city is a private show, new each morning. She arranges her
purse, shopping bag and the gift from Dora on the
outside part of the seat and settles down. There is
always something new to see: one house being built
or getting a coat of paint, another being torn down,
its shameful cracked ceilings and mismatched wallpaper exposed to the world. From the bus you can
look straight into windows, see families talking, couples eating breakfast, people rubbing sleep from
their eyes, scratching their behinds. Outside, people dig gardens, feed birds, in winter shovel snow.
Once Floss saw a woman in a nightdress pounding
on the front door of a house on Freshwater Road,
snow on the ground, fuzzy pink slippers on her feet.
Strange. Bram likes to hear about things like that,
he doesn't seem to notice them himself. She wonders if telling Bram about her morning rides was
what gave him the idea of the two of them driving
across Canada together.

    Pop never owned a car. Floss has been riding
buses around St. John's since she was a youngster.
Golden Arrow Coach Lines they were called then.
She'd liked the name. There were just three routes:
the West Loop, the East Loop, and the Hospital
Route that went back and forth between the hospitals: the Grace, St. Clare's and the old General. The
Hospital Route went out to the Mental every third
trip, which was hard on people who had to visit out
there.

    The very first time she ever set eyes on Bram
was from the window of a bus, one Boxing Day
when she and Marcie Benson were coming home

from Marcie's grandmother's. At Christmastime back then children used to make the rounds of relatives who would let you in to see the tree, give you cake and syrup, sometimes slip you a dime on your way out. Floss had no relatives of her own to visit, so it was nice of Marcie to take her along.

Way out by Mundy Pond the grandmother's house was, its front yard overgrown with dead bushes, its rooms small and dark. The grandmother herself was small and dark, very old, she had hardly any hair and you could see the bones of her skull under the speckled skin. Floss can remember an old lady smell, like raspberry jello mixed with face powder, remember a long black dress, plain and buttoned tightly around the grandmother's corded neck. She'd felt edgy, almost afraid. She had never seen anyone wearing a long dress, never seen anyone so old. But Marcie, not a bit awed, kissed her grandmother and asked why she was not wearing the dress her family had given her for Christmas.

"It's up around me knees, girl. I think I'll get your mother to sew a flounce onto the tail of it," the old woman said. Floss had been surprised that anyone so old could have such a strong voice.

"Sure Nan, you got a grand set of legs." Marcie had actually lifted her grandmother's skirt, exposing carpet slippers and heavy wool stockings.

"You, young maid, are too pert for your own good." The old woman gave Marcie's hand a flick. Nevertheless she smiled, "I changed to long skirts the day I married your grandfather, God rest his soul. That was 1874—I was fifteen and I never changed back—not likely to now."

Not that Marcie's grandmother had anything against short skirts. She told the girls they were lucky to be wearing coats up around their knees; it was a real torment getting around in coats and skirts that dragged on the ground. "In my day you'd dress in your very best to go downtown and when you came back it all had to be brushed, soaked, washed and ironed—took hours! Down on Water Street they had wooden sidewalks, but the street was just dirt and dust. For a penny a boy would sweep a path for you to cross. Still, when you got home you'd be mud up to your knees."

Floss remembers this conversation clearly; she remembers everything about that day. It was sunny but bitter. Cold stung their faces and legs as they stepped out of the warm house. She and Marcie joked that maybe long coats were not such a bad idea, but when they saw the West Loop turning by the foot of the pond they were glad to be able to run for it. Having long legs, Floss reached the bus first and got the window seat, which was how she came to see Bram—only he didn't go by the name Bram then but by Gilly, his nickname.

There was more snow in the forties. Bram tells Floss this is only the way she saw things because she was a child. But she knows there was more snow in the war years. Streets hollowed out between vast towering snowbanks, holes dug around fire hydrants, bus stops and mailboxes—mailboxes were called pillars; they were round, bright red, with flat tops and a royal crest with GR just under the letter slot. That was where she saw Bram, sitting on top of one of the mail pillars.

For all the foolish little things Floss has told
Bram, she's never told him about that Boxing Day,
about the bus easing around the corner from
Pennywell to Freshwater Road, her looking down
and seeing him there—perched cross-legged, he
was, on top of a red mailbox with a bunch of girls
gathered in a semicircle, staring up, adoring him.

It was only four, but getting dark, midwinter twilight laying a blue wash over snowbanked streets.
Without taking her eyes from the handsome boy
atop the mail box, Floss grabbed at her friend's
arm: "Look! Look quick! Who's that fella?"

Marcie leaned across and peered out, "Don't tell
me you don't know who that is! Sure, that's Gilly
Gillingham—Gorgeous Gilly!"

Floss would like to know now if one of the girls
around the mailbox that day was Rosemary, the one
he married. Even then, long before Rosemary started to sing on the radio, people knew her. She
belonged to that crowd whose families had summer
places out in Topsail. Despite wearing the same
ordinary dark coats, the same knitted accessories in
style that winter (bright caps almost like babies'
bonnets, matching mitts and matching knitted leg
bands to show a strip of colour above fur-top boots),
outfits almost identical to their own, Floss and
Marcie saw the girls standing below as mysterious,
exotic creatures. As they pressed their faces against
the cold glass, drinking in the scene, they knew the
words these beautiful girls were hearing from Gilly
Gillingham were more romantic than any words
they themselves would ever hear in all their lives.

Then the bus pulled away and Gorgeous Gilly looked up. He looked right into Floss's face, gave this big grin and shrugged, hands spread, palms up, as if asking, "What can I do? How can I help being so irresistible?"

Floss walked miles and miles that winter trying to catch sight of him. It got so she could recognize his heavy checked jacket, his slightly swaggering walk, from blocks away. She never went up close, of course, never spoke. After a while she stopped watching for him, thought she'd forgotten Gorgeous Gilly. But maybe she hadn't. Floss often wonders, especially when she's riding to work, if it could have been something about seeing him that day, the winter she spent searching St. John's for a glimpse of him, that made her say yes thirty years later, when Bram Gillingham slipped up to her in his mother's kitchen and invited her to his bed-room.

From where Floss gets off the bus it's barely five minutes walk to Furlong's Funeral Home. The streets downtown have a tired look this time of day. Even the cats and pigeons seem exhausted.

It's easy in the grey quiet to fancy you're invisible—like that woman who used to be in comic books. Invisible Scarlett O'Neill, her name was. Floss is not a reader, she never reads books, not even *The Evening Telegram* when Pop had it delivered every day, but whenever her son Rod brought home a Scarlett O'Neill comic she would keep track of it until she got a chance to sit down and read it. Why, she ponders, was she so taken with Invisible Scarlett O'Neill? The prettiness was part of it. Being a plain woman, Floss envied prettiness. And Scarlett O'Neill had such lovely clothes, spent a lot of time in her underwear, changing outfits for some reason. Moreover, and this is what Floss remembers most, Scarlett had this way of letting every garment she took off fall to the floor, toes lifting from a pool of silk and lace. The marvel of that, of just letting things drop, seemed more wonderful to Floss than making yourself invisible.

Floss herself is now invisible. The idea makes her smile. Like Scarlett O'Neill, invisibility is part of Floss's job. "The bereaved do not want to see work being done. They do not want to know that funeral homes get dirty just like their own houses," was what Mr. Furlong said years ago when he hired Floss. He was explaining why she would have to get to work so early. The public areas have be spotless by noon when visitation begins.

Furlong's Funeral Home is a mansion, white with columns; it belonged to some fish merchant before Furlongs bought and renovated it. There used to be more grass and trees, but they extended the parking lot, kept just a strip of lawn and the nice black iron fence out front. Walking up the path, unlocking the big double doors, Floss pretends this is her house. What would it be like, she wonders, to really have a house like this? To sit in the living room and tell a maid to bring tea and toast on a tray? Jam, too; she'd have partridgeberry jam, dark red in a cut glass dish.

Do rich people have maids nowadays? Floss doesn't know; she cannot picture any of the crowd in Housing, the ones with nose-rings and pink hair, being maids. She must ask Dora if she knows of any girls gone into service. Floss's mother was a maid, a nursemaid, sixteen or so when she went in service with some rich man's family. Being a nursemaid was nothing like being a maid, according to Celie. She had talked about parties the family used to give, about the little girl who had a room with elves and fairies and English flowers painted in a border all around the walls. Pop told Floss that when he was growing up even ordinary people had maids. His mother, Floss's grandmother, always had a maid, two sometimes—girls in from outports, little skivvies who worked just for their keep, slept in the attic and got one afternoon off a week.

Once inside Furlong's, Floss switches off the security system and relocks the doors behind her. Then she takes off her walking shoes and pads downstairs in stocking feet. In the cubbyhole under the stairs where the cleaning supplies are stored, she puts her purse and the gift box on a shelf; she will open Dora's present later, as a treat during her coffee break. After hanging up the cotton bag and her rain coat, she pulls on a pair of worn sneakers and is ready for work.

The downstairs sitting room and kitchen are always the worst mess. It's down here people come to escape from the corpse, from relatives, from the thick smell of flowers, air freshener and death you get upstairs. Mourners bring in cookies and sandwiches. Down here they change babies, chew gum, eat, smoke and drink coffee. In between eating and smoking, they cry into Kleenex. The Kleenex and coffee are provided by the funeral home. Floss thinks some of them must be embarrassed to be caught eating—others, the men probably, are embarrassed to be caught crying. Anyway, there's always balled-up Kleenex, along with half eaten sandwiches and cookies, stuffed down behind sofa cushions.

Well before seven every cushion has been pulled out and brushed off with the little hand brush that works so well. When that's done she starts on the kitchen, but first she cleans out the big coffee perk, refills it and plugs it in.

On a good morning Floss can get the kitchen, sitting room and the two downstairs toilets cleaned before the coffee is ready. Then she pours herself a cup, good and black, sits down in the corner chair for five or ten minutes and flicks through yesterday's *Evening Telegram*. Pop used to read bits of the paper out loud to her and Rod, strange interesting things the like of which never happened in Newfoundland: stars falling onto dinner tables, people vanishing, taking off in UFOs and reappearing years later, people building houses out of beer bottles or pearly buttons or popsicle sticks. Once Pop read a bit about this man from India who'd carried his father's bones all over the world in a suitcase.

Floss can never find such stories. Nowadays everything is about movie stars or war, war and starvation. So mostly she just drinks her black coffee, lets her mind wander, enjoys the soft chair and the tidiness of the room she's just put to rights. That newspaper story about the young man carrying his father's bones from country to country she remembers especially, so strange, no country would take him, it seemed, because of the bones. Her father sounded sad just reading about it. Floss had wondered if he was thinking of his own dead sons, thinking he only had her, a daughter, to care what happened to his bones. Rod must have had the same thought. "I'll put your bones in a suitcase, Pop. I'll take you everywhere I go," the child said. About seven Rod was at the time, his grandfather still in his sixties, all three of them young enough to laugh at the idea. Her son now lives on the other side of the continent, thousands and thousands of miles away, and here she is going away too, leaving Pop's bones up in Mount Pleasant—not a soul left even to cut the grass on his grave.

It's a foolish thought. Her father wouldn't have minded; he was never the sort of man to lay a burden on anyone, certainly not on her and Rod. Floss knows she's only looking for excuses—she's tormented about going off with Bram to a place she's never seen, trying to make up some reason not to go.

Mr. Furlong couldn't credit it, tried to talk her out of giving up such a good job. He's told her that he'll hire a temporary cleaner for one month, just in case Floss changes her mind. She can hardly credit it herself. Hardly believe that tomorrow this time she will not be sitting here drinking coffee. Tomorrow she will be somewhere else, somewhere in Ontario with Bram.

Mr. Furlong doesn't know anything about Bram of course. Well, he knows Bram. They went to school together—but he doesn't know about her

and Bram. First when she got this job, Floss wondered if he might suspect because of Bram giving
her such a good reference. She need not have worried. Bram Gillingham, owner of Gillingham
Jewellers (Est. 1886), and Floss, the cleaning
woman, sleeping together was not a thought likely
to cross the mind of anyone in St. John's. It certainly didn't cross Mr. Furlong's mind.

Floss used to hold that against Mr. Furlong.
After all, she was only in her mid-forties when he
hired her—a good bit younger than that one who
was up before court for having three husbands,
younger than the teacher she'd cleaned for who had
a man in every weekend. Floss took to standing in
front of her mirror nighttimes, studying herself,
wondering what was wrong with her. She could see
she was a bit big, a bit awkward—but still and all,
she thought, in fair shape for a woman her age. It
hurt to think that no one ever saw her as a woman
capable of having an affair. For a while back then
she had started putting things on her face—foundation makeup, blusher, eye shadow—but she never
got the knack of it and after a time she stopped.

"Let's take a vacation together—get away—get
to know each other," Bram had said the day after
Pop's funeral when he brought up the subject of a
trip. He gave an uneasy laugh. "Try spending some
time together with our clothes on."

It was not a bit like Bram to say such a thing. By
then they'd been having their Wednesdays together
for twelve years, and Bram had never once said anything you couldn't print in the *Evening Telegram*.
The question, and the way he smiled and leaned

towards her as he asked it, made Floss see him again
the way he'd been that day sitting on the mailbox.
She was so surprised she laughed out loud, for all
they were standing beside Pop's grave and the second before she'd been afraid she was going to bawl.

Up on the hill in Mount Pleasant Cemetery you
can see across the city and out through the Narrows.
While Bram waited for her answer, Floss stared out
at the ocean she'd never once been on, at the hill
with its grey tower. Far away as heaven, Signal Hill
seemed that day, though it was right there and she'd
seen it ever since she was born. Looking across at
the hills and sea it came to Floss how often in life
things happened you have no say over—like when
you wake up and find it snowed in the night, the
world gone from black to white and you sleeping
through it. This time, this moment, she was awake
when something was happening. This time it was
possible for her to choose. "Yes," she said, "Yes, I
think I might like that."

~ ~ ~

Before he even opens his eyes Bram Gillingham
hears the foghorn. A bad omen, he thinks, a bad
sound to hear at the beginning of a long voyage—
or what he hopes will be a long voyage.

He has no confidence that Floss will not jump
ship, abandon him in Ontario, fly home. He's
promised not to make a fuss if she does.

"Just think of it as a week in Toronto," he told
her, "then you can decide if you want to drive out to
British Columbia with me." After selling jewellery
for thirty years, Bram knows how sales are made,

slowly and carefully—introducing the idea, showing the goods, raising the ante.

This is Bram's plan. To beguile Floss with the wonders of Toronto—wonders he's seen many times—then to rent a car and drive clear out to the Pacific. Listening to Floss describe a bus ride across St. John's, he can picture her reaction to a real trip: to the Pacific coast, to Chinese gardens, to Italian mansions, driftwood shacks, to mountains and forest. Bram has imagined the two of them driving up to Lillooet, to Bakerville. They might cross to Prince Rupert, come back down the coast through abandoned goldrush towns and little woods towns, places he'd hitched into in the fifties. Golden years, the fifties had been, him young and free, saved from a war that had killed his older brother; cheap travel and indulgent parents had given him eight years. Eight years of freedom until his father died, until he came home to take over the store, to marry Rosemary.

It is Bram's theory, one he's given a lot of thought to, that Floss missed those post-war years completely. He has never heard her mention them—as if student riots and love-ins and the Beatles had never happened, or Kennedy's Camelot or the Cold War either. Bram knows this has something to do with her mother's getting locked away in the Mental that night the war ended. Since then Floss hasn't taken the world into account, hasn't noticed time passing, not the way other people notice its passing. Which is strange, Bram thinks, because she notices small things: people's gestures, stray dogs, a newly planted garden, a house being painted—as if by concentration on details she can ignore the surrounding world with its untidy, moving history.

Floss's world is a preserved pre-war St. John's, a town with upper and lower levels, with gradations of levels as you climb upward from the waterfront to LeMarchant Road, as you roll over the crest of the hill, meander into Freshwater Valley, into the valleys of Waterford and Rennie's Mill. Floss speaks often of her town's vanished landmarks, of an ice-house beside Long Pond, of red post pillars with royal crests, of a red fountain where pink tongued horses and dogs slurped up water on hot days.

Floss can recall levels below her father's store where children played in dusty unpaved alleyways between rows of unpainted houses whose occupants went to a pump for water, put out buckets of slops to be picked up after dark—and sometimes came to houses further up the hill begging for a loaf of bread or a tin of milk. She can name streets bordering the hilltop just above where she lived, give the names of shopkeepers and shoemakers, railway workers and clerks and carpenters who lived in detached and semi-detached houses, tradesmen who were considered lucky and blessed, but who had to keep civil tongues in their heads if they wanted to stay in the good graces of their bosses and customers. These bosses, government people, merchants, owners of large stores, shipping companies, insurance companies, lived in the valleys beyond the higher levels. These people had big houses, kept horses, had gardens and greenhouses, had gardeners, chauffeurs and nursemaids.

Floss's own mother, Celie, once lived in such a house as nursemaid to the owners' children. Sometimes, on warm moonlight nights, when the older children were back from English schools, servants like her were told to accompany parties of young men and girls out to Octagon Pond, to Topsail Beach, to Middle Cove. The younger servants would carry baskets of food and wine, fill carryalls with napkins and glasses, with musical instruments and blankets and pillows. They were directed to spread these things out on the moonlit grass, unfold chairs and tables, lay cloths, pour wine. With everything arranged for the comfort of the party the servants were told to withdraw, to wait nearby until called. And so they would. Well back in the shadow of trees, silent as trees, Celie and the others would wait, wait and watch while the young men and girls—and sometimes the not so young—ate, drank wine, listened to music, danced, took boat rides and sometimes, if it was very warm, went swimming.

Those nights constituted much of Celie's education; memory of them became the source of her songs and dances, of the stories she later told her three children at bedtime. Bram envies Floss these bits of memory stirred into her childhood dreams. He has never met Celie, knows her stories only from Floss, through Floss's ambivalence, love, envy and resentment.

He wonders if his parents could have been among the young guests at those summer parties. Not his mother, not the daughter of an accounting clerk, but maybe his father. The owner of a small

jewellery store, his Newfoundland accent and educ-
tion would have barred Gus Gillingham from being
welcome into the homes of these people. But still, a
well-spoken, passably handsome young man might
have been invited to such a party on impulse, as an
adventure, or to balance out numbers. Bram likes to
think that his father and Celie almost met, might
have exchanged glances.

According to Floss, no allowance was made for
servants who had been up all night. When it was
almost dawn the rich would call out, tell them to
pick up the remains of the night's revelry, to collect
glasses and cloths, to help guests, their white suits
and dresses damp and grass stained, into waiting
cars and carriages. After the ladies and gentlemen
were driven home, led to rooms, placed between
freshly ironed sheets, the chauffeur and serving
maids, the kitchen boy who was nine, and Celie, the
nursemaid, would report for their day's work.

Floss knows that St. John's, accepts as reality
that place where the rich were as separated from the
poor as men are from animals, where servants could
be ordered to work all night, where store clerks
could be fired for getting married, for selling to a
family member, for buying a car, for not holding the
door for Mrs. Walwyn. There were benevolent rich
people, of course. Celie's stories were sprinkled
with kind mistresses who gave their maids used
clothing, with masters who arranged a special mort-
gage so that a servant could buy a house or a piece
of land.

Bram also knows that narrow, tight world. He
had run away from it, had come back during its dis-

integration, had seen it pass. He does not regret its passing. Floss, he thinks, has not noticed its passing.

Bram lies in bed in a house which had once been on the edge of a green valley, listening to the fog horn, musing about untaken journeys, uncrossed borders, musing about Floss, wondering what would have happened if his father had met Celie, if he himself had met Floss years ago, wondering how their journey will turn out, wondering what life with Floss might be like, imagining her at work on her last shift. He glances at the clock. She'll be having her coffee now, getting ready to begin on the upstairs part of the funeral home. When they marry, if they marry, Bram plans to have an old fashioned announcement printed—like the cards his father used to send to prized customers inviting them to a private viewing of his Christmas stock. Only his father never called it stock, but "a unique collection of fine gems."

Bram vows he will send the card out, send it to every friend and business acquaintance he has; Hubert Furlong will be on top of the list. Bram thinks he will have the announcement printed on heavy cream coloured paper, in copperplate script, very simple. It will say: "This is to announce the marriage of Florence LaFosse (nèe Hayward) daughter of Rodney and Celia Hayward to Bramwell Gillingham son of Augustus and Mathilda Gillingham."

It tickles Bram to make up variations he might have embossed on such an invitation. He could describe himself as "a romancer" (the tab his moth-

er often gave him) or as an "ex-jeweller" or "the for-
mer husband of Rosemary Sullivan." He might
describe Floss as "the delightful Floss LaFosse." He
teases her about her name, says it sounds like the
name of a can-can dancer in the Yukon gold rush
days.

He showers, shaves and, back in his bedroom,
walks to the big window overlooking his weed
infested garden and the side of Velda's Videomart
where Badcock's garden used to be. Maybe the
announcement should be an invitation to a recep-
tion, a garden party. They could have it out there.
Bram remembers his mother entertaining in the
garden. There was no video shop then, of course,
just the shadow of Toby Badcock's birch trees falling
on white table cloths, on silver teapots, on crystal
and china. When it was no longer possible to get
full-time servants, his mother would hire neighbourhood girls by the day to stand holding plates of
sandwiches, passing teacups, pouring tea. The
birches are long gone, alder and thistle have taken
over his mother's roses and rhododendrons. Before
giving a party he would have to cut things back,
have flowers planted, have grass re-seeded and
rolled.

He imagines Floss at such a party, sees her wearing a wide-brimmed straw hat, a long flowing skirt,
brightly coloured—the kind of thing she never
wears. She would feel a bit awkward at first among
his friends, never knowing, for all he's told her a
dozen times, how her absent, dreamlike quality will
intrigue them. Floss has that not-quite-there air
even when she's scrubbing floors, especially when

she's scrubbing floors. Which was where he first saw
her. Even then Bram felt he had known her, looked
into her face before—in another life perhaps.
Sleeping Beauty, he thought, and what was she
doing down on her hands and knees washing brown
inlaid linoleum in his mother's hallway?

"She's Rod and Celia Hayward's daughter. They
once owned a little bulls-eye shop at the top of
Barter's Hill," his mother said when he asked. "Poor
as church mice. Her married name is Florence
LaFosse. I heard her husband was French Canadian,
used to represent some Quebec chocolate company,
came down here selling to small stores. She's a
widow now, with a son—why?"

"I don't know; there's something odd about her,
as if she lives in a dream world." Bram had spoken
casually, avoiding his mother's appraising look.
This was three years after his divorce from
Rosemary, a time when mention of any woman was
dangerous.

"I'm not surprised. The parents were always a
bit eccentric—never belonged to any church.
During the war they lost two sons. On the night the
war ended the mother went berserk, attacked her
husband with a knife. Everyone in town knew about
it. Got herself locked up in the Waterford, Celie
Hayward did. The daughter left school. Father lost
the store. Drink." His mother was not a storyteller,
she had never spoken of her own parents, of the
grandfather Bram discovered in a old photo
album—a dark seaman who wandered off some
ship, discarded his past and settled down in Brigus.
When pressed, his mother's sentences became

shorter and shorter, as they did that day. She did
not want to discuss her char's family any more than
she did her own. "Hopeless," she said, and that
ended it.

Bram and his mother never spoke of Floss
LaFosse again. By the time he and Floss began
sleeping together Mrs. Gillingham was bedridden,
past being concerned about what went on every
Wednesday in her son's upstairs apartment.

It would amuse Floss to know that he sometimes
thinks of her as Sleeping Beauty, blatantly ignoring
the fact that she has married, has had a son and
earned her living by scrubbing floors for thirty
years. "Bit on the thick side for Sleeping Beauty,"
Floss, who prides herself on being clear-sighted,
would say.

Bram thinks Floss is the only woman he's ever
met who has never really looked at herself, never
coolly appraised her features, never enumerated
her own defects and assets. It is one of the things he
likes best about being with her; there's no patting of
hair, adjusting of clothing, redoing makeup, no
flicking little glances at her own reflection in windows and mirrors.

He is still staring down at the garden when a
truck rattles up the driveway. Adam and Lori
Tucker, his new tenant-caretakers, arriving early. In
the back of the truck, pacing between two suitcases
and a lot of sound equipment, is a full-grown Lab
Retriever. The dog had not been mentioned in the
interview. Bram points this out a few minutes later
while escorting the young couple upstairs. They
assure him that the animal will live in the garage.

Bram doubts it. The garage, which hasn't been used since his father's day, looks fine from the street, but the back wall has fallen in on stacks of mouldy account books.

He has made it clear to Adam and Lori that they must live in his apartment, must not use the rooms down below, only go into the area he still thinks of as his mother's house to check on things, turn back the heat when the days start to warm up. Before leaving, Bram goes over it all once again: in exchange for free rent the Tuckers will mow grass, pay the light bills, and, tomorrow, bring his car back from the airport.

Before getting into the car, he stands for a minute looking up at the old house which was built by his grandfather. Bram had been born in the big bedroom on the second floor, the same room where his father was born, where his mother died.

Bram hopes Adam and Lori will not burn the place down—or maybe he does hope so. He's not sure. The house is becoming more and more of a burden. It is huge, uninsulated and in what has become an increasingly slummy part of town. Bram wonders why he's held onto it for so long. Certainly not for Floss. Floss thinks the house ugly and uncomfortable.

"The only good thing about this house is the view—and you can only see that from up here," she said one Wednesday. She'd been standing in the circular window of what his mother used to call the tower room, now his bedroom. Floss had been wearing his wine bathrobe at the time; sun coming in the

window, making her usually brown hair look
bronze.

On the road hours early, Bram ponders how to
fill in time until noon when he is to pick Floss up.
Their flight leaves at two-thirty. He gets gas, runs
the car through a car wash and, because he doesn't
want to meet anyone, goes way in to Kenmount
Road for breakfast. Then he drives downtown, drives up Water Street and down Duckworth Street
studying the few small shops that have managed to
survive, ignoring the concrete and glass office
buildings he cannot learn to like. Each time he passes the store—where workmen are unscrewing the
old wooden sign that says "Gillingham Jewellers
Est. 1886"—Bram has to force the car to keep moving. Like a horse that's been taking its owner along
the same path for forty years, the car wants to turn
into its usual parking place in the lane. It is still only
ten-thirty when he pulls up to HavaJava for a take-
out coffee, drives up to Signal Hill and parks facing
the sea. He sits there staring towards England and
drinking his coffee.

Maybe that's where he should be taking Floss—
to England's green and pleasant land or, even better, to France. France would be a new place for both
of them—fairer that way. He'd been to England
once, twenty years ago, with Rosemary. But they
hadn't gone to France, hadn't seen Paris. He recalls
unpleasantness, his wife sitting on the edge of a
hotel bed, crying, accusing him of something, some
lack of thoughtfulness, lack of planning—details
fade but guilt remains.

Oh that trip! That long ago, disastrous trip! Recalling it, Bram wonders at his nerve in suggesting to Floss that they go away together. Maybe this dream of showing her Canada, of beginning a new life together before easing her slowly back towards St. John's, back towards the future, is one of those things best left to the imagination—like his childhood fantasy of sailing a barge up the Yangtze or exploring the desert with a Bedouin. Does he know Floss any better than he would have known the Bedouin or the Chinese bargeman? Or Rosemary? He has no clear idea what Floss enjoys, is pretty sure she doesn't read much, rarely goes to movies, has noticed that she likes good food—he sometimes cooks for her. Apart from that he doesn't know her taste in anything. What have they talked about all these years? Vignettes she sees from bus windows, stories her mother told, stories about people who come into the funeral home, about Dora next door, and about houses. Floss likes houses, likes them in an appraising yet quite specific way. "I'll never own one, of course," she said once, with that detached acceptance he cannot understand.

It's one of the few things he knows for sure about Floss, this love of houses. Genetic, Bram supposes; her father and grandfather were carpenters, and her son, it seems, would like to be an architect.

Floss has often mentioned playing house in the big field behind Hayward's shop when she was growing up. On summer evenings men and boys used Martin's Meadow for soccer, but in the afternoons small girls, Floss and her friends, made houses—stone outlines of houses on the short grass.

Neighbourhoods of houses divided into rooms. Floss can still recall the arrangements of those rooms. She and her friends would play in the warm, quiet field for hours, hanging imaginary curtains, sweeping floors, preparing meals, calling imaginary children in to supper, careful never to step through walls, always using the imaginary doorways.

Bram is fond of this picture, of Floss as a thin tidy child in a print dress, laying down stones in careful lines, frowning as she enlarges her living room, adds a fireplace or a sunroom. She has told him that sunrooms were very much in then because a rich man on Rennie's Mill Road had built one for his son who was dying of TB. Floss can still describe the white latticework that enclosed the sunroom's north side.

Although she has never voiced any desire to own a house, has never spoken resentfully of others who own houses, it is one of Bram's dreams to give Floss a house. Someday he will take her to a field, a rolling field overlooking the sea. He knows just the place, down in Gallows Cove. He will ask her to outline a house for him, will sit watching her make her dream house in the grass with rocks. Then he will tell her the house is hers, he will build it for her— for them. It will have a sunroom looking out over the bay. He and Floss will eat breakfast there. Another fantasy but, unlike the trip, one he has so far left unspoken.

The trip had seemed like a good idea that day up in Mount Pleasant, Floss's father just buried, lying underground near their feet, her son off to the mainland, his own mother dead, Rosemary long gone and the store signed over to a national company—the crowning glory of his grandfather's life soon to be absorbed with hardly a ripple into Bangles and Baubles Incorporated. That day in the cemetery, it suddenly occurred to Bram how free both he and Floss were. Wasn't there some sad song about freedom "being just a word for nothing left to lose"? Standing in the sun, surrounded by gravestones, it didn't seem such a bad thing to have nothing left to lose.

He had opened his mouth to say so, but was stopped by Floss making a noise, a terrible indrawing of breath, as if she was sucking sorrow into herself, swallowing grief. They were alone, just two of them in the vast bleak graveyard, yet she would not let herself weep. Her control seemed like a rebuff, a denial of their years of sexual intimacy. Why couldn't she put her head back and howl like those grief stricken Arab women you see on television? Or better yet, why couldn't she lay her head on his shoulder and cry the way women in movies cry? Then he could put his arms around her, rub her back, pull her towards him. To hell with restraint, he thought and reached out for her.

Wearing heels, Floss was that day, a bit unsteady on her feet, unsteady and slightly taller than Bram—she had fallen towards him and he found himself looking right into her eyes. Her height surprised him, made him realize how seldom he'd seen her dressed up—twice only: today and at his mother's funeral. Regret came, followed by a reckless desire to take her somewhere else, somewhere warm and foreign, to dress her in bright scarves and swishy skirts, to see her with bracelets on her wrists, sandals on her feet. "Let's take a trip together," he said, "let's see each other with our clothes on." Floss had laughed; he could feel the laughter rippling up through her body; then she'd said yes.

Bram sighs. It's done now, mistake or no. He drains the last of his cold coffee, gets out of the car, walks to the low stone wall and sees that he is float- ing in a vast sea of fog, afloat on an island of asphalt. He breathes in the salty greyness, tasting it. No flights will take off from Torbay today—perhaps no flights will ever take off, ever again. Perhaps everyone still on the island ("those of us who remain," as the Bible says) will be marooned, left to wander like ghosts over bog and barren. Bram half likes the idea. He lets it drift, following it up and out over the bowl of St. John's harbour, across to the bleating foghorn beyond the gun battery on the South Side. He imagines Newfoundland adrift, Newfoundlanders once again abandoned, left to live or die, to beget and breed—to start all over.

"Romancing again!" his mother's voice rings in his ear—not from paradise but from some dim dis- tant day Bram can almost recall. With an effort he pulls himself back to reality. If their flight is can- celled where will they sleep? The Tuckers and their Labrador Retriever now occupy his apartment. Floss will certainly not take him to her place, to what she calls "the Housing," a place joined by cardboard walls to neighbours she has refused to let Bram meet. To Bram—who thought he knew some- thing of pride from his parents and grandparents, from his wife Rosemary—Floss's pride, the pride of the poor, has been a revelation.

"I'll not step in through that door, not have some hootie-flootie bellhop look down on me," she'd said once outside Hotel Newfoundland. It had been her birthday, and they'd gone for a rare drive down to Ferryland and back. Just after dark, without a word, Bram had swooped up to the front of the hotel, waved at the bright foyer, announced that he'd booked a table—they could have supper, could perhaps spend the night. "No," she said, but he'd walked around, opened the door, ordered her out. Knowing her weakness for food he even described what would be on the menu.

But, "I'll not have people wagging their tongues about us," she said and refused to budge. Useless to tell her that they would not be noticed and, if noticed, not remarked on. In the end he'd gotten back in the car and driven her to a bus stop because she even refused to let him drive her home. She hadn't turned up the following Wednesday.

It was the same whenever he wanted to take her anywhere, to the Burns Night dinner his parents had always attended, to a concert or club or dance. Floss would not even go to a movie with him. And she'd firmly refused to take him home—to the Housing to meet her family. "That I will not. Pop got enough to worry about without trying to think of things to say to you—without knowin his daughter's been sleepin around."

"You haven't been sleeping around—you've been sleeping with me," he said, then told her about the first Gillingham, the one who went door-to-door in the outports, who sold brooches and beads out of a suitcase.

"Ah, but he was a foreigner. It's all right for foreigners to be poor—that's different. Different altogether!" Floss said sounding foolishly triumphant, refusing to explain.

No, if their flight doesn't leave this afternoon he will have to go alone to some hotel. And Floss will go back to the Housing, will probably go back to work at the funeral home, will accept the fog as divine intervention, will refuse to step through any doors no matter how glittering he makes the other side seem.

Bram looks at his watch. It is eleven-ten; their plane might already be in, might be on the ground out at Torbay airport—just waiting for him and Floss. If the plane is in, it will get out—it only has to be in. The sky over Torbay may be invisible but it is wide and empty.

Greatly cheered, he drives down Signal Hill and up Water Street. Watching out for a telephone from which he can call the airport, he forgets completely to check and see if they've finished installing the new sign over Gillingham's. By the time Bram reaches LeMarchant Road he's decided not to bother with a phone call; he just knows their plane has landed, knows it's out at Torbay, sitting there waiting for him and Floss, knows it will take off. Why shouldn't it? There's nothing up there to collide with.

After her coffee break Floss tosses yesterday's newspaper into the garbage—not one interesting thing
in it. She washes her cup and unplugs the coffee
pot. She will plug it in again just before Mr. Furlong
is due. He likes to smell coffee perking when he
comes through the door.

Now she has to start in on the main floor where
the chapel and visitation rooms are. Rather than go
through the mortuary to the elevator she uses the
stairs. It always takes two trips, one lugging the
heavy-duty vacuum she'll not be sorry to see the
back of, and one carrying two mops and all the
cloths and cleaners in a bucket.

Upstairs she begins with the entryway so that
the marble floor will be good and dry before people
come tracking across it. Because the funeral home
is open late every night, the staff take turns working
overtime. Only Mr. Furlong gets in before noon; the
others will arrive much later.

Floss likes washing up the black marble. It is not
something she would tell anyone, but she enjoys
scrubbing floors. Has ever since she was a young
girl helping her mother on Saturday mornings.

She and Celie would scrub the entire flat and
the steps too—fifteen wooden steps that led down
to Pop's shop. Floss can remember her mother
turning the radio up and singing—songs about
sailors and soldiers going off to war, sweethearts
promising they'd be true, "...forever and ever, my
heart will be true..." Celie would sing as they moved
from room to room surrounded by the smell of
Jayes Fluid. Her mother had a sweet voice. Still has,

for all Floss knows. She hasn't heard her sing for years.

They would always start on the kitchen floor, crawling backwards from bright cream and green squares to the canvas hall runner, to the brownish flowers—an imitation carpet design—that covered the floors both in her parents' bedroom and in her own room at the end of the hall. The attic where her brothers slept, where her grandmother's maids had once slept, had painted wooden floors that were scrubbed only two or three times a year.

It would take most of the morning for the mother and daughter to scrub their way to the bottom of the stairs, Celie doing the treads and risers and Floss the spindles. When they got down in the store where her father was, Floss would go outdoors and scrub the two front steps with a wire brush before emptying both buckets out into the concrete gutter. It was very satisfying to watch the black water swish down Barter's Hill—all that dirt rushing downhill towards the harbour.

While the floors upstairs dried, they would have a little lunch in the shop: orange crush and apricot or raisin squares. In winter Pop would put the kettle on and three of them would eat in by the store stove. But summertime they ate outside, Floss and Pop sitting on the front steps, Celie sitting on a chair her husband would bring out from the shop. Floss remembers that Pop even cut pieces of wood to go under two of the legs so the chair would stay steady on the sidewalk.

Her father and her brothers were always waiting on Celie, doing little things to please her. She was a beautiful woman, small with curly hair. It matters. Celie did something Floss used to think of as twinkling—smiling up at men so they tripped over each other being nice to her. Floss never had the knack of twinkling; she took after her father, tall and ungainly.

This was early in the war when her brothers were still safe. On Saturday mornings they'd be off with the old handcart delivering orders, so it would be just Floss and her parents sitting on the sidewalk outside the store.

They were modern people, Celie said, a modern family where everyone had to be treated as equals, even children. Because of this Floss and her brothers called their parents Rod and Celie, something no one else in the neighbourhood did. Undercooked meat, not going to church, even Celie's smoking was all part of being modern, connected in Floss's mind to the rich family her mother had once worked for, the big house she had once lived in.

After lunch her mother and father would light their Players and talk in low voices about customers who had come in that morning—who had made unusual purchases, which families had paid cash, which were running up bills. Floss would pretend to be deeply interested in peeling bits of paint off the steps. If her parents remembered she was there they would break off talking, warn Floss that she mustn't repeat a word outside the house, begin talking to her in a teasing way they thought she enjoyed. Her father would smile and ask if Floss thought she'd earned her ten cents; Celie would wonder if her daughter really was old enough to go to the Star or York with Marcie that afternoon. They might ask one another if the shop could afford to let Floss take a bag of chocolate mice and Mary Janes to the matinee.

Steve and Kenny always knew when their parents were joking. They joked back, the four of them, childishly, happily tossing words around the way Jimmy Webber juggled balls down at the Races— bright and shining and just above Floss's head, just out of reach. No matter how many Saturday mornings this happened, Floss never caught on, never understood that Rod and Celie were teasing until they laughed.

"Florence Hayward! WHEN are you going to learn to smile?" her mother would shake her head, smiling herself—as if her daughter's lack of humour was a delicious secret she and her husband shared.

The terrible things that came later have probably changed Floss's memory of those Saturday mornings, made them seem more pleasant, happier than they were. Scrubbing the funeral home's front porch, the thought crosses Floss's mind that in a few years time she might be somewhere else remembering how happy she once was kneeling here making wide circles of cleanness in the black marble.

In Furlong's chapel, and in the hallway leading to it, there are rose coloured carpets to vacuum and a lot of dark furniture to polish. Floss polishes half of the woodwork one day and half the next. It takes time to clean wood properly, to wipe the carved armrests on the pews, the neat dovetail joints and little shelves in the low pulpit. She always goes over it all a second time with lemon oil and a soft cloth.

Pop made furniture years ago. Not for sale in the store like he did storm sashes, but for the family. When she was small Floss would catch ribbons of wood that fell from his plane, clip the cream coloured curls on top of her straight brown hair. Pop built Celie a sideboard and Floss a bed. She still has them both.

The second year Rod was in university she and Pop were desperate for money. Her father got so worried about bills he wanted Floss to advertise the sideboard for sale. According to Pop, people were paying hundreds of dollars for handmade stuff. But she wouldn't hear tell of selling it. "I'm glad now, the bed and sideboard are the only things left out of the house on Barter's Hill—the only decent sticks of furniture I got," she told Bram. She has decided she will give the bed and sideboard to Rod's wife when he gets married. Of course the bed is a hard size to fit a mattress to, and not much use for a married couple—what they used to call two-thirds size.

Pop made the bed specially to fit into Floss's room, which was really a trunk-room off the hallway. The only place to hang anything was on the door-knob and the only place to lay anything down was on the window ledge. But you could see the harbour out of the window, and the walls were covered with pictures she'd cut from calendars. Suppliers used to drop off the calendars. Her brothers got the ones with ships, cars and motorcycles, hers had darling babies who ate Pablum and healthy families who drank cod-liver oil. The pictures Floss loved, the ones she kept for years, were of women gazing into mirrors, beautiful women marvelling at what Cashmere Bouquet soap or Pond's Vanishing Cream had done for their faces.

Floss's childhood room was warm, even on the coldest nights, because there was a grill to catch heat rising from the store stove—and not just heat, but voices, low conversations, laughter, smells. A wonderful safe and private place her room was— except for those uncomfortable nights when Celie invited one of her sons' girlfriends to sleep over.

Celie was always so tickled when Steve or Kenny brought their girls around. Unlike Floss, the girl-friends were pretty and small, always small—what a difference being small and pretty makes to a woman's life. The girlfriends giggled, tied chiffon scarves over their pin curls. In the mornings they would twitter in the kitchen, drinking tea, nibbling toast, polishing their fingernails, embarrassing Steve or Kenny who, having forgotten all about the girl he'd brought home, would stumble down to breakfast unshaved and blinking.

No question in those days, of course, of the boys taking girls up to their room. Not even Celie and Rod Hayward, for all their being so modern, would have stood for that. Besides, there was babies, the danger of having babies. Her mother was very frank about that. "All right for you!" Celie would tell her sons, often right in front of some horrified young woman, "It's her who'll pay for your bit of fun, end up in the Anchorage havin a baby and some old bat holdin back on the ether, telling her to suffer for her sins!" Floss grew accustomed to these grim references to childbirth out of wedlock, usually made as Celie marched one of her brothers' girlfriends into her room to spend the night.

"Move in against the wall, ducks," Floss's mother would say as she bundled the girl into the two-thirds size bed. Having saved the girl, Celie would sit herself down on the edge of the bed and the two of them would talk, often until dawn, a quiet murmur that threaded though the night, that made Floss wake feeling tired, out of sorts, harbouring a sense that something more than a night's sleep had been stolen from her.

Furlong's visitation rooms, when Floss finally gets to them, do not take much time—a few petals here and there, fern or bits of ribbon to pick up, drapes to open, a thermostat to turn up—then it's done. The coffins are closed at night. But it wouldn't bother Floss if they were open. Dead people all look pretty much the same, like wax models of dead people. Except for dead children. Dead children she cannot abide—and dead young people, especially young men Rod's age, like the boy two months ago who made away with himself. Poor young mortal, she pitied him. Pitied his parents even more.

Waiting outside they were. Sitting in a car in the parking lot when she came in one morning. Leaning against one another in the front seat, huddled together. First off, Floss thought it was two young ones—a pair of the ne'er-do-wells who were always dropping beer bottles, and worse, on the parking lot nighttimes. She'd flicked her hand at them as she unlocked the door, thinking they had better take the hint and be off before Mr. Furlong came in.

Instead, they got out of the car. The man first, scrawny and wiry with thin sandy hair and moustache. He was wearing one of those dark suits you used to see a lot around St. John's, probably the same suit he'd been married in. It was a mild morning, but the man pulled a beat-up old windbreaker out of the back seat and put it on before walking around to help the woman out. It took him a while to get her on her feet. As they crippled across the parking lot to where she was standing, Floss could see that the woman had been given something, something to dope her, something that hadn't completely done the job.

By rights, the visiting rooms are not opened to the public until noon, but Floss let the boy's parents in. The man said his son's name, not another word, just the dead boy's name. "Mark LaFosse," he said.

The woman started to crumple, but Floss got hold of one arm and himself the other. Being a mother is more dangerous than going to war, Floss thought as they shuffled into the room where the body was. They stood tight alongside their son's coffin, staring down at the polished cover as if they could see him. Floss let them stand awhile before easing them down onto the couch. She didn't turn on the lights or open the drapes, just left them there, bunched together like Halloween people made out of old clothes stuffed with dead leaves.

She knew who they were of course, knew soon as the man said his name. He had faded like a old snap, skin and hair gone putty colour, but his features had hardly changed from the day he drove her up to the hospital in his taxi. All that morning, while she cleaned, Floss kept thinking she should take some coffee or a cup of tea up to the man and his wife. Mr. Furlong didn't like people bringing food or drink upstairs. Still, she would have taken something up to those two if she thought it would help. It wouldn't—they couldn't have held onto a cup, either of them.

They must have had the dead boy late in life. He was not much older than her Rod; maybe he'd been born the same year. Maybe the woman upstairs was pregnant the same time I was, Floss thought. Perhaps that was why the taxi man had called her darling—my darling—when he helped her through the door of the hospital. Maybe he had been thinking about his wife as he held her arm— her bent over with labour pains, sobbing, a nurse running for a gurney.

Floss had had it all worked out. In the fifth month, after she admitted to herself there was a baby inside her, she set her mind to the problem of where it would be born. She knew you had to be a married woman to get into a real hospital. At the Grace, which was Salvation Army, and at the Catholic St. Clare's they wanted to know your religion and get your husband's signature before they let you in to have your baby. Otherwise you were sent to the Anchorage, the home for unwed mothers, the place Celie used to warn the girlfriends about.

Floss's first idea was to get some man to go over to the hospital with her. But reviewing the men of her acquaintance—the policeman (now married) she'd gone out with for a short time, the flirty fellow (name unknown) who took tickets at the Paramount, the nice French Canadian who came into Pop's store, even Pop himself (going through one of his blindly happy times because Celie was temporarily home)—she had realized the impossibility of such a plan. Her baby's actual father, the man who had impregnated Floss in an act so unpleasant that she'd almost succeeded in removing it from her consciousness, was out of the question. If she was going to keep this child and love it, it must be completely hers, separated forever from Toby Badcock's grunting and heaving, from the rough pressure of brick at her back, from his red-faced warning, her silent humiliation.

Late in her seventh month, with her mother once again locked in the Mental, Floss had finally told Pop she was expecting a baby. "A baby!" her father said, surprised, if not shocked. Nothing could shock Pop when he was depressed and drinking. He didn't ask who the child's father was. No use to torment the poor girl, "You'll always have a home here," he said, "and the baby too."

And that was about it. Floss had gone down town and bought ten yards of flannel at Bon Marche, a sweater and cap set at The Arcade. In Gillingham's Jewellery, probably from Bram's father, she bought a five dollar wedding ring, which she put in her coin purse against the day it would be needed. Searching through her mother's bureau, hoping to discover a wedding certificate she could somehow change the date on, Floss found only two ration books and a war savings account book made out to Mrs. Rodney Hayward. These would have to do. In the flurry of late arrival the hospital might accept even this slim evidence as proof she was a married woman.

On a morning in mid-June Floss felt the first pain. She got dressed, put her mother's account and ration book in her purse and told her father she was going down over the hill to look for a crib. She had walked up and down Water Street for three hours, thankful it was not winter, wondering how long it was possible to stay upright, wishing she could remember more about childbirth from the book she'd read down at Gosling Library.

At four o'clock the pain suddenly stopped. She went into Bowrings' Cafeteria and got herself a cup of tea. Sitting in the corner table Floss slipped the wedding ring on her finger. It was her own name and her father's name she would be using, what harm in putting Mrs. in front of it? At least her baby wouldn't be born hearing someone call its mother a fallen woman. Mrs. Rodney Hayward—she was whispering the name to herself when the first big contraction hit; like running into a wall, it was. She held onto the edge of the table, waiting. When the pain receded she opened her eyes, looked down and saw water pooling around her feet. Somehow she managed to get to the door and out into the street where she leaned against the building, wait- ing, hoping the child would not be born here on the sidewalk.

Thank god for Mrs. Cornish! Thank god for obliging taxi drivers! Floss was thinking fifteen minutes later as she was lifted onto the hospital gurney. She waved a limp goodbye to the taxi man, watched him stop and speak to the woman in the little cubbyhole beside the hospital door. "I'm parked out in the street," he said, something like that.

The office woman shouted after him, "Sir, Sir— I need your name, your last name for my records...."

"LaFosse," he said, "the name's LaFosse!" With that he was gone; gone with only his name left behind, and the woman in the office typing, click-clack, on her black machine, and the gurney rattling down the long hall, porridge coloured ceiling tiles passing overhead. The taxi man's name was still there next morning, typed neatly on a strip of tape around her baby's arm, typed on matching tape around Floss's arm when she woke up. "Florence LaFosse." It didn't go well together, but beggars can't be choosers.

When Floss told him about letting the LaFosse couple into the room where their son's casket was, Mr. Furlong asked if they were relatives of hers. Floss hesitated; she hated to lie, always had. Finally she said, "No, no they're not relatives." It was true, of course. Only she felt it wasn't, felt related to the old couple, to the young man in the coffin. She had stayed behind, sat at the back of the chapel for the service. The place was full; he'd been popular, the LaFosse boy. Thinking about her own son, Floss had cried, hoping Rod was safe, praying he'd never do what this boy had done.

She'd told Bram about the couple, about them waiting outside in the morning. Only she never mentioned their name; that would be too dangerous, too near home. Bram asked how Norm Furlong felt about her letting people in before visitation hours. Floss senses that Bram doesn't like her working for Mr. Furlong. At first she thought this was because he was worried they might be found out, a bit ashamed, perhaps, of the way she talked, of who she is. Floss knows now that's not it—Bram would take her anywhere, was hurt that she never invited him to Christmas parties Mr. Furlong and his wife give for the staff. She's not sure what's behind his resentment of Mr. Furlong. Floss has found the man to be a decent boss. He's only the second man she's ever worked for, of course. The first one, Toby Badcock who owned the bakery Floss worked in for years after she left school, wasn't decent. Toby is another thing she hasn't told Bram about.

Old Toby was on city council but that didn't stop him from feeling up the young ones he hired to work in his bakery. Nowadays he'd be charged, Floss thinks; back then girls wouldn't even tell their parents, just whisper amongst themselves after he caught one of them. "Badcock by name and Badcock by nature," they would say, making out it was all a joke.

When Floss first started cleaning for the Gillinghams the Badcocks were their next door neighbours, sharing the same back garden. Mrs. Badcock was one of the women who used to play bridge with Mrs. Gillingham every Wednesday night—which was why she started having Floss in to clean on Wednesdays. Before going home, Floss used to help Bram's mother (only then she didn't know Mrs. Gillingham was Bram's mother) set out the tea things.

After Mr. Gillingham died Mrs. Gillingham began talking to herself, creating a continuous murmuring undertone that required no response, although Floss would say "Yes" or "Well!" as she arranged crustless sandwiches and iced cupcakes on glass plates. Sometimes, Mrs. Gillingham went on about her good friends the Badcocks, about how long the two families had known each other, about how kind Ethel Badcock was, how generous Old Toby had been. Floss would listen to every word and bite her tongue.

She remembered the little game generous Old Toby played on paydays. He used to make each girl who worked for him go into his windowless office and stand quietly by his desk while he added up her hours in the ledger. When he had the total, he would come out from behind his desk and squeeze past her so he could get a steel drawer out of the brick wall. He would lay the drawer on the desk and take money out. Floss thought the bricks must have been part of the oven because your wages, a few bank notes, half-dollars and quarters that he slowly counted into your hand, would be warm. The old bugger would push right up against you, always managing to rub his hand along your breast.

"Private business," he would say in that deep, holy voice of his if two girls tried to come into his office together. The bakery girls were not supposed to be friends, not even supposed to talk to each other, not supposed to tell each other how much they made, not supposed to tell anyone what went on inside the old wooden shed that was Badcock's Bakery. The building is gone now, torn down, a big Irving Service Station built in its place—all white plastic and coloured stripes outside, but Floss would never go in there.

Her work done, the funeral home gleaming and spotless, Floss takes the vacuum and cleaning supplies back downstairs, stacks them neatly into the cubbyhole and turns the coffee perk back on.

There is still no one about. Good! she thinks and, taking her overnight bag, she walks down the hallway, through a door marked "private" that leads to the shower and dressing room used only by the embalmers after their night's work. It amazed Floss when she first met these men how ordinary they were, people who told jokes, fished, showed you pictures of children and grandchildren. Despite this, despite the cheerful pink tiles, the bathroom gives her cold shivers. She showers quickly, using reams of paper towels to dry herself because she's forgotten to bring her own and will not leave a damp funeral home towel behind.

The slip has been a mistake; the lace scratches (she should have resisted the influence of Scarlett O'Neill, brought the usual unadorned slip), but she's pleased with the fawn skirt and cream blouse—"Smart but not gaudy," Celie would say.

She bundles her black slacks, her white blouse and worn sneakers into the old cotton bag, stuffing it all well down into the garbage container before glancing at her reflection. "God, girl, what are you doing?" she asks the dull, plain faced woman in the mirror. She wishes now she'd thought to bring lipstick to brighten up her face, wishes she had Tums or Gravol, something to make her stomach feel less queasy.

She almost forgets Dora's gift, has to return to the cubbyhole under the stairs and retrieve it from the shelf. The box is large but light, unwrapped, just tied with a ribbon which she slides off. Inside are yards of deep green cloth, silky shimmering stuff Floss first takes to be a tablecloth. Unfolded, it turns out to be a rain coat, long, with gores flaring from the yoke and wide sleeves. Where in the world had Dora bought it, how could she afford such a gift?

Floss takes off her brown raincoat, hangs it up and tries on the beautiful green coat. She remembers one of Dora's sons, Winse—the one who was Rod's friend—singing a song all one summer, a song about green. "All in green my love comes riding," the song went. Winse sang it for months, practicing on that guitar Dora bought down at John D. Snow's. Eventually Dora started singing the song herself. Floss would hear the words through the thin walls and sometimes she would sing back. "All in green my love comes riding/ riding down the dusty dawn…" they would sing as they ironed or washed dishes.

Floss is sure her friend chose this gift because of the song. The coat is a kind of blessing from Dora. Floss whirls around, turning fast so the coat swirls out touching four walls of the little room. Then she goes upstairs.

Mr. Furlong has not come in. Floss has the impulse to turn back, to look at every room in the funeral home, to take in all that neatness, the order she's created, to go downstairs and sit quietly in the little room she's just left, the room where the vacuum cleaner is stored, where her old raincoat now hangs.

Holding the thought of the abandoned vacuum and the brown raincoat in her mind, Floss makes herself go to the door, makes herself open it, walk through. As she steps outside the silky coat unfurls, lifts, swirling around her like the skirt of a can-can dancer. She waves to Bram, wishing she was wearing high-heeled shoes, wondering if he would like to be called Gilly again.

Earlier versions of some stories in this collection have been published in the following:

Not A Face You Know
TickleAce

Moments of Grace
Pottersfield Portfolio

Touch and Go
A Way With Words

Unfinished Houses
TickleAce

Secret Places
Grain Magazine

Folding Bones
Home For Christmas (anthology)

Vain Deceit
TickleAce

Poems in A Cold Climate
Fiddlehead
Digging Into the Hill (anthology)

Cautionary Tales
Fiddlehead